SINFUL PLEASURES

AN ANTHOLOGY OF EROTIC TALES

JANINE ASHBLESS   ELLA SCANDAL   SONNI DE SOTO
JO HENNY WOLF   LILY HARLEM   LADY DIVINE
GAIL WILLIAMS   SAMANTHA MACLEOD   TONY FYLER
ELLIE BARKER   LISA MCCARTHY

SINFUL PRESS

First published in 2016 by Sinful Press.
www.sinfulpress.co.uk
Compilation Copyright © 2017 Sinful Press
"The Pier By Night" © Janine Ashbless
"The Dream Weaver" © Ella Scandal
"On The Line" © Sonni de Soto
"The Black Orchid" © Jo Henny Wolf
"Fireworks" © Lily Harlem
"The Man In The Mask" © Lady Divine
"Taking It" © Gail Williams
"On Selkie Beach" © Samantha MacLeod
"Lazy Sunday" © Tony Fyler
"Miss Blue Hair" © Ellie Barker
"The Butterfly Waltz" © Lisa McCarthy
Cover design by James at GoOnWrite.com

A CIP catalogue record for this book is available from the British Library
ISBN-13: 978-1-910908-15-0

NB: Poetry extracts in "Lazy Sunday" are taken from the original versions of
Victor Hugo's Demain des l'aube and Le Roi s'amuse, and Francesco Petrarca's
Era Il Giorno Ch'al Sol Si Scolaro. All others are the authors own work.

CONTENTS

Foreword   v

1. The Pier By Night   1
2. The Dream Feeder   24
3. On The Line   38
4. The Black Orchid   64
5. Fireworks   89
6. The Man in the Mask   114
7. Taking It   126
8. On Selkie Beach   159
9. Lazy Sunday   171
10. Miss Blue Hair   192
11. The Butterfly Waltz   204

About the Authors   241
Other Sinful Press Titles   247

FOREWORD

Sinful Press welcomes you to lose yourself in Sinful Pleasures.

For Sinful Press's first anthology, I wanted to keep the guidelines as open as possible so that I could see the extent of writing talent and imagination that exists within the erotica genre, and I wasn't disappointed. From established authors to first time writers, submissions rolled in by the hundreds – some a variation of a well known theme, others a step in a new direction through voice, characterisation or plot. What they all had in common was a passion and creativity that makes erotica the choice of readers the world over.

Having to pick a selection of stories from such a vast array of talent was one of my most difficult tasks to date, and after months of deliberating, the final line-up for Sinful Pleasures was completed. Working with the chosen authors to fine-tune their stories has been a dream, and I wish to thank each and every one of them for their professionalism. I'd also like to thank those whose stories weren't accepted, and to wish them luck in their future publishing endeavours.

And here we are, at the end of this amazing process, with a finished and polished anthology that offers something for everyone, from mainstream erotic romance to surreal sex-filled dreamscapes and everything in between.

I do have one last message of thank, and that is to you, the readers. Without you, there would be no authors or publishers. Your love of reading keeps us doing what we do, so please, talk to us, whether it's through a review or by contacting Sinful Press directly, and let us know what you think. Is there something you'd like to see us publish more of? Is there something we're getting wrong? Your voice matters and we will listen.

Lisa Jenkins
    Sinful Press

THE PIER BY NIGHT

JANINE ASHBLESS

W ell, since I'm stealing your husband for the day," said Shauna, "you'd better take mine. James can keep you entertained until teatime, Maz."

Maz smiled, accepting the off-colour joke in the manner it was intended: another witty Shauna pronouncement. "I'm sure," she said.

She glanced at Daniel to make sure he wasn't flustered by the innuendo, or wanted to say anything to her, but Daniel was too busy gazing at Shauna. She was always worth looking at—tall and blonde and golden-tan. But it was her confidence everyone really noticed. There aren't that many women high up in particle physics, and Shauna did her damnedest to stand out. She'd made a career out of not being a spectacled man with bad teeth and a tendency to mumble. The go-to girl for media appearances, she'd even had her own TV series on BBC4. And today she was one of the key-note speakers at the conference.

Daniel was on a couple of panels, too. He'd not done too

badly, and Maz thought he was looking very smart in his new jacket. But he stood in Shauna's shade. Hell, everyone did. Shauna shone like a star.

"Where shall we go?" James asked, as they exited the hotel, wending their way past the delegates drifting in.

Maz took a deep breath of Brighton air, hoping for a scent of sea. Instead all she got were traffic fumes and fish 'n' chips. "I don't know." She glanced at James. "What do you fancy?"

"How about the Pavilion? It's within walking distance. Lifestyles of the rich and tasteless."

"Okay. Sounds good." She opened her handbag and started rummaging within. "You don't mind if I smoke as we walk?"

He shook his head, but couldn't resist looking disapproving. "That's not good for you."

"Yeah yeah."

James and Shauna were into clean living, she knew. They'd both been sporty at university, back when Shauna was Daniel's lab-partner and James was the guy every girl in their college secretly—or not so secretly—wanted to get off with. Rugby had been his big thing then, Maz remembered idly. That might all be behind him, but the two of them still went for a run every morning, the mad sods. It kept Shauna slim and young-looking, she supposed, but she couldn't imagine doing it herself.

James wasn't slim; he was broad and tall, like a standing stone. A square frame went with his square name. Despite the keep-fit, his mobile, expressive face was growing lined, but only in a good way. His dark eyes still glinted with the same sardonic humour, even though his thick curls were touched with early grey.

He should dye his hair, Maz thought. They were all the same age, but James was starting to look older than his wife. Still stupidly handsome, just older.

"It doesn't bother you, Shauna hijacking Dan like that?" he asked as they walked.

"Bother me? Why should it?"

"I dunno." He shrugged. "It bothers a lot of people. She doesn't have many female friends. In fact, I think you're the only one left."

Maz blew out smoke. "Does it bother you that she's always got every guy in the room hanging around her with their tongues out?"

"God, no. If it did, would I have stuck it out this long?"

They both laughed.

"Well then. The thing is…" The coastal breeze was an irritant and Maz brushed back her long brown hair from her face, considering. "Shauna's brilliant. I mean, she's smart and dynamic and generous and…a bit crazy, sometimes. Just enough to be exciting, you know?"

"Oh yes."

He hadn't taken offence. She was glad of that. She was fairly sure James wasn't uptight, but she didn't know him well enough to be sure that calling his wife 'crazy' was within acceptable bounds.

Actually, this was probably the first time they'd had a conversation anything like this personal.

"And she's beautiful," Maz continued. "She's so *totally* out of Daniel's league. And mine. It's not like I could ever hope to compete with her."

"Hoy!" James turned, frowning. "Why'd you say that?"

"It's true. I'm no competition for Shauna, so why get jealous or snarky or anything? I might as well enjoy her company. Other women don't like her because she makes them feel defensive. But I know I've got nothing to defend."

"That's bollocks."

"No, it isn't. It's not like she's going to run off with Daniel, or any of those other geeks. There's no point in taking it seriously when she's sitting in his lap, or whatever. People pair up with the most attractive person they can catch, so they tend to match. We have peer groups based on looks. We don't pair up or down."

"Says the HR manager? I'm scared now."

"I did social psychology, remember?"

"I've seen some ugly men with beautiful girls."

"*Rich* ugly men get beautiful girls. Money puts you in a higher peer group. So, anyway, that means Daniel got me. Shauna got you."

He smiled in a slightly baffled manner, the lines around his eyes creasing charmingly. "I think you're doing yourself down, Maz. You were always one of the hot ones at uni."

"Bullshit." She rolled her eyes. "I was the wallflower type."

"Okay, not in a flashy way. But, you know—really cute."

"Not like Shauna though. Not in her league."

He stuck his bottom lip out and admitted, "No. But no one's in her league. *I'm* not in her league."

Maz didn't answer that, because he was sort of right. James was a history lecturer nowadays. Reasonably successful, and well-liked, and still a looker…but not a media personality like his wife.

"Anyway," she said after a pause. "Thank you."

"Thank you for what?"

"For what you said. That was sweet."

James opened his mouth as if to say more, and then visibly thought better of it. Instead he bestowed one of his trademark twinkly winks that said nothing, yet somehow conveyed a conspiratorial warmth and approval.

I bet his students adore him, thought Maz, not for the first time.

They spent several hours exploring the Royal Pavilion. James enjoyed the historical ambience. Maz enjoyed the deranged Regency excess of the decor, particularly the dragon chandelier. They both enjoyed lunch in the restaurant upstairs, and each other's company.

It was funny, thought Maz, that in the fifteen years she'd known James, she'd spent so very little time in conversation with him. Shauna had always been there as an intermediary, and as the centre of attention. James talked to Daniel about guy things, of course—mostly complaining about work politics. Which, given that she worked in Human Resources, had more often than not left her implicated in their barbs and complaints, until she wrote herself out of all those exchanges and wandered off to talk to Shauna about something else.

Now, with James on his own, she was rather disarmed to find him such a genial companion. They talked about the gap year he'd spent in South America, the psychology of driving in different countries, and their family backgrounds—a labyrinth of topics, veering off at every explorable tangent. He was curious and witty. He also insisted on paying for lunch.

Washing her hands after eating, Maz looked at herself in the bathroom mirror, checked her lipstick and smiled to herself. She was feeling bubbly and enlivened, and was already looking forward to more time with James. Wrinkling her nose at her reflection, she acknowledged that she was enjoying his company just a little too much. She'd had a bit of a crush on him, way back at uni, and it looked like that seed wasn't entirely dead. A little attention, a little time basking in his company, and she could feel green shoots of pleasure sprouting from that dry old husk.

Returning to the sea-front, they walked up the length of the huge Victorian pier, skirting the gaming arcades and the booths selling virulently coloured sweets, the seafood stalls and the machines that would squash a coin flat for you. At the end of the pier was a small fairground with a Horror House and a helter-skelter, and rides ranging from the tame to the terrifying.

James nodded at the Booster—a towering two-armed thing that swung its passengers vertical and upside down, right out over the sea. "Fancy a go on that?"

"Not on your life!"

They settled on the Crazy Mouse ride, which they both thought they could cope with.

"You must scream," Maz told him, as they were strapped into their swivelling carriage.

"Why?"

"It raises adrenaline levels, so you enjoy the thrill more."

"I didn't know that. I'm not usually a screamer." He

grinned at her. "Are you?"

Her jaw slackened, the blood rising in her cheeks to tell him she'd caught his drift.

"I mean, I've heard the odd noise through the walls over the years, but you are usually pretty—"

The carriage lurched violently into motion at that point, interrupting his description. Maz didn't have time to dwell on the tease either, because the ride was somewhere between exhilarating and completely horrific—every switch in the track seemed to threaten to hurl them off into the sea—and she was too busy shrieking. James followed her advice and yelled too, especially when she grabbed tight onto him.

They were both still laughing as the ride came to an end. James held out his hand to help her down, and then pulled her into a hug. Maz buried her face in his chest, returning the embrace—and though every motion was irreproachable, the intent was not. She breathed in deeply and he smelled warm and wonderful, a mix of fresh laundry and baking bread. As they pulled apart their eyes met, and she could see the knowledge in his face, in the way his eyes shone so warmly. He kept one arm lingering around her shoulders—gently, gently—as they turned away from the ride.

"Enjoying yourself?" he asked.

"Yeah." She smiled up at him, her insides doing complicated gymnastics that felt hot and wet and fizzing. "This is great."

"I'm…" He looked abashed. "Having a really good time," he finished, carefully.

"Good." She couldn't stop smiling; it seemed to well up from inside her breast. Her face felt flushed, but she couldn't care. She couldn't bring herself to think of anything negative.

They ambled along the shingle beach, chatting, enjoying the autumnal sunshine. Swimmers hobbled down to the waterline and dashed in and out of the sea, splashing bravely and shrieking. Gulls flashed white, diving for fallen chips. Every so often their hands would brush together, and each touch made something inside Maz thrill like a plucked wire.

"What do you want to do now?" James asked, as they came level with another set of concrete stairs leading back up to the promenade. The question was lightly posed, but it seemed to carry an unconscionable weight. Maz looked sideways at him, rearranging the tickling strands of her hair back from her face one more time. Her body knew exactly what it wanted to do. Her body seemed to belong to some other person—someone with no memory, no ties, no guilt. Somebody who had lived all her life here, in the sun, on the beach, far away from any home or husband.

How easy it would be to do something irrevocable. Something that would tear down their carefully ordered world.

"Do you think they've got an aquarium?" she heard herself ask. "I like them."

"It's a seaside town. Of course they've got an aquarium."

They did.

Indoors, it was surprisingly quiet and empty. The sun must be keeping everyone else outside. After the blaring pop music of the pier and the excited children on the beach, the dimly-lit faux-rock tunnels, with their windows onto pellucid underwater landscapes, seemed like another planet.

Maz and James took their time. She hadn't been kidding about how much she enjoyed displays like these. The glowing pools drew her, and the fact that James was beside her only heightened the sense of dreamlike intensity. He would touch her occasionally—a hand on the small of her back, a finger brushing her wrist, the gentlest of clasps upon her upper arm as he pointed out a delicate seahorse among the reed grass. There was a quiet intimacy to it that made her shiver and blush and lose focus.

She could feel her whole body thrumming, as if she were lambent with arousal.

She enjoyed every moment, from the starfish in the touch-and-feel pools to the huge Japanese spider crabs from the bottom of the Pacific, their span of spindly legs metres across, that lurked in ultraviolet darkness. But her favourite was the jellyfish display. This room was dimly lit with glows of red and blue, the tanks bare except for their denizens pulsing delicately as they rose and fell like phosphorescent thistledown in the gin-clear water. No other tourists were around. She came to halt in front of one tank, fascinated by their alien beauty, their slow dance emptying her mind like a meditation.

She felt James come up and stand behind her. He put his right hand on her waist, then the left found its place over her other hip. He stood quietly, so close that she could feel his body warmth on her back. They were in perfect symmetry.

Her mind was empty, and her body felt like it was shining in the dark.

Without a word, she covered his right hand with her own,

and slid it up to cup her breast.

She heard him sigh under his breath. Then he moved against her, his chest to her back, his face stooped to her hair. And both hands on her breasts, squeezing softly, hefting their slight weight, thumbing her nipples. That friction through her clothes sent burrs of pleasure dancing across her skin, all the way to her core. Ridiculously, she wished she had more tit for him to caress—but it was a fleeting fancy, nothing more than a shadow of her sense of inadequacy. The hands that were supposed to touch Shauna were upon her, now; his body was warm against hers, his breath was shallow and pent against the whorls of her ear. She could feel herself melting under the heat of his regard, the warmth running right through her to escape in a trickle between her thighs. Her whole body softened into one thrilling ache—all except her nipples, which somehow, perversely, were pebbling as he teased them, until he was able to take each point between thumb and finger and roll them with exquisite boldness.

"Hhhhh," she gasped.

The jellyfish hovered before her blurred vision, like angels falling through an alien heaven.

When he moved one hand around and trailed his fingers down the cleft of her cleavage, her legs nearly gave way beneath her. She relaxed back into his embrace, surrendering. Then he turned her in his arms and pulled her close.

She lost sight of the jellyfish. His shadow engulfed her and his lips moved over hers. Soft and warm, he kissed her. It was almost chaste, at first. Then he broke the seal of her lips with his tongue and their kiss, though gentle and slow still, became something not in the least platonic. Through his clothes, she felt the press of his hardening cock.

A natter of voices warned of approaching tourists. They pulled apart like they were tearing skin from skin. Her head was filled with the smoke of their kiss. She felt drunk.

"Wow."

"That was…"

"Yes."

He pursed his lips. She could feel the heat burning in her cheeks. For a moment, the silence hung between them, fizzy with promise.

"Um. We need to head back to the other two. I suppose."

She looked at her watch, theatrically, not even seeing the numbers. "Yes. I suppose. They should be finishing soon."

Humbly they slipped from the jellyfish room. James' hand lingered at the small of her back, that tiny pressure making her want to arch her spine. In the gift shop on the way out, he bought her a mouse-sized fluffy octopus to hang from her bag, presenting it as they left the building.

"What's that for?" she giggled.

"To remember the visit by."

"Oh…I think I'll remember," she told him, mock-rueful.

They were back at the hotel by 6 p.m., and rode the creaky old elevator to the fourth floor. Slightly self-conscious now, they stood at right angles, a little apart. Maz glanced in the wall mirror and caught James grinning at her. "What?" she asked, arching an eyebrow.

"Oh…I just love the way you don't wear a bra, and your nipples stick out through your clothes," he said with disarming candour.

She looked down at herself. Her nipples studded her soft cotton tee like buttons waiting to be pushed. "It's the sea-breeze," she excused herself, a little embarrassed. "It was a bit chilly…"

"Oh rubbish. They do it all the time." He smiled beatifically. "It's *great.*"

She couldn't help giggling. "Stop it!"

"What? Looking at your breasts?"

"Making me blush!"

"So I *am* allowed to look at your breasts?"

"Oh!" She mocked a slap at his arm, and he faked a flinch. "That's not entirely up to me, is it?" she warned him. "Shauna might have something to say about it."

"And Dan."

She sobered abruptly and looked away, nodding.

The plan was that Daniel would join them both and they'd go find a nice Italian restaurant or something in The Lanes. They'd have three hours before the official presentation ceremony started, which they were all due to attend that evening. Shauna, they knew, had been invited to have dinner with some Very Important People and wasn't going to be up for pizza.

But Daniel wasn't in the hotel room when Maz got back. She wasn't sure whether she felt disappointed or not. She slipped into the bathroom for her shower and concentrated hard on the minutiae of her toilette. Soap, razor, shampoo. Underarms, hair, pussy, legs, feet. She didn't let herself think about what had happened during the day.

But afterwards, she paused at the sight of her bare body in the misty mirror. It looked so ordinary, to her eyes. Not bad, but not good. And yet he'd…

She couldn't help picturing James' big square hands on that canvas; gliding over her skin and cupping her small breasts. He had blunt fingers and solid wrists and darkly-haired forearms—she knew that, because she'd studied them today. She imagined him standing behind her, a shadowy halo embracing her body as they both watched each other in reflection. She pictured him pressing her against the tiled wall of the shower cubicle and fucking her under the spray. His body would be darkly furred too, she guessed; combed to stripes by the water. In her imagination, his cock was enormous, like a pornstar's: a veined monster, as hard as stone, that made her squeal with shock and pleasure as it plunged into her split.

She felt the scrubbed whorl of her sex fill with moisture again, no longer pristine.

"Don't be stupid," she mouthed at her mirrored self, but her eyes were loaded with secretive delight.

It occurred to her that she hadn't had a cigarette since just after lunch. Not since the ride on the Crazy Mouse, in fact. It was as if her body had changed in some way. She touched it cautiously, running her fingers across her pubic mound. Her flesh felt electrically charged, her blood effervescent. It was lust—pure, incandescent, explosive: lust that was like the sun coming out and filling the world with colour. She was a fuse that had been lit, and was now burning its way towards its inevitable end: the whoosh of a rocket, perhaps, or some colossal detonation.

She hadn't felt like this in years. After over a decade with one man, she'd actually forgotten what it was like, and she was a little shocked to rediscover the sensation. Oh, she and Daniel got on great, and they still had sex regularly, and it was fun and pleasurable and all that. She loved him. But she didn't feel this crazy, burning ache for Daniel.

One day with a hot man—that was all it had taken, she chided herself.

Daniel still wasn't there when she re-entered the bedroom and began to dress in her evening attire—a short teal dress that showed off her legs...and yes, made it clear she wasn't wearing a bra. She pinched her nipples through the chiffon until they stood out proud. James would notice, she thought. It hadn't been deliberate until now, but here she was, flaunting herself at him.

The door rattled, and Daniel burst in looking flustered. "Sorry," he said, diving straight for his suitcase. "We got talking with the vice-president."

He seemed to assume that she knew 'the vice-president' of what. Maz turned to face him, bracing herself for the guilt she was sure she deserved.

She felt nothing—only a rather maternal concern for him as he rummaged frantically for his formal clothes. She came over to help him.

"Listen, Maz," he said, yanking out ties and discarding them on the bed. "You don't mind, do you? Shauna's managed to get me a place at dinner with her. The Director of CERN's going to be there!"

Oh, Maz thought, her expectations—of an evening of unfulfilled titillation, safe under the umbrella of her husband's protective presence—imploding. "So we're not going out together?"

"Is that all right?" He looked at her beseechingly. "Oh—You look so good in that dress! I'm really sorry, love, but this is such a great opportunity. Shauna totally stuck her neck out to get me on board. It'd be crazy to miss out."

She blinked, nonplussed. *Asking permission, flattering me, explaining.* Well, he was ticking all the right boxes, even if a little fast and not actually pausing for a reply between.

"James can still take you out to dinner," he added, as an afterthought.

"Right. Okay." Her voice sounded thin. It felt like Daniel had just taken down the safety cage between her and a tiger. Not that James was predatory. Maybe she was a tiger too. But in that situation, how do you stop *something* happening?

Her misgiving must have communicated itself to Daniel. He leaned over and pecked her on the cheek. "I'd love to take you too, Maz, but it's an all-nerd thing. We're just going to be talking shop."

"That's fine," she said, and this time her voice did not betray what she felt: the hot bubble of excitement rising inside her.

I love my husband, she reminded herself. It was quite true —and it made not a speck of difference.

They met up with Shauna and James in the hotel lobby. The physics elite were dining at a restaurant a little way down the seafront, so it seemed politic that James and Maz would walk with their spouses that far, before going to look for a restaurant of their own.

Maz saw James glance at her dress, but he said nothing.

"Maz…you're okay with this, aren't you?" Shauna asked loudly, giving her a hug that enveloped her in a cloud of expensive perfume. "I just thought it would be such a chance for Daniel…"

"That's fine," said Maz. "No problem. Thank you for looking out for him."

"It's my pleasure." Shauna was wearing a very short, bright red dress—much shorter than her own, but cheongsam-style so the neckline was eminently respectable. She looked fantastic. Those scarlet stiletto heels didn't hurt either. Maz acknowledged that she couldn't blame Daniel one bit. She didn't blame Shauna either—any more than she blamed the moon for causing the tides. Shauna was a force of nature.

James held Shauna's cashmere wrap for her to put on, and Daniel took his cue and at the last moment helped Maz with her grey suede jacket. Maz said nothing much as the four of them walked out and strolled through the gathering dark. She was happy to listen to the others chattering. She was glad that the breeze had dropped and it was unseasonably mild, because her legs were bare. The cool air only sensitised her hot skin, making every movement of fabric against her feel like a caress.

Inside her the tiger paced back and forth, waiting for its moment, burning bright.

They said goodbye to Shauna and Daniel outside the restaurant, and promised not to be late for the ceremony and presentations. Then she and James were alone.

"What shall we do, then?" she asked.

"I don't know." He ruffled his curls with a broad hand. "I'm…well, this is all new to me."

He wasn't talking about looking for a pizza restaurant. "Really?" she asked, with a slightly cynical smile.

"Yes. Really. D'you think…?"

"Well, you're…you know."

"A man? Incapable of keeping it in my pants?"

She joined in with his smirk, and settled for a diplomatic, "You're pretty cute."

"So are you." He looked pointedly down at her open jacket and suddenly complained, "Oh good God—you're doing it again!"

She looked, saw that her nipples were angry points protesting the night air, and tried to cover up. James grabbed her in a sudden hug, squeezed her hard and then released her just as abruptly, laughing.

"Sorry."

"I'm not. Do you want to go eat, then?"

She considered. "Um…to be honest I usually eat really late at home. I'm not hungry yet."

"Okay."

She made one last valiant attempt at virtue. "I think we should avoid going back to the hotel though."

He pulled a face. "Yeah. I think you're right. Want to walk, then? See the pier by night?" He indicated the line of golden lights stretching out into the sea.

"Is it open?"

"I think so."

"Okay then."

They turned back up the street, talking inconsequentially, walking close together but not quite touching. James had his hands jammed in his pockets. Maz felt so thrilled, simply being alone in his company, that it left her breathless.

Then they turned onto the pier, and she was hit by a wholly unexpected emotion.

Walking the pier by night was nothing like doing it by day. *Nothing.* By day it was bright as a wedding cake, a hectic mix of stylishly traditional and grotesquely brash. The white-painted buildings floated against a blue sky and the sweep of the beach below and to either side. Electronic voices beeped and buzzed and hectored, and children ran wide-eyed among the glittering temptations.

At night, the stalls aimed at children were all closed. The strung lights were golden-yellow, and so brilliant that they blanked out all fainter illumination, so that the pier seemed to march off into utter darkness—no lights on the sea, no stars, no moon. It was like a gantry hung out into the void. Not even the beach below them was visible. Yet the unseen surf was terrifyingly audible—it pounded the pier struts beneath their feet and sucked at the shingle, far louder than during the day, and it had a hungry, angry sound.

"Shit." Maz grabbed at James' elbow.

"What?"

"That noise! The waves!" She looked down at their feet. The floor was made of narrow planks with dark gaps between. For the first time she realised how old the planks looked—almost rotten in places. The wood sagged and bounced beneath their weight.

"It's calm tonight."

"It doesn't sound it!" She couldn't bring herself to imagine what it must be like out here in a rough sea. Clinging to James' arm, she pressed against him. "It's scary," she admitted.

"Don't worry. It's not going to fall down tonight."

She didn't think it was. It was no practical terror that had seized her, no nervousness about the structure. It was a deeper, atavistic vertigo. "I know, but…"

He turned, putting his other arm around her. "You want to go back?"

Oh, he smelled just as good as she remembered, with layers of sage and mint over the warm-bread scent of his skin. His bulk seemed to hold the vastness of the night at bay. "No," she said into his breastbone.

"You okay? You sure?"

"Yes. I'm good."

"You feel good," he agreed, in a lower voice. His arms slid around her, pulling her closer. She could feel his heat all down her front. She could feel her body moulding against his, her spine arching to push her breasts up against him, her bum lifting to the descending clasp of his big hand. Even over the roar of the surf, she could hear her pulse pounding in her ears.

"Oh," she whispered, long and yearning.

The breath caught in his throat, a tiny laugh. "We should probably keep walking."

"Why?"

In answer he moved his hips, and she felt the unmistakeable jut of his erection.

"Oh!" she said, louder, lifting her gaze to look him in the face. He bit his lip.

"That's what you do to me," he told her—still playful, but with a gravelly edge to his voice now. Heat flooded her from skin to core.

"Then you're right," she said weakly. "We should keep walking."

Reluctantly he pushed her back to arm's length, then

wrapped her forearm over his and turned them both up the pier. "This is turning into an...*interesting*...day."

"Yeah," she agreed wholeheartedly, matching his slow pace hip to hip. Once they were beyond the surf-line, the roar of the sea dropped to a less menacing grumble. She pictured the black water below them, licking at the legs of the pier.

"I've never seen you scared before." His hand was folded warm over hers, his fingers rubbing the back of her wrist as if he couldn't stop himself. "By the sea, I meant."

She ran her tongue over her lips, moistening them. "Don't you think this is an unnerving place? So bright, and so dark? We're on the edge of the world here. It's like we're about to fall off into space."

He understood. "No climbing back, once you fall."

"You could swim to shore, maybe."

"Maybe."

Music swelled to greet them as they approached the last third of the pier: some pounding techno-style beat. The arcades were shut, but the fairground at the end of the pier was still open. The twin crane-arms of the Booster swept around and around, golden against the inky sky. The swoosh as it passed overhead made the hair stand up on Maz's neck.

"Is that better or worse in the dark, d'you think?" James wondered, squeezing her hand.

"I don't know." Just the sight of it hurling its passengers overarm like that, far above their heads, made her feel dizzy. She shuddered and leaned into him. "Is it better if you can see how far it is to fall?"

They were standing still again. James took the opportunity to put his hand on her waist. "What are we going to do?" he asked, his voice low. He might have been talking about funfair rides, or not. "Maz. What do you want to do?"

She looked up into his face. This was the moment of choice. "I want to stand right at the edge," she told him.

The strings of bulbs had created pools of dense shadow behind the odd angles of the pier buildings. He led her to a shadowed area on the east side, and right up to the white-painted railing over the drop. There was no one else around. Maz put both hands on the metal. It felt colder here, but James stepped in close behind her, his chest to her back, his body a shelter. She looked down, but couldn't see anything, not even the white crests of the waves. Just illimitable black.

"Shit," she said, awed.

"It's okay. You're safe. I've got you." He demonstrated by putting his hands on her hips, and she felt her whole body surge with gratitude. She pushed her ass into his crotch, and felt it at once—he was massively aroused, his hard cock rubbing against her softer flesh. He made an inarticulate noise: surprise, perhaps. He shouldn't have been surprised, though, she thought. Hadn't her complicity been clear all along?

Her dress hung only to mid-thigh, her jacket shorter than that. It was easy for him to get his hands up under her skirt and onto her smooth bare thighs. Easy for him to reach around and caress her through the silky fabric of her panties. She whimpered with pleasure. The cloth was already damp enough to allow him to outline the cleft of her sex.

"Oh…that's nice," he whispered. Teasing more insistently at where the nub of her clit was hidden, he sent an electric jolt through her from sex to fingertips and made her twist and arch against him.

"Open your legs," he growled in her ear.

She shifted her stance to part her thighs. His hands, hidden under the fold of her skirt, danced across her most intimate parts, front and rear. They explored under lace and elastic, they played with the satin shapes of her flesh. She closed her eyes, forgetting the yawning darkness before her, and let his touch set her on fire. When she realised he was sliding her panties down to mid-thigh, she was so aroused it didn't shock her at all. The coarser fabric of his jeans and the cold teeth of his zip rubbed her bare bottom as he moved against her, breathing hard.

"Oh God. Your hand feels so hot!" she moaned, as he scorched the cold skin of her bum-cheeks.

He wrapped both arms around her, snuggling up, his lips against her ear. "That's not my hand," he told her, making her start and hiccup.

"Shit! James!" Her giggles were stifled, knowing that they dare not draw attention.

"Is that bad?" His throaty, panting whispers made her sex run wet. "You make me want bad things, Maz."

"Aah!"

"Would my hand be better?" He eased away from her, not enough to reveal her, not enough to make a true gap—just enough to slide one hand down between them and, from behind, run his fingers the whole length of her sex and cup it in his hand. She felt the open mouth of her vulva kiss his broad palm.

"God," he whispered. "That's beautiful."

"I…"

"You're so wet." His voice ached with longing. "It would be just so easy to…"

"*Yes.*" The word came out as a groan.

For a moment, he went absolutely still. He was so close she heard him swallow.

"Step up one rung," he said, and Maz felt her sex spasm in guilty delight. "It's okay. I'll hold you."

She obeyed, mounting the lowest horizontal of the fence. He was a tall guy, after all, and she wasn't tall, even for a woman. The extra six inches gave him the angle he needed. The head of his cock sought and found entrance, nudging into her, shy at first, then bolder. She had a moment's panic as she thought he was *too big*—that he really was the priapic monster of her fantasy, that he couldn't possibly fit—and then he snaked one arm around her and *pushed*. She gasped. He made room. All the way. Not fast—they couldn't be seen to be doing anything blatant in public. He didn't thrust. There was almost no visible movement.

He simply embraced her, pressing close, a bear-hug that both engulfed and filled her. She was pinned against the fence, held between the light and dark, his cock inside her like a burning brand. His thighs were so tense they trembled. But she felt *everything*. Each shift of his hard mass within her, the slow-motion slip and slide, the gather of her muscles, the swirl of her climax spiralling in toward the black hole of her need—closer, closer, closer.

"Oh," whispered James. "Yes. Yes."

And as she started to come she turned her head to the right and saw the arm of the Booster sweep down in its huge arc, gold against the infinite darkness, like a vast hammer falling above her into the void, over and over, without end.

THE DREAM FEEDER

ELLA SCANDAL

J ust as the wax from the single white candle in the middle of the dining table spills over the sides of its tarnished silver angel holder, the clock on the wall behind me begins to click and whir. A soft rattle of opening doors is followed by a strangled cuck-crackle as the broken cuckoo takes pains to announce that it's nine o'clock.

I sigh, staring at the porcelain plate in front of me. It's empty—the food that should have been served up on it still sitting in the oven dish on the kitchen counter. A chip on the edge of the plate catches my eye and I stroke the smoothed-out ridge, wondering why I'd even bothered. Amira is always late; it's her thing. The only times she isn't late are those times she doesn't show up at all.

My puff of disappointment snuffs the candle, sending swirls of white smoke snaking through the air. I stay in my seat, quiet and still, until the hot red glow of the wick fades and blinks out. There's no point in calling her because she won't answer.

I think about my girlfriend as I pad out of the dining room and up the uncarpeted stairs. We've lived together for almost three years now, but lately we've been having problems. Our jobs keep us apart more and more these days, and the separation is starting to tell. Her brother, Vikram, suggested that she might be hiding another lover in another city, but Amira swears she isn't.

Me? I'd have believed her six months ago, but now I'm not so sure.

After throwing my clothes into a pile on the floor, I drape one of her dirty t-shirts over my pillow and pull the bed covers back. The sheets are cold and the bed altogether too big, but I snuggle in anyway. Maybe she'll be home when I wake, maybe she won't.

Staring out of the creeping taxi window into the pouring rain, I bite my bottom lip. I jiggle my leg, peer down at my watch, and then stare out of the window again. My nails drum against the screen of my mobile phone. The temptation to open the window and hurl it at the knife-jacked lorry that caused this damned traffic jam is almost too strong. Of all the times the crappy thing could have gone flat it chooses the worst time to do it. I need to call Neeta. I need to tell her why I'm running late—again—but I can't because of this stupid phone. She's going to hate me this time for sure.

If only Vik hadn't been winding her up at the club last month. Telling her I was seeing someone else in the city where I work was cruel of him, and entirely untrue. I adore my girl, and always have. Vik likes to stir the shit pot, though, and has done ever since he discovered that my new 'boyfriend' is a doe-eyed entomologist called Anita.

I once overheard him telling our brother that he couldn't decide what was weirder, a woman fucking another woman or a woman with a passion for cockroaches and moths. Ravi had called it when he'd said the only weird thing going on was Vik's archaic attitude toward sexuality.

The taxi picks up speed amidst a cheer that emanates from the other cars on the road. It takes almost twenty minutes to get home, and my heart sinks when I see the time. Almost eleven. I pay the driver and stand on the pavement outside of the garden gate, staring up at the house. It isn't anything grand. It's always been a bit poky and rundown, but it hasn't ever seemed this unwelcoming before. Neeta always leaves a light on for me, but not tonight.

I let myself in, closing the front door quietly behind me. Lingering smells of coriander and cardamom make me flinch. With any luck, she won't have gone to too much trouble. A peek into the dining room makes me feel sick. I only leave the light on for a few seconds, but it's long enough for me to see cheap champagne standing in a bucket of water, empty plates and—devastatingly—white wax dried to the side of Neeta's favourite angel candle holder.

"Shit."

My legs feel leaden as I drag myself up the stairs. As much as I want to climb into bed beside my love, I don't hurry. I'm too scared that I'll find the bedroom door closed against me, shutting me out. When I get to the top I exhale, huffing out a quiet, relieved laugh. The door is open.

From where I stand I can hear Neeta snoring softly. I

want, no, I *need* to be in that bed beside her. Need to feel the warmth of her soft body, smell the mouth-watering scent of her fresh sleep sweat and her faded sweet peach perfume.

As soon as I slip beneath the covers she wriggles back, pushing her round ass into my groin, her shoulder blades against my breasts. My arms wind around her and I smile as she sighs, the subconscious knowledge that I'm home lulling her into a deeper sleep. She isn't still, though. Her limbs twitch. Her head jerks in tiny movements every few minutes, making her hair tickle my nose.

Neeta is a dreamer.

Some of the tales she tells me between our good morning smiles and wet, lazy finger fucks are worthy of print. Many people have grown bored of her recounting her nocturnal adventures, but I always listen with rapt attention. She's my partner so everything she has to say interests me, but that isn't the only reason her dreams intrigue me. I work in a sleep centre—dreams are part of my livelihood.

I lie quietly, listening to Neeta breathing. Inhale... exhale...inhale...exhale with a rattling snore. I can't help smiling, but it's only a half-smile. A distracted smile. My mind is wandering back to a conversation we had not a week ago.

Neeta had taken an unusually deep interest in an area of my work. It's a new thing, and last week was the first time I told her about it. She'd listened, wide-eyed, while I'd explained the idea behind it, and once I'd finished she joked about being my subject one day. Except I'd known she wasn't joking. She was serious.

She shifts in my arms. Snuffles a little grunt then jerks, a sharp burst of giggles turning her snore into something so adorably cute my heart aches. Maybe I could give it a go. I could turn it into a treat, one I know she'll love me for when I tell her about it tomorrow. The poor girl is way overdue some attention from me, and an unsuspecting subject should yield much greater results than one who knows what's happening to them.

Even though I know I can't possibly garner any results whatsoever, I decide to go ahead.

Leaning close, letting my lips skim her peachy soft earlobe, I start to whisper.

"*There's a hedge in front of you. A high hedge, twice as tall as you, and it's so dark it looks like all of its leaves are of the deepest black. There's nothing else around you but the hedge, everywhere you look, there it is.*"

Neeta stiffens, pushing herself closer to me. It is working already. With just a few suggestions I've turned her apparently amusing dream into something dark. I'll have to be careful. All it will take to turn her dream from a fantasia of our joint creation to a nightmare I'll have to pull her from is one miscalculated word, and that would be a disaster.

I stroke her hair, making sure my touch isn't heavy enough to disturb her.

"*Right opposite where you're standing there's a gate. It's golden and pulses with a warm, welcoming light. Your feet carry you toward the gate. You show no resistance, because you know that on the other side, something incredible will be waiting for you. Something magical. Walk to the gate, Neeta. Walk through it…*"

The golden gate shimmers as I pass through, encouraged forward by a beautiful, familiar voice. Warm sparks of light dazzle my eyes, and every time I blink, lingering white flashes blind me. I hear something. Lots of things, in fact. Close up I hear whizzing sounds, the pattering of many light feet and the fluttering of wings. Soft whispers and hushed giggles seem at odds against a background of something loud and vivacious.

Arms extended, palms out, I take a few steps. The ground is soft and cool. Something tickles my feet. I stop, but the tickling continues, moving over my ankle bones, itching my calves, my knees, my thighs.

"*Take a deep breath,*" the familiar voice whispers. "*Smell all of the wonderful scents of this magical place you've entered into.*"

Hand flat on my bare stomach, I shiver at the tickles on my thighs and draw a greedy breath into my lungs. My chest expands, my stomach tightens and I start to salivate. Flowers. I smell flowers, grass and something syrupy.

The tickles carry on, shifting up my hips, some moving over my ribcage and chest, others fanning out to trace over my arms. Bumps rush over my skin, making all the little fine hairs prickle and stand on end. I don't know what they are but it feels lovely.

"*Your eyes are clear now,*" the voice says.

It's right, I can see everything. I listen to the whispering, seeing things I don't notice until they're pointed out to me: Lush green grass littered with clumps of purple clover, pretty white daisies and glowing yellow buttercups. Tall orangey dandelions sway in the breeze, little seedlings breaking off the clocks around them and rising on a soft breeze.

Moss covered boulders sit in beds of bright tulips; daffodils bend and sway. A gust of wind blows over me, sending the dandelion clocks into a frenzy. They billow around me, moving me forward, brushing against my tingling skin.

"Half a dozen of them drift past your face and you gasp."

They aren't dandelion seeds at all! All of the tiny fuzzy things floating around me are women. The fluff is their hair and the tickles are coming from their fingers. They smile at me, whispering, singing, stroking my skin. I lift my arm, watching them dance over my hand, some of them weaving in and out of my fine hairs, others bending over to kiss me and standing up again with blushing cheeks.

"This is so beautiful," I murmur.

When the dandelion women are blown away by the breeze I'm left standing in a space all of my own. I want to stay right where I am. The massive white flowers in front of me are on stems that tower over my head, and I can tell from the gorgeous, huge bluebottles that fly into the undergrowth but don't fly back out again what they are.

Venus Flytraps.

I'm so reluctant to move on, but the familiar voice is soothing me. It's telling me to walk forward, to pass beneath the pretty flowers. That I'll be safe because I'm not alone.

I trust that voice, so I do as it says. I take a few cautious steps, coming to a stop just before the first clump of plants. I look up, watching bees land on the petals, seeing them crawl toward the stamen. The droning buzz makes my mind feel sleepy, but my body is alert, my nerves tingling with anticipation.

Right here at my feet are a dozen closed leaves. They aren't still, though. Rhythmic, pulsing movements warp the shiny green surface as they visibly shake on their stems. Curiosity chases away my fear of those snapping pods and I get closer. A hushed sigh catches my ears just as one of them shivers, and slowly it starts to open.

I cry out in surprise, startling the bees above me into flight.

What I'd thought to be a bluebottle isn't. It isn't even a fly. Oh, it has wings alright, but it's the size of a coconut, and just like the dandelion clocks, it's a woman. Dark skinned, green haired with opalescent blue eyes. Beautiful.

When she stretches her wings and takes off, she zips right past my face, winking at me and licking her lips. It's such a suggestive gesture I feel my eyelids lower, my stomach muscles tighten. She circles my head once, twice, and again, whispering as she passes by my ear for the last time.

"*Get on your knees and taste it.*" It sounds so much like that familiar voice!

Casting my eyes down I shake my head in awe. It's not a Venus Flytrap at all. I laugh. That's why the blue bottle had looked so smug! She had been sandwiched between two plump, wet vulvae.

Watching the clitoris of one spasm and the opening of the other pulse, I can't help but mimic the blue bottle. I lick my lips, wondering how soft that skin might feel, how the slick clear fluid that's trickling from each and running down the channel that separates them might taste.

Without even realising I've moved, I'm on my knees. My hand comes into view, reaching, fingers outstretched. With the lightest touch, I trace a lazy circle around the still twitching clitoris. It's warm, wet and so ready.

My own clit starts to press against my labia as I reach for the other leaf. This one expands, drawing my fingers inside of it. It's just as warm and wet as the other, but where that one seems to be happy to stay still and let me caress it with gentle strokes, this one expands and contracts. It's encouraging me to move within it, to feel out its walls, to fill it and fuck it.

I can feel my clit parting my labia now. Can feel myself getting wetter and wetter as the two vulvae I'm fingering start to quiver. The one I'm knuckle deep in snaps over, pushing the backs of my hands together. They're forced to the bottom, below the vaginal openings, as the leaves form a spiky seal around my wrists.

This is what the bluebottle girl had felt. She'd been right at the centre of this. Right there, watching and feeling these two wet cunts rub against each other. I feel the seal tightening, feel both sides start to violently shake. Contracting, oozing, sucking at each other as they come over my hands.

Then, with a soft sigh, the sides part again. I pull my hands away. Each of my wrists are partially ringed with evenly spaced red spots. They feel good when I stroke them with my silvery wet fingers. A sweet scent catches my attention and, without hesitation, I raise my fingers to my lips.

Closing my eyes, I suck, making sure I get every last drop of that delicious nectar in my mouth. I like it so much I'm tempted to do it all again, but the familiar voice is back.

"Your cunt is throbbing," it tells me. *"You want so much to find something that can touch it, lick it, fuck it…something that will make it feel like the centre of the world before it soothes that*

ache. You look around, trying to find the perfect thing, but what you see is an orchard. Take a walk beneath the trees."

In less than a minute, I'm exactly where I've been told to go. The scent here makes my belly rumble. Apples, pears, plums, and a lovely layer of sweet pea. I'm still sucking my fingers, but what I want is something to bite. Something I can sink my teeth into, tear apart, and swallow.

My eyes scavenge the ground, looking for windfall fruits, but not all of what they find matches the scents, or even the trees. Covering the grass, everywhere there's a shaft of sunlight, lies mounds of plump, ripe fruits. Strawberries, blueberries, blackberries, grapes. To my delight, they're all things I can pick up and put in my mouth.

On my knees, I gather handfuls. I dip my head, squashing them past my teeth, onto my cheeks, lips and chin. Flavours burst over my tongue, juices slide down my throat. I can feel them dripping onto my chest, running over my breasts, dripping off my nipples. As I chew I touch myself, spreading the red and purple liquid over my skin, pulling my nipples, squeezing my breasts with one hand while I feed myself with the other.

The familiar voice suggests that eating this way is sexy. The whispers are strangely sensual, and make me want to fuck all the more. *"You hear the sound of churning water and tumbling rocks coming from the other side of the orchard,"* it whispers. *"Go and find it."*

My feet mulch berries into the grass as I walk through the dusky silence. The Picasso bugs, which aren't entirely bugs, that dash across my path don't startle me. I can hear the water loud and clear; nothing is going to stop me from reaching it. I want to know what awaits me there.

As soon as I emerge from beneath the trees the scent around me changes. Gone are the sweet aromas of spring flowers and summer fruits. They've been replaced by something heavier. Orchids, lilies and roses, with a maddening undertone of spice and erotic musk. There's an edge of the masculine here, too, and that makes me wonder.

I reach a stream. It's only shallow here, the bed dotted with polished stones. My smile hurts my face when I catch sight of Ebony Jewelwing dragonflies skimming the surface. There are dozens of them, concentrated at this spot because movement picks up further downstream. When I get a good look at one I laugh. Little men playing chase and taking each other in hand with much enthusiasm when they manage to either catch or be caught.

Following the stream, I pick up pace as it does. The noise that's been in the background the whole time is revealed to be that of a waterfall. It's a lively one with a sharp but short fall. The bank that runs down beside it isn't steep, although I still have to hold on to my bouncing breasts as I speed down it.

Once the ground levels out again, I pad through the grass. I still have my tits in my hands, playing with my nipples. I love the zing I get in my clitoris every time I squeeze.

I wander leisurely, stopping to rest my toes on one of those mossy boulders so I can run my fingers over my vulva. Oh, I want to stay here by the stream, to push my fingers inside of me until I spray the ground with a messy orgasm.

"*Neeta*," the familiar voice whispers at its quietest yet. "*Look up and see me*."

I do look up. A few metres away is the most beautiful thing I've ever seen, and I know it immediately. Holding my breath I close the gap, moving painfully slow so I don't frighten it away.

Splendid pale green wings edged in bright purple. Soft green tails trailing almost to the ground. A Luna Moth! I'm only a few feet away from it when a twig snaps beneath my foot.

I look up in dismay, expecting to see my favourite insect flying away from me. But it hasn't flown at all. What it has done, is grown. I shake my head, wondering at the beauty in front of me. The Luna Moth is my height now. It starts to turn and I hold my breath again, eager to see the creature itself.

What I see is a long leg. A thigh, a hip and curve of a breast, and the softness of a rounded belly. An arm comes into view, then a shoulder, ear, jaw and cheekbone. By the time the woman comes to a stop I'm almost crying. Joy, astonishment, lust and love all wage a war inside me.

But then Amira smiles and I'm left with just two emotions; peace and love.

She holds out her hand and I go to her. Silently, she turns around again, leading me to a forest of deep green leaves. Her fingers twine with mine and she strokes the back of my hand. Just that one small motion ignites a fire in me and lust becomes everything.

Now we're among the leaves, walking quickly. Waxy red cups bow over our heads, dipping, lowering until two stop right in front of us. Amira urges me closer, whispering that the need in my groin will go once we get there.

Rounding the enormous flower, I come to a halt, gasping at what's revealed to me. Amira has let go of my hand and is already fluttering down onto her Peace Lily. I watch her wings vanish, watch her place her hands on her butt cheeks and pull them apart. She's looking at me, so I know she's done it so I can watch the almost black cock disappear into her cunt.

I keep my eyes on her, stroking my clit as I watch her ride it. Her moans make my legs shake. They make me slide my fingers down, make me push them into my aching vagina. My gaze snaps to my flower. I lick my lips, scrambling up the rubbery petal and wrapping my hands around the pale yellow dildo right at the centre. Amira likes cocks, but I don't, and somehow these plants know that.

I waste no time lowering myself onto the gloriously bumpy length. My lips part, my opening stretches, and then my pussy is filled so much it can't take anymore. I start to move, coating the hardness I'm fucking with my juices. Watching Amira fuck her flower while she watches me fuck mine with lazy, lustful eyes makes my breath catch in my throat.

Desperate thrusts, loud grunts, the slapping thud of heavy tits against breastbones. Butterflies that aren't butterflies flutter their multi-coloured wings over our skin, wasps that aren't wasps nip and sting our nipples until we both cry out. And then I'm stiffening, screaming my orgasm into the wind, rolling off the wonderful thing I just fucked and falling backward off the petal.

I sit up, stunned.

The bedroom curtain is fluttering in the breeze coming in from the open window. My long hair, free of the band I'd been wearing when I came to bed, tickles my skin. Amira shifts behind me. The scent of her floral perfume mixes with the lingering smells of the meal I cooked earlier in the night, making my mouth water and my still spasming cunt hungry for more.

"You came home," I breathe as she sits up and cups my cheek, tipping me back until my head sinks into her pillow.

Just before her lips touch mine, she whispers, "I always will."

ON THE LINE

SONNI DE SOTO

Chris Carey sat in front of his computer, trying like hell to take notes on the article he was reading. But his mind was on the phone sitting silently on his bed.

It was 9:13.

Danielle usually called at 9:00.

She was probably busy. He knew that. She had a heavy class load this semester. And, still struggling through her sophomore year, she was about half a year behind schedule at a university that cost more per semester than his entire four-year college education. Not to mention, she was also president of the kinky youth program for all the local colleges. She was busy. He should leave her alone.

But she usually called at 9:00.

He snuck a look at his phone again, the blank screen dark.

He bit his lip and his shoulders slumped in on themselves. Should *he* call her? She always called him. But, if she was busy, it might have slipped her mind.

But, if she had lost track of the time, didn't that mean that she probably didn't have time for him?

Maybe he should just wait. He didn't want to disturb her and she would call him when she was ready, he was sure. So he dragged his eyes back to his computer and the notes he wasn't taking, trying not to mentally will his phone to ring.

But he could feel each minute tick by—fourteen, fifteen, sixteen, seventeen—each sixty-second increment making more of an impact than any of the words in front of him.

With a frustrated grunt, he set aside his laptop.

This was ridiculous.

Danielle was his girlfriend.

If he wanted to call her, he could call her.

He didn't have to wait for her.

Decisively, he reached for his phone and began to dial.

She answered on the first ring. "Twenty minutes past nine." Danielle tsked. "I always wondered how long it would take for you to call me." Even over the phone, he could practically hear her shrug. "Twenty minutes sounds about right."

"So this was a test?" He raised an eyebrow, not sure he liked the idea of that.

"Not a test, per se." Her throaty voice was a soothing purr that, despite his efforts, did calm his irritation. Which was kind of irritating in and of itself. "More of an experiment. To shake things up a bit."

"Shake things up how?" He harrumphed back against his headboard.

"We're in a rut, Christopher." She sighed with an audible shake of her head. "We've got to Columbus our way out of this."

JANINE ASHBLESS

A rut? They were in a rut? Chris frowned and adjusted his glasses. He supposed that, sure, they'd both been a little tired lately. A little overworked and stressed. But a rut? "How are we supposed to do that?"

"Close your eyes," she urged into the phone.

He huffed a bit, pouting, but did as she asked. It was, after all, a simple request. "Okay."

"Imagine us," her voice whispered in his ear. "Imagine us in your room. On your bed."

Chris let out a sigh and tried. His mind focused, picturing her painted and so-mobile mouth forming her words. He thought about her tongue, slick and sly, as it slid across those lips, leaving a sheen in its wake. Chris let his mind remember the taste of her kiss, an utterly illogical mix of heated want and cool mint.

He imagined the familiar flush that always swept over her cheeks right before he took her mouth, that visible sign of her excitement that never failed to fuel his own. He knew that a blush like that could travel down her neck, her shoulder, her spine in a tickled shiver with the simplest touch.

And then there, in his room, on his bed, in his mind, like magic, she was laid seductive and stretched-out before him. He imagined the dark fall of curls that clouded around her face and shoulders, framing bared, bronzed skin perfectly.

His hands itched to grab the curves of her body. The swell of her sweeping hips. The pointed tips of her delectable breasts. The length of her long legs. The soft spread of sun-ripened skin, that always held the sweet scent of citrus, over the generous lushness of her body.

He could hear his own breath rasp as his mind transported her from her dorm room to the foot of his bed.

"Good," he heard her coo in his ear. "Now that you have me there, whatever will you do with me?" Her mockingly naïve tone left him feeling provoked and promised.

"I want you naked."

It had just slipped out without him realizing it. To be honest, he hadn't even noticed that he'd conjured Danielle wearing her favourite pair of rubber duck covered panties, those tiny, yellow quackers taunting him in his fantasies.

He heard her laugh. "I'm not already naked?" Her chuckle lowered. "What am I wearing?" she asked in a husky tease.

"Silk stockings, stilettos, a lace thong," he grumbled, not about to tell her what his mind had actually given her.

"All right." Her tone sounded like she approved of his costume choice. "So take it off," she told him. "With your teeth."

Chris paused, his face heating.

He didn't actually know what she looked like naked.

Not completely.

They hadn't done that yet.

He'd seen her topless. He'd seen her without her pants on. Once, during a matinee movie, he'd spent one-quarter of a film with the knuckle of his left index finger slowly stroking the cottony crotch of her panties, covered only by the darkened theater, her knee-length skirt, and his coat.

"Am I naked yet?"

Oh, yeah.

"Um." He coughed and ruffled his short, red hair. "No, not yet." He pushed his glasses further up his nose, feeling his face flush a shade closer to his hair.

"Good," she said breezily. "I want you to tell me when you do it. Tell me *how* you do it."

41

How?

He paled.

How was he supposed to tell her how he would strip her when he'd never actually done it? And wasn't he supposed to be doing this with his teeth? He couldn't talk if his mouth was full of lace and silk, could he?

He swallowed hard. Uh. "I go up to you and I take off your clothes." He hated how it sounded almost like a question.

"Jeez, slow down, speedster," she scolded. "Get in the game. Phone sex isn't a *wham-bam, thank you, ma'am* sport. Go slower. Describe it to me."

He sighed and squirmed. Jeez, he didn't know how to do this. Talk dirty. It was one thing to read stuff like that. Much different to watch it in a video or imagine it in his head. But right now, with all this expectation bearing down on him, he felt stupid, choking on all these unsaid words piling up at the back of his throat.

"Okay, fine." She sighed. "I'll start us off. But," she added, her tone haughty as a grade school teacher, "while I describe me getting naked, you have to get naked too. Like in real life. Right now. Okay?"

He bit his lip. He looked around his empty attic bedroom. He knew his parents and sister were somewhere downstairs. Probably watching TV or something. He had privacy. No one would know what he was doing. He sucked in a steadying breath. "Will you get naked too?"

She paused as if shrugging. "Sure, why not?"

He nodded. "Okay." He'd do it. Like she'd said, why not?

"That's the spirit! Okay," she said, sounding eager, "so I'm sitting on your bed, kicking off my heels."

Chris winced and quickly adjusted his initial image to fit the one she was describing. And, though a part of him ached at the loss of those cheeky ducks, imagining Danielle slither and sway in silk and lace definitely held its own appeal.

He fought a grin as the small swath of lace that covered her mound hugged her hips in bright, happy yellow. He did smile at the jaunty orange bow that stared daring back at him with fowl defiance.

"You climb over me with that look in your eye," her breathy voice continued. "You know, that one you get right before you're about to do something really naughty. That *I've got an idea and you might not like it, but I sure will* look. You start to reach for your belt to undo it." She paused. "Are you doing it?"

Chris peeked down at himself. He was wearing drawstring sweatpants. No belt.

But he supposed, if he could re-dress his fantasy version of Danielle, he could do the same with the fantasy version of himself. He shrugged. "Yep." He reached for the drawstring of his sweats, struggling with the double-knotted bow.

"Good," she said, sounding as if she were settling back on her bed, settling back into her story. "As you tug at your belt and pants, you lean down to grab the edge of my panties with your teeth, tugging them down my hips. I have to lift my hips and wiggle a bit while you pull, but you get them down my thighs and knees and ankles before tossing them off to the side."

He heard rustling on her end and wondered if she too was taking off her clothes. But before he could ask, she continued, "By then, you have your pants kicked off, leaving you in just your shirt and boxers."

He wore briefs but, as he'd always kept his pants on, he didn't expect her to know that. And, at the moment, as he lifted his own hips to slide his sweats off, he really didn't care about the details.

"You grab my hips in your hands and forcefully flip me onto my stomach," she said, her voice hitching a bit. "You run your hands over my back and ass before bending low to kiss and nip at the curve."

Oh yeah. He could practically feel all that full, supple flesh in his hands and on his lips. "Then what?"

There was a pause that stretched into a smile. "Then," she said smugly, "you lean over and bite the clasp of the garter belt open."

His mind stalled for a moment.

Could he even do that?

Did people do that?

That seemed to take an oral dexterity that he didn't think he possessed. It just seemed awkward and physically tricky. "Couldn't I just take it off with my hands?"

"No," she snapped at him. "You can't use your hands because you're stroking yourself with one hand and holding me down on the bed with the other. So you have to bite it off."

Chris shrugged. All right. He still didn't quite understand why he couldn't just take the two seconds to strip her with his hands, but why not? If this was her fantasy, who was he to question it? So he adjusted the image in his head as he tried to figure out whether her garter would have a taste—maybe salty with her sweat or rubbery from the elastic—or not.

"Now stop talking, pay attention, and start stroking yourself," she added, her tone demanding and a little breathy.

He wondered if she was doing it too. Touching herself. He wanted to ask, but didn't know if he should and didn't want to risk ruining the mood.

So instead, he reached down and palmed his half-hard prick through his briefs. It was oddly arousing, this strange bedtime-story game. It was as if two distinct images of Danielle existed in his head. The one he'd conjured, lying helpless and hot beneath him. And the one he knew to still be lounging in her dorm room, controlling the scene and its players like a puppeteer.

His hips jerked involuntarily into his hands. "Now what?" His voice sounded rougher, touched with a little impatience.

"As you pull down one stocking with your hand, you take the other one off with your teeth, tonguing and nipping at my leg," Danielle told him while he pictured her thick thighs, dimpled knees, and strong calves in his hands, against his lips.

He reached inside his briefs, gripping his cock surely in his hands before stroking himself. He moaned. "Then what?" he asked, getting lost in her voice and the images it evoked.

"You tell me," Danielle Atali murmured into the phone as she lounged back in her bed and plucked at her nipples. "I got me naked, just as you asked. What do you want to do to me now?"

Maybe it was mean—it really kind of was—but she wanted to know what he'd say. She knew that Carey wasn't terribly experienced. Not that she was either, but she had more experience than he did. She hadn't had all that many partners, but she hadn't been a virgin in quite some time.

And she honestly wondered what he would say. Was more than a little curious if he would even say anything at all. Carey had problems expressing himself sometimes.

Most of the time, really.

Whenever they would talk about sex or kink or their relationship or where to freakin' eat lunch, he would mumble and stutter before looking to her for answers. And, while she didn't necessarily *mind* making the decisions, a part of her could never really tell if he didn't know how to say what he wanted or if he just didn't quite know what that might even be.

"Tell me." Her voice lowered into a murmured coax. "I want to know what you want."

"I," he muttered into the phone hesitantly, "I don't know."

There was a pause.

A long one.

She opened her mouth to say something, anything, if just to fill the silence. She didn't even know what she would say, but that pause was nearly unbearable.

"I," he hedged, "I want to see you. To look at you. I guess." She could hear him swallow hard. "Send me a pic. So I can see."

Danielle's breath caught.

He wanted a picture?

Like, a nude shot?

She'd never sent one of those before.

Never taken one.

Never even thought about it.

It wasn't like she was ashamed of her body—she was all about body positivity—but, even empowered as she was, there were definitely bits that she was never quite content with. And they all hovered roughly in the vicinity of her naughty bits. Thighs that wobbled and rubbed together when she walked. Hips that jutted awkwardly and never seemed to fit the rest of her. A tummy that seemed pudgy and pooched further out than she'd like.

Even her boobs were weird, cone-ish and small, rather than round and full. She guessed, in her bra, in her clothes, she looked all right. Maybe even reasonably attractive. Hey, after all, she did catch Carey in the first place, right? But that was different than naked.

Naked, all the tricks she'd learned over the years—padded bras and chunky tops to add more balance to her bottom-heavy body—would be gone.

Typically, when she did finally get stripped down with a guy, it tended to happen in the dark with rushed hands and a flurry of lust. They were too busy getting off to notice much of anything.

But, with a naked picture, Carey would see everything. She could hide nothing.

She bit and worried her lip.

"Danielle?" she heard him ask over the other end.

She sighed.

But this was what he wanted. And she had wanted to know that. Wanted to give him what he wanted. Didn't she? Hadn't that been the whole point of this game?

"Gotta make everything complicated, don't you, Carey?" She huffed more to stall than anything. "Well, I'll have to hang up to do it. Call me right back, when you get it," she told him sternly before disconnecting the call.

She could just leave him hanging.

Go to sleep.

Or try to anyway.

But did she really want to?

She knew what he wanted; what did she want?

She held out her phone, letting the image of her face in the phone's camera stare unsurely back at her. The lines of her face were curved and carved in uncertainty. Her mouth moved with a dissatisfied worry that seemed to warn. Even the flush in her cheeks seemed embarrassed for her, for the folly a simple click of her camera could hold.

But, when she looked into the wide, dark eyes that looked back at her on that tiny screen, there was an excitement there that dared her. She had never taken a dirty picture before. Would never have. If he hadn't asked for one.

But he had.

He'd finally asked her for something. And she knew— knew it when she'd hung up her phone, knew before he'd even asked—that, whatever it was, she would give it to him.

Taking a deep breath, she lowered the phone. It was weird, trying to take a picture with her phone like this. No matter the angle she tried, she couldn't get the right one, ending up more often with a mangled zoom of a few parts that never quite looked human, much less like her.

Getting up, she walked to her roommate's full-length mirror. Yes, that was more like it. Striking a pose, she tried again, pushing out her breasts and sucking in her tummy. Did she look at the camera, maybe pouting or giving some come-hither expression? Or did she look off into the distance mysteriously? Or did she just smile like some lecherous yearbook picture?

Maybe *that* was the real reason why people sent so many

headless nude photos. Sure, anonymity was all well and good, but it also meant you didn't have to worry about having a dumb expression plastered all over your face. She already felt like an idiot, exposed and aping at being a pin-up girl while second-guessing every inch of her body in front of someone else's mirror; was it too much to ask to at least be sure her face looked all right?

Fuck it! Fuck all this. He'd just asked for a picture, not some primped-up, perfectly airbrushed porn mag spread. She was sure he'd be happy with whatever she sent. He wouldn't judge her. Not like that. He really ought to be grateful she was doing it at all.

Right?

Taking a deep breath, she steadied the camera, struck her pose, and snapped the picture.

There.

Done.

She took a quick look at it, just enough to be sure all the requisite parts of her—face, tits, mound, and legs—were in it, and sent it off without analysis or judgment. If she looked too hard at it, tore it apart with a dissecting eye, she would never send it off. It would just sit accusing and damning on her phone, never appreciated by anyone other than her.

But, even as her finger pressed *Send*, she longed to snatch it back.

Too late, she thought as she watched her phone's screen grow dark again, waiting for a call she both feared would and feared wouldn't come.

Chris stared at the photo on his phone. Cursing the size of his screen, he tried to enlarge it as much as possible, but all the details were scrunched and fuzzed on the hand-held device.

But she was beautiful.

Curvy. Tanned. So soft and full. His hands gripped his phone harder, imagining the ripeness of her trapped somewhere inside. He squeezed his device as if maybe, through it, he could reach her.

He should call her.

She'd told him to call her *right* back.

But that would mean he'd have to stop looking at her.

And, try as he might, none of the images he could conjure in his head quite matched up to the reality of her.

So, as quickly as he could, he committed the image to his memory, tried to hang on to every curve and line, every texture and weight, of her body. Her nipples, jutting and just a few shades darker than her skin, made his mouth water. Her hips and the barest hint of that big, beautiful ass made his hands tense, made him want to study the slope and scope of those globes. He wanted to explore and map every inch of her, the dramatic dip of her waist, the sturdiness of her limbs, the sweep of her shoulders and the mystery of her mound. He shut his eyes and filled his mind with her, letting his previous image of her fill and round out.

Then he dialed her number.

She answered. He could almost feel her on the other end of the line, but she didn't say a thing. It made him feel uncomfortable, being thrown into the thick air of expectation crackling through the phone.

He coughed.

Then swallowed.

Hard.

"Thank you." He winced. That sounded really stupid, didn't it? Jeez, he should have told her how beautiful she was. How much he wanted her. All the things he wanted to do to her. Do with her. But all he could think to do was thank her.

"Was it okay?" Her voice sounded funny this time. Quieter. Less clear and definite than he was used to. He checked his phone quickly, sure there was something wrong with the connection or something. "Did you like it?"

"Yeah," he told her. "it's great."

There was a long pause. He checked his phone again. There had to be something wrong with his reception or something. "Great," she said finally. There was another pause. "So now what?"

Uh. "What do you mean?" He shrugged.

"Was that all you wanted?" she asked, her voice snapping back into a more familiar tone. "Just to get me naked? Just to look and nothing else?" Her voice wavered a bit as she wondered, "Don't you want to do anything else?"

He wanted to do everything. Everything a person could do to another person, *that* was what he wanted to do with her.

He just wasn't entirely sure what that was. Exactly.

And he certainly didn't know how to say that to her. How did he tell her that he wanted to know the texture and taste of her skin? Wanted to test the taut swell of her flesh with his teeth? That was weird. Wasn't it?

It felt weird. Like desecrating the sacred space of her skin with the slobbering profanity of his tongue. He swallowed again. "What do you taste like?"

"Excuse me?" He blushed when he heard her laugh,

bubbling up surprised and a little bemused.

Was it a strange question? He thought it was valid. It wasn't as if he knew.

"What do you taste like? You know," he shrugged as he let his voice lower pointedly, "there." It was something he'd thought about. A lot. He'd always imagined that a woman would be wet and warm there. Maybe sweet, the way porn always made it sound, like honey that lingered thick and rich on his tongue. Or salty perhaps. He wondered if she would taste bitter, the way his own come had been the times he'd tried it.

"I don't know." Her almost chiding tone made it sound like she did think it was an odd thing to ask. Maybe it was. Though why it would be, he couldn't understand.

He wanted to know. "Taste it."

"What?" she all but shrieked into the phone.

"Taste it." Well, she'd asked him what he wanted. "I want to know what you taste like." He always figured that you shouldn't ask questions you didn't really want to know the answer to.

Which was, maybe, why he didn't tend to ask a lot of questions. Didn't wonder too many things too much or too hard.

But she'd asked him. Gave him permission to question. And now he had to know.

"Do it." He gripped his dick more firmly. "Touch yourself." Letting his mind imagine, he stiffened in his hand. "I want you to come and then I want you to taste it. All while you describe it to me."

"Christ, Carey!" Danielle sighed into the phone, trying for an exasperated tone but just sounding turned on. "Give you an inch, huh?" That breathy hitch in her voice made his cock jerk and his body tighten.

"Okay." He heard her twist and settle on her bed. "But you have to strip down too then," she added as if that was a hardship. As if that wasn't precisely what he wanted. He'd been losing patience with the cotton impediment as it was.

Gratefully, he tore off his shirt and kicked off his briefs. "Done," he told her. "Your turn."

There was more awkward shuffling before she picked up the phone again. "Okay," she said, "I'm touching myself."

"Where?" He stroked himself too. "How?"

He could hear the telltale stir of her sheets as she squirmed. "Uh." She swallowed hard. "Um, my right hand is touching my nipple—"

"How?" He wanted to know. To the most exacting detail.

He heard her choke again, the sound strangled as prickled shock stuck in her throat. "Well," she said, "I guess I'm rubbing them. No." She cut herself off. "No. It's more of a flick."

He nodded. Flick. That was good. He could imagine her fingers flicking over her flesh, making the soft, tan peak pucker. "What does that feel like? Is it good?"

"Mmm-hmm." He thought she might have her head thrown back. Maybe she was pressed against the pillows with her neck arched like she did when she was really excited. "It's good," she told him. "I can feel it everywhere. It's making me hot. Wet."

Yeah. He squeezed his dick in his hand, holding himself hard while he fought for control. "How wet is it?" His voice was a gruff grunt. "Your pussy," he corrected, liking the feel of the word on his tongue. The way it felt a little wrong—

uncertain and unsteady—but somehow right too. "Touch it and tell me."

There was another lull on the other end. A heavy hesitation that seemed to stretch on. In his mind, her teeth worried her lip, a familiar and endearing display of indecision before making up her mind. "Okay."

Chris closed his eyes and imagined her hand sliding slowly down the soft swell of her belly, over the curved crest of her hip, across her thigh, and the barely sketched out secret between her legs.

"I'm wet," she told him, her voice reedy and thin. "Very wet."

"What else?" He began to stroke himself loosely again. "Tell me what you feel like. As if," he paused, thoughtful, "as if I was the one touching you."

God, Carey! Danielle bit back a moan and her thighs clenched around her hand. Where the hell was this coming from? Where had he been hiding this?

"Danielle?" His voice was rough with wonder on the other end of the connection.

She bit her lip before taking a deep breath. "Uh." She tried to focus her thoughts on her fingers, what they were doing and what they were feeling, rather than her other more insistent parts. "I feel fuller."

"Fuller how?"

Blushing, she felt herself throb beneath her fingers. Jeez, why was this so hard? She knew the words. She wasn't some repressed priss who shied away from her body or sex or anything. She liked to think of herself as liberated. As a free spirit. This shouldn't be a big deal to her.

But it was.

Made her feel embarrassed. Made her feel vulnerable and unsure.

And aroused to a point beyond all those liberated, unrepressed words.

Her fingers flexed before she curled them over and between her slick folds. "My labia," she began, "are full. Hot and so sensitive. I can feel every touch. Every brush feels so good." Like a sizzle along her spine or a lick of fire over her skin.

"That's good," he told her, his voice an ushering push. "What about your clit?"

Her middle finger grazed her hungry nub, making her hips jerk into the brief glance. The erect flesh sent a jolt, raw and ragged, along her senses. She licked dry lips and gasped. "I'm excited." Maybe even a little too excited. Too sensitive.

"How do you like to be touched?" Over the phone, his voice echoed in her head. "Tell me. How would I touch you."

Oh God! Umm. She squirmed a bit before taking a settling breath. She widened her legs, bending them butterfly-style against her bed. She slid both hands down, one parting her open while the other dove deep. She closed her eyes and imagined.

She imagined Carey, the *real* Carey, as he really was. On his back. On his bed. His glasses slightly askew. His smile, always a little lopsided like he wasn't quite sure if he should, a little wider on his freckled face. His hazel eyes would be hot and hungry, even though he lay back, waiting for her. Hanging on her every word.

He was naked. She knew it even though she couldn't see him. Knew he would be. Because she'd told him to.

She smiled.

She'd never *actually* seen him naked yet, but she'd imagined him so before. A lot. So she knew exactly what he looked like in her mind. Pale and hairless, his chest was sleek. In real life, he always looked skinnier shirtless than she imagined him, but that was okay. If she recalled, his skin was always softer and warmer than she imagined too, inviting her to run her hands along, to hold tight to, and to nuzzle close to the sweet flesh.

His arms were long—his legs too—lanky and firm to the touch. She loved to wrap her hands around his arms and feel his muscles move in her grasp.

Biting her lip with carnal curiosity, she wondered, as she often did, whether the length of him stretched to places she'd yet to see. She'd brushed up against him before. Felt his erection press into her as they kissed. She'd even let her fingers graze him from hilt to tip once, while they lingered in her car parked in front of his parents' place, feeling his firmness while she teased with the idea of just full-out copping a feel, fully testing his dimensions.

So, yes, she was pretty sure she could estimate his proportions with reasonable accuracy. She might be a little off on length. Maybe a little generous on girth. She knew enough and had enough experience to have at least a rough idea on color and shape.

Mostly, she liked to think about what he would feel like. The heat of him as he rubbed against her. The weight and pressure and push of him inside her.

Though, so often, when she watched him, he moved so

stiltedly. Awkwardly, really, as if he were always on the verge of one action before quickly switching to another. Like he was never quite sure what he was doing until he was actually doing it.

But, in her head, in her dreams, he was any way she wanted him. Did whatever she wanted.

So what did she want?

"Danielle?" he asked. "Are you still there?"

"Of course." She flushed a bit at where her thoughts had been and how flustered they made her. She shook her head. "Now hush," she sniffed as she hid her embarrassment beneath some sass, "you're interrupting my train of thought."

"Sorry," he apologised quickly. But she thought she might have detected a bit of a laugh touching his tone.

Ignoring it, she cleared her throat. "Where was I?" She nodded. "Oh, yes." She continued their collaborative fantasy. "I'm still on the bed. Face down, right?" For accuracy's sake, she flipped over onto her stomach on the almost-too-firm dorm mattress. She shimmied down to hang half off the bed, her feet touching the scratchy carpet of her room, before settling into the image. "You grab your belt from the floor and look at me with that *you're gonna get it* look in your eyes and say…"

"You've been a very bad girl."

She rolled her eyes. "Way to be unoriginal, Carey." She playfully groaned. "That was so predictable; everyone says that."

"For a reason." She listened to him rummage on the other line. "Classics are classics because everyone loves them."

She laughed. She liked that he could make her laugh. She heard a crash coming from his end. "What are you doing?"

"You said I grabbed my belt," he answered as if it should have been obvious. "So I'm grabbing my belt."

God, she shouldn't be so excited about the fact that he was playing along, but she couldn't help it. All right, she thought, let's see where we can go.

"You fold your belt in half, holding the two ends in your hand." She wiggled her fingers in place beneath her, pressed between her mound and the mattress. "You swing it back," she said, her voice climbing like some demented baseball announcer while her fingers began to play over her labia and clit, "and smack me across the left cheek of my ass."

She jerked when she heard the echoing crack from the other end of the line.

She lost her breath.

She knew that sound.

Intimately.

The arousing sound of leather meeting flesh.

Suddenly, the image of him on his bed, with one hand on his cock while the other slapped the folded belt against his thigh superimposed itself into the fantasy she'd created. As if the two scenes were happening simultaneously, feeding into each other.

"You smack me again." Her fingers rubbed faster and harder against herself, seeking even more friction, more sensation. "Again and again. First one cheek, then the other." With every word, she could hear that belt strike in her ears, her mind remembering the feel of that sound on her body, filling her with its rich memories.

"Do you beg me to stop?" His voice was a gritty grunt.

"No." She shook her head. "I beg for more."

"So I give you more." Then the line filled with the crack of that belt and its connecting sound.

"Oh God." She moaned while the images in her mind collided as surely as that leather. That was so hot. "Keep going." She felt every strike on his body like an echo in the heart of hers. "What comes next?"

What came next?

Chris bit back a chuckling moan and tightened his grip on his cock. "I set aside the belt," he said as he did so, despite her disappointed sigh, "before I grab your ass in my hands." Her cheeks would be warm, burning beneath his touch. He pictured his fingers sinking deep into that firm flesh while she moaned, pushing into his grasp. "I grab you by the hips and pull you closer, so your ass is flush against me. My cock grinding against you."

God, he wanted to fuck her. Just sink deep inside and find his release.

But he reminded himself with a shake of his head that this fantasy wasn't about his release. He wanted hers. Theirs. Together.

He cleared his throat, trying to refocus his thoughts. "With my hands still on your hips, I pull you onto my lap, so you're bent over my knees." So that ass would be upturned and accessible.

He wondered if her tummy would feel soft and vulnerable against the strength of his legs. Or if her nipples would jut and poke his thigh.

"Have I been bad again?" Her voice was filled with husky humor.

Oh yeah. "Very. Sending naked pictures." He tsked. "Talking dirty. Getting wet."

"Jeez, I *have* been naughty. Well," she said on a sigh, "in for a penny…" She giggled. "I wiggle on your lap, sliding a bit so I can give your cock a lick before wrapping my fist around it."

Fuck.

He gripped his dick a little harder. Like any other guy, he knew the feel of his own hand on his cock very well. But the sound of her voice and the image of her hand, her tongue, on his dick made the familiar feel completely different. Better than the times he'd fantasised about it before. Closer to what he imagined that would really feel like.

"Slowly, I slide the entire length into my mouth," she continued, "sucking deep."

Damn. Much as he didn't want to do it, he had to stop this. He needed to get a hold of himself. He needed to take control of the scene again.

"That feels so good." With one last, regretful tug, he let go of his penis, letting it lay hard and wanting against his stomach. "But don't think that'll make me forget how naughty you've been."

He reached out a hand, holding his fingers tightly and cupping his palm. "With my cock in your mouth, your cry gets muffled while I spank your ass." He brought his hand down, just as he'd practiced for maximum sound and sensation. The hit left his skin burning; he could practically feel the outline of his hand like a brand on his thigh.

It shouldn't have turned him on—he wasn't a bottom—

but it did. The idea of feeling what his fantasy Danielle felt, even as he imagined himself as the reason for it, was inexplicably, almost illogically arousing.

He struck again, this time higher, climbing the length of his inner thigh. He snapped the skin with just the fingers of his hand, held loose so they stung where they connected. He hissed and tensed. "Your whole body jerks every time my hand lands on your flesh." He imagined her supple form wriggle and writhe on his lap. "You always gasp, like you're surprised by the strike, right before you moan." The lusty sound always betraying how much she liked it. "Moan for me." He needed to hear it.

God, the sound she made over the line was almost enough to push him over the edge. Staggered by that sound, the sensations, and the intensity of the scene they'd created, Chris stiffened, reining himself back under control.

He wondered if that sound would have a feel against his cock. It would have to. Even over the phone, he felt it run hot and sharp through him.

Hell, even the short, shallow pants he could hear coming from her struck him like rapid fire. Like the swift, hard charge of her orgasm approaching. Threatening to damn near barrel over him.

He had never seen, never heard or experienced, her coming.

He'd seen her excited. He'd even seen her replete and satisfied. But this was her first climax that he would know. He wanted to know it completely, and worried, if he spoke, he might miss it. "Your turn. Tell me what you need. What do you want?"

"Your fingers." She panted. "I want you to fuck me with

them. Over your lap." The request was short and clipped as if the snipped words were a strain. "With my ass sore. And my pussy wet. You put one hand on my back, between my shoulder blades, then shove two fingers into me." He imagined her on her bed in her dorm room doing just that, punctuating every phrase with the push of furious fingers. "Over and over. No easing. No mercy."

"It's a punishment." Awe and surprise touched his voice at her desire unfolding. "As much of one as the spanking."

"Yes." She moaned as she came, the sound distinctive and unmistakable. Like pain and pleasure and release trapped together. Like an undeniable force moving through her, freeing her.

"Taste it." He kept his voice quiet, reverent, not wanting to miss a single sound. "I want you to suck your fingers and tell me what you taste like."

There was a pause, heavy and thick. As hot as he imagined her body to be. He heard her lips, her tongue, her throat work, a slick slide that felt like a stroke on his skin. "It's hot," she said, her voice a throaty rasp. "Thick. I can feel it smooth on my skin, on my tongue. Like liquid heat."

"What's it taste like?" He had to know.

"Salty." Her husky breath stuck in her throat a bit. "A little earthy. The way I imagine sex should taste like. Like sweat and skin and silk and heat."

Yeah. Chris shut his eyes and imagined it, wrapping his hand around the base of his cock again. Yes, that was how she would taste.

There was a pause as she caught her breath. "So, Carey," she said breathily, aiming for but not quite reaching flippancy, "what do you taste like?"

Chris stared at his still hard cock. Fueled by the kind of daring only a horny dick can provide, he coughed awkwardly. "You could, uh, come find out?"

He heard her nervously chuckle. "Right now?" She laughed again, but the sound was almost rueful. "I can't right now. It's late. And I still have to study."

He knew that. Of course, he did.

But he could hope.

"This weekend then." He'd take the day off work—he could call in sick or switch shifts with someone—and come up to campus to see her. "We could make a day of it."

There was a pause on the other end of the line.

A long one.

He imagined her teeth worrying her pretty painted lips before banishing the thought. It really wasn't helping his situation by dwelling on her mouth at the moment.

"Danielle?"

"I have a biology paper due on Monday and a bunch of stuff that still needs to be done for the kinky market we're holding for the munch next month," she said in a rush. "But, if you're free Saturday night..." She let her words linger between them.

"I'm free." For that, for her, of course he was.

"Good. Then I can't wait to find out for myself." She laughed again, relief as well as amusement tickling in the sound. "Good night, Carey," she said before she hung up on him.

Chris lowered his phone and leaned back on the bed. He let his mind wander and wonder over next Saturday night before gripping himself in his hand again.

Yes, it had definitely been a very good night.

THE BLACK ORCHID

JO HENNY WOLF

The killer followed Poppy Baines into the jungle of Baines' Orchid Conservatory, and the nape of his neck prickled as if death were breathing down on him. It was warm inside the greenhouse, the air humid and mossy. As it crept into his lungs, he could already feel algae sprout up inside him.

It was different from any greenhouse he'd ever seen in any nursery. There were no orderly rows of plants on long tables, no clusters of plants grouped in squares with others of their variety. This was chaos, and he was following Poppy Baines on a narrow path straight to the heart of it. Butterflies fluttered like fragile jewels between trees and tall plants. The inside of her conservatory resembled a rain forest, but the stuffy silence —the missing sound of birds and mammals—turned this into an eerie imitation. There was a mucky undercurrent in the air. It was like following Poppy Baines into the green, shadowy underworld.

He should have listened to his gut and brought his gun.

But this was the British countryside, and he was only going to talk to a gardener. The common cliché saying that the killer was always the gardener was just wrong. Donn knew, because he was the killer. But then, he didn't look like one: too smooth and open in the eyes, with an easy smile, despite looking sharp as a blade in his suit. You just couldn't trust appearances, and maybe there was more to Poppy Baines than met the eye, even if what met the eye was rather gorgeous. Besides, Donn felt more like a watchdog than a hitman at the moment. Someone had made Al Cutrone's son disappear and this was the last place anyone knew he'd been, so Donn had been sent here to track him down.

It had gone against his instincts to leave the gun in the car. With his trigger finger itchy at the thought of leaving it behind, he'd grasped the neck of the bottle of pomegranate tea sitting on the passenger seat instead. It had travelled with him all the way down to Eden at the heart of the Great British Nowhere, a last reminder of the civilization he'd left behind when he came looking for Al Junior. He'd also packed his jackknife. You only send a hitman when you expect a certain amount of dirty work.

Baines' Orchid Conservatory was a Victorian greenhouse in the park of an old manor, and it didn't look like a business. It didn't look like much at all, apart from the jungle showing through the milky glass. He'd rapped his knuckles against the outer door and waited, tapping his finger on his bottle. At long last, a blurry shape had approached the inside door, shrouded with condensation, at the other end of the entry passage.

65

The redhead opening the glasshouse had been unexpected. Too young to be either an orchid collector or the reason he had been sent to this godforsaken place in the middle of nowhere. Too fragile to take anyone out.

"Can I help you?" Her voice, dark and throaty, had momentarily stunned him.

"I'm looking for…Baines?"

"Poppy Baines, that's me."

"You're quite hard to find, Poppy Baines. Your house isn't on the map." He'd taken a sip of tea and waggled his eyebrows. Insolence made him look innocent and cute. And it had worked: she had laughed, a sound that warmed the cold air like a shot of whiskey.

"Well then, you found me. How can I help you?"

"I need a black orchid."

"And why do you think I would give you one?" Tilting her head, she had looked him over.

"This is Baines' Orchid Conservatory, isn't it? I thought you sell them." Donn had pointed his tea bottle at the greenhouse before sucking on the straw again.

"I *breed* them. There's a difference."

"And you do this with your own unlimited funds, I'm sure."

"I don't just give them away to anyone. That's like a death sentence, and I want my plants to live."

Donn could have told her a thing or two about real death sentences, like the one looming over whoever had done away with Al Cutrone's son while he'd been off on a wild hair about black orchids. "So how do I get a black orchid, then?"

"Order one by mail. There's a nice breeder in the

Netherlands, and he has no problem giving his plants away." The smile hadn't left her lips, but she'd moved to close the door.

"How long will that take?"

"A week, maybe two? Really, it should be quick."

"Getting a mail order orchid is like getting a mail order bride, though. If you're okay with not getting the real thing, they're great. But I drove all the way out here to get the real thing." And Al Junior hadn't gone to the Netherlands, that much they knew.

"Old-fashioned *and* into mail order brides? You're a real keeper, aren't you?"

Donn flashed a grin. He liked her gall. "I'm up for grabs, if you're interested."

"Not a chance." She said it firmly, but the corners of her mouth had twitched.

"Your loss. At least share some of your expertise then. I can't be trusted to find the right plant on my own." In truth, he couldn't be trusted at all.

Poppy Baines had looked him over from head to toe as if she was weighing the pros and cons of letting him inside. Pro: he looked good enough to eat, in his prime, and probably less antiquated than the orchid collectors she got to deal with on a normal day. Cons: he was a stranger and a killer. Of course she didn't know that.

"Come on in then," she said, but stopped him as soon as he lifted a foot to step inside. "Don't bring that sticky stuff in here. No sugary drinks in my greenhouse! And careful at the door." She'd watched his every step like he would start smashing pots the minute he was through the second door.

"Watch where you walk. If you step on any of my plants or insects I will make you pay."

"Insects?" he asked, already so deep inside the greenhouse now that the light had turned green and gloomy. He took three large steps to catch up with her. "Like, spiders?"

She stopped and looked at him over her shoulder. "Didn't you pay attention in Biology class? Spiders aren't the same as insects."

"If it crawls and bites, I don't care what it is. I hate it on principle." He halted close to her, pulling his shoulders up to his ears as he examined his surroundings, scanning for anything that fit that description. Between all the green and brown, some smaller pots shimmered white as bone.

"Well, I'm sure there's a black widow somewhere around here…but I wouldn't worry. Most of my minions just hunt down the pollinators. In here, I'm the only one pollinating my orchids."

"I imagined the thing with the birds and the bees going differently," Donn murmured, following her deeper into her green hell. He was almost sure now that she wasn't his target. No killer of any kind would drop hints like she did. He started sweating beneath his wool coat. Poppy Baines just wore jeans and a flimsy cardigan over a tank top, which was much more fitting for the summery temperature in the greenhouse. The jeans shaped her ass nicely, but they were covered in muddy stains and could probably stand on their own when she took them off. Donn wiped his hands on his coat to get rid of the dirty feeling he got from just looking at her jeans.

At last they reached a potting table close to the back (or

so he presumed), and here Donn recognised structure amidst the chaos. The table stood like an altar or a pagan site of worship, flanked by two trees covered in black flowers. Some of them were growing directly on the trees, in hollow or forked branches, some grew in oddly shaped pots hanging from the boughs. Poppy went on tiptoes and carefully plucked one of the plants from its seat, leaves and root ball and all. She set it onto the table and gestured for him to step closer.

"You won't find an orchid like this anywhere in the world," she said in a hushed voice.

Donn bent closer to examine the plant. At first glance, it looked just like any other phalaenopsis, except for its black flowers. Donn had never seen a flower of such a deep, velvety black. The blossoms swallowed light, and it became hard to look at them after a few moments. Donn closed his eyes, and it was then he noticed the quality of the air had changed. There was something old in it, primal, and as he inhaled, it circumvented his brain and went straight into his blood. He blinked.

"Does it…have a scent? I thought orchids were scentless?"

"You're clearly an expert." She rolled her eyes. "Go on, smell it."

Donn obeyed, taking another deep breath. There definitely was a scent. It was familiar, somehow, yet at the same time ancient and wild and unexpected.

"Do you know what it is?" Donn flinched as she spoke near his ear. He hadn't even noticed her coming so close, and her voice, husky like the purr of a cat, was hot on his neck.

"I'm not sure." He straightened. Her closeness made his

blood rush hotter. As she straightened as well, he detected a blossom that must have fallen from above and was now tangled in the coppery thicket of her curls. His fingers itched to comb out her hair and bring it into some kind of order.

"Oh, you will know soon enough." Poppy smiled. Donn's eyes were still fixed on the blossom in her hair. It looked like a misshapen orchid, pale and sickly—and then it moved.

"Um," he said. Poppy Baines tilted her head, and the creature caught in the tangle of her hair crawled towards her ear. She was still much too close to him, and since Donn was at a loss of words, he reached for her hair, but paused before touching it. "You...there..."

Knitting her brows, she looked at his hand, then back up. She didn't step back. "Yes?"

"There's something in your hair...is it okay if I remove it?" At least he'd found his voice again, even if it was hoarser than usual. Poppy grinned, amazingly relaxed for someone with a mutant flower crawling through her curls.

"Go ahead. Try not to squash it though."

It stunned him that she agreed, but not as much as the jolt of electricity as he touched her hair and felt it slide through his fingers. Delicately, he caught the thing in his hand, caging it between his fingers. He extracted it with his breath held, biting his lip as he turned his hand around and presented his catch on his open palm. "What is this?" The heady scent of the flower was still in his nostrils, fogging his brain and turning things fuzzy. It didn't even cross his mind that he was holding onto a monstrous creature, its legs tickling his palm. He longed to feel her hair again, longed to rake through the thick strands and fist them at the back of her head while he pulled her in and crushed her against his chest.

He shook his head. This wasn't right. He never mixed business and pleasure.

"Hymenopus coronatus. It's a flower mantis. I have them to hunt other insects." Carefully, she took the creature from him, leaving his skin prickling from the tickle of her fingertips. She held it up to a branch above her head and patiently waited for the mantis to crawl onto the bark.

Donn cleared his throat. Back to the reason for his visit. "Your orchids are really stunning. I didn't believe it when my friend told me about it. Al Cutrone Junior, ever heard of him?"

Poppy narrowed her eyes, following the slow climb of the mantis as it crawled deeper into the thicket of leaves above them. "He didn't respect my flowers. Didn't come back." She craned her neck and a satisfied smile fluttered across her lips. "There you go, little friend. Eat those naughty little bees!"

Donn had to draw his gaze away from her ass when she turned back to him. He said the first thing that came to his mind—and it had nothing to do with Al Junior. "So if you don't let the bees have their fun with the flowers, how do you propagate?"

"Would you like to watch?"

This shouldn't sound so dirty, yet his body reacted with an unmistakable heaviness in his groin. He cleared his throat again. Flashes of images flitted through his mind. Poppy, naked except for the occasional streak of soil hastily wiped across her thighs, writhing in a bed of flowers. Him, tracing paths along the constellations of her freckles with his mouth. The image was as inappropriate as it was erotic and Donn found that he couldn't unsee it. It trailed across his sight like the streaks of dots you get from looking at the

71

sun too long. He swallowed heavily. "Please," he rasped at last.

Poppy smirked, with a sparkle in her eyes that made him feel transparent and naked. He stuck a finger into his shirt collar to get some air onto his heated skin. It was entirely too hot in this hellhole of a greenhouse.

"Maybe you should take off your coat before you collapse," she prompted gently. Donn's cheekbones burned right through his skin as he followed her suggestion and shrugged out of his coat, folding it and depositing it out of the way on an empty rack attached to the table, while she plucked another black orchid from her tree shelf. She placed it side by side with the first plant. "Mostly, I just split them into clones, since I have already reached perfection with this breed. I used to pollinate though, to get this dark black."

She waved him closer, and Donn followed her order. It was like a reward when she placed her hand on his arm, and another jolt of electricity tingled through him, sizzling hot in his lower belly. The heaviness in his groin increased.

"Give me one of the toothpicks from over there, please," she murmured, leaning closer, and Donn sucked in air like a drowning man who'd broken through the water. His lungs only filled with more of the orchid's earthy fragrance. As he reached for the toothpicks she had indicated, his head was swimming, as if the orchids had wrapped their roots around him like mangroves to pull him under again. His hand, so steady usually, shook. Poppy let her fingers slide along his much longer than necessary when she took the toothpick he offered. He wished she would touch him even longer.

"Alright. Do you see this little thing at the centre of the flower?" Poppy pointed the tip of the toothpick at a black blossom, and Donn bent down to look at it closely. "That's the column. You have to insert the toothpick here, carefully…" She demonstrated it to him, but Donn had a hard time concentrating. "You have to push the tip into the stigma to get it sticky, then pull it out along the anther cap… here. Do you see those little yellow dots? They're called pollinia. The gonads, basically." She pulled the toothpick out of the column and showed him two tiny yellow blobs sticking to it. "Now comes the fun part." With a grin, she moved to the second plant.

Donn swallowed. Poppy's voice turned throatier with every word, softer, and he leaned closer so he wouldn't miss a single syllable. "This time, you want to get the pollinia to stick to the stigma. So you gently—gently—push your pick into the column, all the way to the back…and there you deposit your load." The toothpick came out clean, and she turned her face to smile at him. Her breath tickled against his cheek, warm and damp. Squeezing his eyes shut, Donn tried to get rid of the images of Poppy on her knees, her mouth hot and wet as she sucked his cock into her throat.

"Do you want to try it?" she asked, and Donn wasn't sure if she meant pollinating an orchid or fucking her throat. The answer was the same for both.

"Absolutely."

"Good. Take a toothpick." Poppy indicated a flower and Donn tried to replicate her steps. It was even harder to concentrate now, for Poppy had stepped so close to him that he imagined he could feel the pebbled tips of her breasts against his back. She wrapped one arm around his midriff and slid the other hand along his arm to guide his hand, more like she would show him the perfect stance to fire a gun, not to pollinate a flower. She was almost as tall as he was and her breath condensed hot against the nape of his neck. Donn could hardly breathe, his hands shaking more than ever. He wouldn't even hit a target like this if it was a foot in front of him. Shiver after shiver raced down his spine.

"Just like that," she murmured against his ear, "gently…"

Donn pushed the toothpick with the pollinia deep into the column of the second flower, grinding his teeth to hold back a groan. He tensed his abs against her hand on his stomach, hoping she wouldn't notice him trembling. Tendrils of heat shot out from where she touched him, wrapping around his insides and suffocating him. If she moved her hand just a little bit downward, she would find his hard-on pressing up against the zipper of his pants.

"Good boy," she whispered as he pulled out. The toothpick was clean. "Now you have to come back in six months when the seed pods are ready."

"But…" Donn's thoughts were hazy, but he knew that he couldn't wait six months. "I need the black orchid now." *No, dumbass, you need to find a killer.* Somehow, in his mind, both things had become one, circling endlessly around each other.

Poppy didn't give him room to think. Instead, she dropped her hand to the buckle of his belt, tapping her nails against it. Donn had no time to process this, for she slid her other hand from his arm up to his neck, dragging her nails over his scalp as she raked through his hair. Her lips moved against his ear. Donn was helpless to stop his hips from bucking. "Maybe we should play a game. If you win, you get a black orchid."

"And if I lose?" Fuck, he was hoarse. He couldn't

concentrate with her fingers sliding through his hair and slipping around his throat.

"Oh, I'll think of something, don't worry about that."

Donn's answer came too quick and without thinking. "Okay, let's play."

"Perfect." Poppy reached for something out of a tin on her potting table and showed it to him. It was a piece of soft paper string used to bind up flower stems. Not all that impressive, he thought. Then his brain was flushed out the drain as she clasped his wrists and brought his hands behind his back. "I'm going to tie your thumbs together, and you won't break that tie if you don't want to lose the game, okay?" Her fingers were hot as she encircled his thumbs in her grip, and Donn's throat went dry. He would be at her mercy, completely helpless without his hands. This meant offering himself for the taking, and he wasn't entirely sure that the nature of her taking was benign.

"Okay," he rasped. A paper string wasn't that hard to break. At least he hoped so, but when Poppy had tied his thumbs together, he tested the hold of this binding nevertheless. It was loose enough so he could slip out, but that also meant he had to take extra care not to lose it accidentally. Poppy turned him around.

"Did you know that mantises are cannibals?" she asked, looking him up and down as if she contemplated eating him. He nodded, feebly. Poppy continued, "The females eat the males when they don't get away fast enough after mating. But they're still ready to risk their lives for a fuck. Interesting, don't you think?" She traced the bulge of his straining cock with the tip of her finger, and Donn opened his mouth. No sound came out. She tilted her head, an amused smile crooking her lips. Her eyes were as green as the filtered light inside her glass house.

"Your mouth is pretty useless, isn't it? We should give it something to do."

He clapped his mouth shut. Poppy's grin became devious. She stepped so close he could feel her heat burn through his clothes, so close that he could see her skin shimmer. He thought she wanted to kiss him, but she bent sideways and picked something else up from the table.

"Open up..." She twirled a black orchid blossom between her fingertips. Donn hesitated. "Don't worry, they're not poisonous," she said, tipping the flower to her own lips.

"Do you want me to eat it?"

"Of course not. I want you to open up and hold it in your mouth while I do...other things. And don't you drop it, or it's game over."

Donn flexed his hands behind his back. His pants were growing tighter. He would be so vulnerable like that, but his blood simmered, pulsing in his groin, whispering to him to give in and let go. Surrendering, he opened his mouth and allowed Poppy to gently push the blossom between his lips. It tickled his palate, his tongue, filling his whole mouth with its petals. Donn forced himself not to bite down against the fuzzy sensation. The blossom would offer no resistance if he did. It was solely his responsibility not to break it, his responsibility to keep his mouth open no matter what Poppy did to him. Saliva gathered behind his teeth, and he curled his lip inwards to keep from drooling. The scent of the flower filled every hollow of his skull as he inhaled, and on his tongue, the petals were as velvety soft as a woman's sex.

All of a sudden, the odd familiarity of the scent made

sense, and it hit him like a hammer. It smelled of sex. Of cunt. Its taste filled him to the brim and overwhelmed his senses, rushing through his veins and straight down to his prick. Moaning, he thrust his head back, grabbing the edge of the potting table to keep on his feet as his knees threatened to buckle. He made the most ridiculous sound when Poppy Baines cupped his cock through his pants and squeezed.

"Think of that flower," she warned him. Had it not been for that, he would have swallowed the blasted orchid the very next moment, when Poppy undid his belt, then his pants, and worked his cock free of its prison. "Nice."

She stepped back, examining him like the specimen of a rare plant. Something in her eyes had him on edge, and Donn prepared to be taunted for being so easy. His cock didn't care about his humiliation though, jutting out recklessly. Wobbly, he spread his feet apart to keep his pants from slipping down and pooling around his ankles.

Poppy shrugged out of her cardigan and dropped it to the floor between them, and Donn stopped breathing when she sank to her knees. *Fucking hell.* He looked down at her, dripping drool from his mouth and almost losing the flower. She was rigging the game, and not playing by the rules at all...not that they had specified any rules beyond *don't drop the flower*. It had seemed simple enough a moment ago, yet when Poppy parted her lips and breathed onto his cock, then dragged her tongue across the tip, wetting it, it turned into an impossible challenge.

The only thing harder than holding still was his cock. Tension coiled between his pelvic bones, drawing every bit of his conscious mind down into the roiling vortex of need smouldering there. He wanted Poppy's soft, red lips around his shaft, and he longed to push deep into her throat, like she was an orchid and her mouth the vessel to receive his seed.

As Poppy pulled away from his throbbing cock, Donn moaned in protest, but it turned into a gasp when she pulled her tank top over her head and bared her breasts. Her nipples were hard and rose-coloured, and Donn wished he could touch her tits and brush his thumbs across the tips until her lips parted in soft sighs and needy mewls. However, he was condemned to suffer, his mind kindling his lust, forced to remain still if he didn't want to lose the game. He began to wonder if a job was even worth this torture. Definitely not, he decided, when Poppy leant forward again and swirled her tongue around his cock. No torture could be more effective than her mouth. It was wet and warm and commanding, coaxing the first droplets of pre-cum from him in no time.

Donn rolled his hips, willing her to take him in deeper, but no moaning or gurgled begging swayed her. She took him halfway in, sucking hard, then released him again, grinning like a cat while he panted frantically and cursed her in silent, impotent desire. He longed to sink his prick all the way into her mouth, into her throat, holding her there to feel her convulse and heave around him, but he didn't dare to break the string that bound him.

"You like that, don't you?" Poppy said, her voice a throaty purr. She enclosed the base of his shaft with her hand, stroking up and down. Slowly.

Donn nodded hard, tilting his hips to get his cock back to her lips. His jaw hurt from stretching his mouth open for so long, and he was close to spitting the flower out. He wanted to spur her on with crude words, wanted to beg, wanted to sob, and it all accumulated in a ragged growl when she sucked him into her mouth again, deeper this time, to the back of her throat and deeper still. Her tongue teased his balls while she gorged on his length. The tension in his abdomen coiled tighter, white-hot and blinding, and Donn could no longer breathe as his whole body braced for release. Poppy pulled back, releasing his cock, but it made no difference anymore. With a hoarse cry, Donn came, spurting his cum onto her chest while his world went black. His bones melted; the tension washed out of him, and Donn was ready to dissolve into a puddle.

"You made a mess," Poppy said, but she sounded gleeful rather than disappointed. "Come down here."

Donn obeyed, awkwardly, for kneeling when your legs shook like that was not a matter of grace, but damage-control. Face to face with Poppy, he cast his eyes down. Not the best idea, since it forced him to look at his cum dripping down her tits. His face flushed with shame.

"Good boy." Poppy plucked the flower out of his mouth. It left the taste of sex behind, of a cunt unfurling at the height of pleasure. Donn moved his jaw from side to side.

"Now, clean up."

Her order brought him up short, and for a moment he wondered if he was supposed to break the string around his thumbs. Then it clicked.

He'd never licked up his own cum before. The idea should have made him balk, but instead it turned his insides liquid, soft, and he closed his eyes and bent over her chest. Poppy arched up, giving him better access, and she threaded her fingers through his sweaty hair and guided his head as he dragged his tongue over her wet skin. The taste of his cum mingled with that of the orchid, creating a heady mixture.

There was a tangy hint of pomegranate tea in it; he'd never thought it could be tasted in his seed. Donn licked down from her clavicle, down her sternum, licked her tits, until the wetness on her skin was as much from his mouth as it was from his cum. He licked and sucked her nipples until she sighed and pressed his head harder to her skin, and he didn't let go when she struggled to her feet, so that she had to bow over him. At last he had to let go when she fisted his hair and pulled his head back.

"There's more for you to eat," she said, popping open the button of her jeans. Donn licked his lips, dry from the thirst to bury his face in her cunt. He could hardly restrain himself while he waited for her to kick off her shoes and shimmy out of her jeans. He should be spent and tired, close to falling asleep after his powerful orgasm, but he was pulsing with a strange energy, almost as if he'd overdosed on caffeine. His cock was still half-hard, and growing harder by the minute.

Finally, Poppy stood naked, bone-white amidst the green of her jungle, her hair like a flame. With a smile she lifted her leg, placing her thigh on his shoulder and leaning forward, grabbing the table behind him to support herself. Donn groaned. Kissed her soft folds, reverently, struck with awe. Pressed his nose into the thicket of her curls and inhaled, filling his lungs to bursting. Even so, there was still some of the mossy, humid air left inside his chest, and he breathed in her cunt to replace it.

"Lick," she said. As if he would forget. Tenderly, he lapped at her, tracing her labia first, then parting them and dedicating himself to her clit. He called up his complete repertoire, kissing, licking, suckling, until she writhed above him, and he could see a flush creep over her chest when he glanced up. She was holding on to the table with only one hand, the other buried in his hair and urging him on. Her nails scratched across his scalp, his nape, leaving fiery trails in their wake. If only he could break free from the paper string and dig his fingers into her thighs, leaving marks while he locked her in place beneath his lips. Were they even still playing?

Poppy moaned and wriggled above him, increasingly frantic. His face was wet and sticky from her juices. He gulped it all down, drinking her wetness like the water of life. The ache in his knees and in his jaw didn't matter to him. Even the black orchid lost its significance, becoming as irrelevant as his own lust. What mattered was only her pleasure, her wet cunt under his mouth, her taste flooding and drowning him. He kept going even as she tensed up, clawing at his hair, and a hoarse cry broke from her lips. He kept going as she convulsed, bucking against his tongue and pushing his face hard against her flesh, kept going even as his lungs screamed for air and white spots danced in his vision.

Donn gasped when she yanked his head back at last and air streamed into his lungs, every sensation intensifying with the rush of oxygen, so much so that his cock bobbed and his balls tightened, teetering on the precipice of another climax.

"Good boy," Poppy said, breathlessly, patting his sticky cheek like he was a dog while she disentangled herself from him. Donn's hands itched to grab her, to show her that he wasn't some harmless puppy. He longed to drive his cock home, deep into her cunt, until she moaned and begged for another orgasm.

"Are we still playing the fucking game?" he asked, voice

rough with need. Yet his need had entirely shifted away from the black orchid. *To hell with it.*

"Why, not in the mood anymore? Because your cock tells a different story."

"My cock wants to fuck you till you beg for mercy," he growled. The only thing holding him back from pouncing was a last thread of control, more brittle and fragile than the paper string around his thumbs.

Poppy raised her eyebrows, grinning, and brushed her toe up along his shaft. Donn closed his eyes. The thread that held him back, the last straw of restraint, was ripped to shreds by Poppy Baines' toe against his cock. With a feral groan, he pulled the paper string binding his hands apart and reached for Poppy's hips. She laughed, triumphant, and not the least bit afraid as he grasped her, boring his fingertips into her flesh so hard he would leave bruises. He wanted to leave his mark on her. He wanted to claim her.

Struggling to his feet, Donn pulled her against him. Poppy wrapped her arms around him, squeezing his ass and dragging her nails across his buttocks. He would look like he'd been in a fight with a wildcat once this was over. With his cock pressed up against her stomach, his fingers roamed her back, carding through her hair and grabbing a fistful of her red mane. Her lips parted, showing him the white of her teeth as she smiled and let him pull her head back, willingly baring her throat. Donn kissed and licked her neck, planting tiny bites from her shoulder to her ear, and rocking his hips as she whimpered and rubbed herself against him.

She wanted this. There was no protest, no attempt to stop him, nothing to keep him from whirling her around and bending her over her potting table. Donn didn't know where to touch her first, where to press his mouth or where to squeeze and pluck and tease. He wanted to touch her everywhere, so he just turned her in his arms and pressed her to his chest.

"Do you have a condom?" he asked, mouth close to her ear, one hand cupping her tit and pinching her nipple. She bucked her ass against him.

"In my jeans. Back pocket."

Donn was reluctant to let go of her, but his need won over. Fisting her hair to hold her still, he fished for her jeans. Poppy rolled her hips and pushed her firm buttocks against him, driving him almost insane. He extracted the condom with one hand from her jeans, forcing her to arch her back with the other hand in her hair.

"Convenient," he murmured, ripping the wrapper open with his teeth. He no longer cared for reason or caution.

"I use them to gather samples," Poppy said, but she didn't explain further. Donn had no mind to listen anyway. He had to let go of her to roll the condom over his erection, and his own touch was already enough to bring him to the edge. With the condom in place, he lined them up, and drove his cock into her with brute force.

Poppy gasped and bucked like a horse, and Donn grabbed her hair harder. Her curls entangled him, red, silken tendrils, pulling at him like her velvet cunt. He was the one to take her, and he was the one being consumed, swallowed up by her, drowning in her. He was rough and hard and commanding, yet she met every thrust with equal fervour and the jerking of her hips. She even spurred him on, panting "Harder!" and "Deeper!" as his thrusts drove her against the table and her feet scrambled for purchase. There was no art left in this, no skill. Donn rutted against her in pure, animalistic greed. They rolled in the dirt, smeared with sweat and soil, and Donn didn't even care. Poppy knocked over the black orchids sitting close to her head as his thrusts whipped her on.

His climax was a wave of primal force, washing over him just as Poppy's core clenched around him and she cried out, convulsing hard and beyond any control. Donn's eyes rolled back into his skull and he collapsed on top of her, boneless. Poppy still rolled her hips, leisurely and without need, while Donn breathed against her neck. Brushing her damp hair aside, he pressed kisses between her shoulder blades.

"You alright?" he asked, his tongue thick and useless in his mouth, scrambling the syllables of his question.

"Yes." Her voice still had that feline lilt. As if she was still far from done.

Donn pushed himself up and stepped back, discarding the condom and pulling up his pants. A butterfly, glittering in emerald green, fluttered down from above and landed on her naked shoulder. Poppy didn't seem worried about her nudity, and Donn averted his gaze to offer her the privacy to dress.

There were more butterflies swaying in the air around them like drunken fairies. Donn watched them dance, shivering at the thought that it was probably their sweat that attracted them. Butterflies were nothing but fancy scavengers. Donn's skin itched. A large, bright blue butterfly fluttered close by his face and drew his gaze toward the thicket of plants behind him. Amidst all the green and black, there were those dots of white; planters holding more orchids. Donn stepped closer.

He'd noticed the bone-white planters before, on his way

into the heart of Poppy Baines' jungle, but he hadn't noticed what they were. They were shaped like human skulls, with orchids growing out of gruesome cracks in their crania. There were tiny orchids growing from empty eye sockets, and larger ones growing from jaws propped open in silent screams. It was morbid, and despite the heat, Donn shivered. Something about the planters was all wrong. Why bring a reminder of death to a place frothing with life? As if life itself wasn't enough to remind you of its inherent mortality.

Glancing over his shoulder, Donn checked if Poppy was already dressed.

She was leaning against the potting table, still in the nude, letting butterflies feed off her skin. A prickle started at the base of his skull. He flinched when she suddenly moved, bending down and picking something up.

"Huh, how did you get up here?" She talked to her hand like she would talk to a pet, or an old friend. Donn inched closer, against the warning hum of his nerves, and the silent screams of the skulls behind him, urging him to run.

"How did what get up here?" he asked.

Poppy extended her hand, presenting him with a black beetle.

Donn froze. "Are you breeding them, too?" He tried to sound casual. His working knowledge of insects might be narrow and mostly confined to what could kill him, but he knew his skin beetles. They could clean a corpse of flesh in 48 hours.

"Down in the vault, yes. There's a beautiful old vault beneath the greenhouse…interested in a tour? Your friend took one too."

Donn licked his lips. The skulls behind him whispered, a

constant rustling warning him of following Poppy Baines into the Underworld. Down there was a different kind of life. Swallowing, Donn forced his lips into a sore smile. "I think I'm running out of time. I should leave."

"Too bad." Poppy pushed herself up and stepped closer. She was stark naked and as non-threatening as anything, but she held one hand slightly behind her back, and that was enough to set off alarm bells in Donn's brain. His jackknife was stuffed into the pocket of his coat, but it could just as well be on the moon, with Poppy blocking his way.

"I guess I'm not getting that orchid?" He retreated further, inching away from the goddess before him. The skulls' whispering grew into a hiss. Donn resisted the urge to look at them. Taking his eyes off Poppy Baines was too dangerous, even for a second.

"You'll have to come back in six months. Then we'll see if you get one or not." Her voice was dripping with thinly veiled hunger. She was ravenous, and it wasn't his cock she wanted to put on her menu. He took another step back, nearly stumbling over a root breaking through the soil on the ground. For a split second, he thought the twisted root was reaching for him, trying to ensnare him, to capture him for its mistress so she could devour him.

"Maybe you should make a note with my name on it so you remember me. I mean, you didn't even ask for my name, despite…" He trailed off. She hadn't asked for his name. She'd sucked his cock and fucked him into oblivion, and the whole time she had not once been interested in his name. The skulls started screaming again. Something clicked into place, and Donn knew with lurid clarity why everything about those planters was so wrong, so upside down.

They were all distinct.

They hadn't come from one mold and hadn't been artificially made. They were real.

"I'm Donn," he offered, hastily, backing away. "Donn Black." Something as simple as a name wouldn't have kept him from finishing a job, but maybe it would give her pause. In his mind, he saw her already attacking him, naked as she was, and saw them both rolling through the dirt in a fight to the death.

Poppy halted, cocking her head. The butterfly on her shoulder opened and closed its wings like a giant eye, blinking at Donn. "I think I will remember you, Donn Black," she said.

Run, the skulls urged him, but Donn stood rooted to the spot. He'd killed enough men up close, in cold blood, face to face. The rush of adrenaline was familiar, the heightened clarity of his senses, the tension in his every muscle, the intimacy of the moment when he was eye to eye with the man whose life he was going to end. He knew all that, and yet he wasn't prepared. Poppy Baines looked too soft to be dangerous and yet she was exactly like him.

There was something fundamentally different between the two of them, though. It was a job for him. Something he did because he was good at it and it made good money. The bloodlust in Poppy Baines' eyes was more profound. Instinct, running deep inside her veins like an ancient current of water running beneath the ground. His heart beat harder. He didn't want to kill Poppy Baines, no more than he wanted to end up like Al Junior and become one of her orchid planters.

"I'll come back in six months, Poppy Baines. I will."

"I'll wait for you."

She no longer followed his retreat then, and after a while, he dared to turn his back to her as he walked slowly towards the exit. He listened into the silence of her greenhouse, keenly alert for every rustle, every crack of a twig. Only when he stepped out into the late afternoon, did he dare to breathe again. It had been cold when he ventured into the depths of Poppy Baines' orchid conservatory, but now, the air carried the first, warm hint of spring.

FIREWORKS

LILY HARLEM

Alice stared into the distance. The tide was out, and the gentle ebb and flow of waves was only just audible from where she sat on a towel by the pier. She hadn't planned to come to Blackpool this weekend, but Julian was here for a conference so the trip was a free ride and a free hotel, and she'd had nothing better to do.

Plus, as the weather forecast had promised, the sun was shining. The air smelled of ice cream and suntan lotion, and to her right, donkeys plodded up and down with kids gripping onto the saddle handles as if they were on white-knuckle rides. It was an idyllic scene with couples and happy families all around.

She sighed. So why wasn't *she* flooded with happy hormones? Her boyfriend, Julian, was handsome and considerate, romantic at times. She was at the beach, one of her favourite places, and her body confidence was at an all time high after shifting a stone and being a slave to the cross-trainer.

Stretching her legs out, she examined her toenails. She'd had a manicure and pedicure a few days ago, the first one ever, and she liked the scarlet varnish she'd chosen. It was vampish, seductive, sexy, and matched her new bikini—a two-piece was another first.

Something in her heart tugged. After so much effort to look good she wished Julian was with her now, on the beach, to appreciate her new figure. It was all for him. After three years together she didn't want their relationship to get stale. Fall into the trap of being comfortable and letting the weight pile on; become more unfit as the months drifted by. He was a catch. A doctor. 'An eligible bachelor' her mother had called him when they'd first started dating.

A ball skittered over her legs—the blow-up type that could be snatched by the wind and ushered into the distance in a nanosecond. Two small boys raced after it, kicking up sand with their heels. One called "Sorry, miss," over his shoulder.

Alice brushed the sand from her shins and watched them dart between other beach goers, full of excited whoops as they went. Had Julian ever been young and carefree like that? He was always so serious, his mind full of research and drugs, proposals and funding, even at the weekend. She loved him, very much, and would have given up the fancy new handbag he'd bought her to see him like that—building sandcastles, messing about with a ball, playing in the waves. Not a care in the world except the next kick, splash or ice cream.

Lately he'd had a constant frown line between his eyes. She was sure it was permanently etched there like a small crevice. Oh, she knew he had pressure piled on him—funding was never easy to secure and he believed passionately in the life-saving research he was involved in—but still…all work and no play was making Julian a dull boy.

She sat up straight, and swallowed down a bite of bile.

Dull.

Julian was dull?

That couldn't be true. He was serious, yes. He had a serious job, doing something not many people could do. His mind was occupied with important things, not like hers; she just worked as a secretary at a marketing company. He was trying to figure out how to change the world for the better. Pioneering, brave, committed, intelligent, they were words to describe Julian, not dull.

So why did everything feel so colourless? The azure sky above her didn't shine, and the golden sand was muted. Maybe it was she who'd become dull. One of the fifty shades of grey and not in a good sense.

Reaching for a bottle of water, she took a long drink. Although the dullness in her life wasn't nice to admit to, now it had been acknowledged she had the sense of a weight lifting from her, a fog clearing. Alice had no desire to be dull or live a dull life. She wanted rainbows and butterflies, unicorns and fairies. Well, maybe she didn't have to have the unicorns and fairies, but she wanted a life brimming with passion, laughter and adventure. When she was an old lady she wanted to look back with no regrets and oodles of memories.

Feeling fractious and unsettled, she dumped the water bottle back in her bag and stood. She flicked out her towel, sending sand skittering into the air, then rolled it up. After adjusting her floppy sun hat and ramming her feet into flip flops, she made her way towards the pier.

Would Julian be a regret? He was married to his job she

joked with her friends when birthdays, Christmas and Valentine's Day came around each year and an engagement ring was conspicuous by its absence. Joking aside, she was beginning to wonder if it would ever happen.

She stomped through the deep sand, aware of a patch of perspiration forming in her cleavage. Maybe he was simply too busy to take a trip to the jewellers. She'd taken on the job of purchasing his parent's birthday and Christmas presents for him, and booking holidays.

Finally off the sand, she paused at an ice cream van. The long swirl of white sweetness atop a cone and speared by a chocolate flake was irresistible given her mood, and she stood in the queue of three to treat herself.

Besides, a little of what she fancied would do her good. Then perhaps later, when Julian had finished at the conference and they headed out for dinner, her mood would be less bleak.

When it was her turn, she handed over the money, already salivating at the thought of the ice cream melting on her tongue. There was a small commotion to her right; two small dogs had crossed their leads around their owners and there were gasps and giggles as they tried to untangle.

Smiling, she wandered off, licking the sweet treat as she went. She hoped it wouldn't spoil her dinner. Julian had mentioned something, as he'd dashed out of the hotel room that morning, about finding an Indian restaurant.

Curry wasn't her favourite—it used to be, but now she knew the horrific calorie content of the dishes she enjoyed the most she tried to avoid it. But at least she'd have just his company tonight. Last night, at the hotel restaurant, they'd had a drug rep with them. He'd had wonky teeth, a shiny balding head and been full of his own importance. His conversation had drained her, and she wondered if it had drained Julian, too. It had certainly put a dampener on any thoughts of sex before they went to sleep, despite the lavish top floor room and the decadent four-poster bed.

She tugged the flake from the ice cream and poked it into her mouth. After sucking, she pulled it out slowly and indulgently, savouring the chocolate as it swirled over her tongue and the flavour spread. She fluttered her eyelids and sighed.

"You enjoying that, love?"

"Got one here you can suck if you're in the mood."

A group of four men were walking past. Each had on the same t-shirt embellished with the words *Barry's Epic Stag Do*. They were all grinning at her. One put his finger in his mouth and pulled it out slowly as he groaned and clutched his groin.

Alice hurried on, a flush travelling over her cheeks. Really? So immature.

They dissolved into laughter as Alice turned the corner to her hotel. She tutted but then stopped. God, when had she turned into such a prude? It was only a bit of fun, and she had been asking for it, sucking on a flake as though it were a cock as she wandered along the street in her bikini.

A giggle burst up from her chest. She pressed her hand to her sternum, surprised at herself. And then it hit her. When had she last sucked a real cock? Julian's cock? Pausing, she looked up at The Grand Hotel with its long windows, two turrets and russet stonework. She couldn't remember. Certainly not this year. And when had he last...

Crunching into the cone, her belly tightened, and it had nothing to do with the cool ice cream now filling it. A sense of sadness swirled within her and one word screamed into her brain…dull.

It wasn't Julian who was dull, or her, it was their relationship. More to the point it was their sex life.

And that just wouldn't do.

Here she was in the prime of her life, feeling physically great, certainly not a prude, and sex wasn't just not in the cards—the cards weren't even on the damn table.

She dropped the last of her cone into a bin, knowing a seagull would likely grab it sharpish, and pulled on her sundress. There was a parade of shops just down the street, and she had an idea.

Julian would have to forget about going for an Indian meal; she had other plans.

Half an hour later, Alice was back at the hotel. She had two bags with her: one full of tasty nibbles from Marks and Spencer and another with a couple of items from a souvenir shop.

Julian might have wanted spicy food for his evening meal, but he'd be getting spice of a different variety. Alice had reached her limit. Her tolerance for being dull was all used up. Boring was no longer on the menu. Her mother had always told her, if you have a problem, don't complain about it, fix it.

And that was what she was going to do.

She filled the bath, tipping in the entire contents of not one but two of the little bottles of bubbles the hotel had provided. It smelled expensive and citrusy and soon the bubbles reached the top of the tub. Stripping naked, she wandered around the room, her feet sinking in the plush carpet, and feeling confident their room was totally private as it was so high. After putting music on, an old Adele album that always made her feel good, she poured a glass of wine from the mini bar.

Sinking into the bath, the bubbles caressing her skin, she started to form her plan. Julian was expected back in an hour but he'd be late as usual. There always seemed to be one last thing to do. Another meeting, phone call or set of data to record. But that was okay. She accepted this about him and had long since learnt if she didn't let him get the last thing done, the knowledge it needed doing would irritate him all night. A bit like the princess who slept on a pea, he'd toss and turn and be up early with even more things to do because he'd lain in bed thinking about them.

So she had a little over an hour. That was good. She reached for a razor and slid it up her foamy leg. The sun had kissed her skin and the golden glow was pleasing. She repeated the process on the other leg and thanked her lucky stars she'd packed the skimpy new black lace nightdress she'd treated herself to. Tossing the razor aside, she sipped her wine. Had she subconsciously known things needed taking in hand? That her sex life had to change, as did Julian's preference for a cuddle and sleep after a long day?

Well, this was make or break. He'd either accept her plan and surrender to her, or he'd shun the idea and refuse to remove the professional veneer he showed to the rest of the world.

Alice couldn't deny there were butterflies in her belly as she lifted from the bath and dried off. It was a risky plan, but she had to go through with it. Continuing in this colourless relationship wasn't an option, and as it was, she didn't know if she wanted the longed-for ring to be slipped onto her finger. If this was their honeymoon period, the time in their relationship sex should be exciting and fun, then what did the future hold?

Yes, she was going to take the matter in hand, literally. She could only hope their love was strong enough to survive having their sex life thrown up into the air and seeing how it landed.

She slathered cocoa body butter onto her legs and torso, rubbing it into her buttocks, too. Her skin tingled from the hot water and the sun as she smoothed the cream across her chest and over her nipples. They were tight and pointed. Thinking about sex had created a chain reaction within her body.

Perhaps she'd instruct Julian to rub cream over her breasts later.

Would he do as she told him?

Would he surrender to her and let everything else in his world slip away, leaving his submission to her the only thing on his mind?

God, she hoped so.

Before long, Alice was dressed in the new black negligee. It was silky against her skin, the lace bra section doing nothing to disguise her hard nipples and the frill around the base only just hiding the fact she wasn't wearing underwear. Glancing in the full-length mirror, she went up onto her toes, elongating her legs. Damn, she'd look better in heels.

After a quick rummage she found what she was looking

for—the sexy stilettoes with the silvery heels she'd worn with jeans the night before.

Perfect.

But the look wasn't complete. She needed to fully transform from a ready-for-bed-girl to a woman who was going to take what she wanted and demand obedience.

With a fluttering stomach she battled with a desire to throw the whole idea out of the window and hide her purchases in the back of the closet. Steeling her determination, because she hated the thought of failing to do something she'd set her mind to, she grabbed her makeup bag. It only took a few minutes to add a sweep of powder, a stroke of mascara and a slick of *To Die For* red lipstick.

A pack of bobby pins called to her, and she swept her hair up, stabbing in the pins haphazardly to create a tousled up-do. Gone was the slick shoulder-length brunette hair, and in it's place was the just-fucked-look.

She smiled and downed the rest of her wine.

As she poured another glass, she heard a click.

Julian.

He was back sooner than she'd expected.

Quickly she turned off the bright over-head light and sat in the plush plum-coloured chair by the window with her legs crossed. She assumed the relaxed position just as he opened the door.

"I'm sure it will be fine with Alice, she always enjoys meeting my overseas colleagues."

Fuck.

He had someone with him. A colleague. Of all the times...

Alice's heart skipped a beat, heat roamed over her chest, neck and cheeks. Fight or flight?

Of course she did neither, she just sat here, dumbly, looking like a sexy nympho awaiting her boyfriend.

Which, of course, was exactly what she was.

Julian's eyes widened when he saw her. His jaw dropped open and he scanned his gaze from her toes to her head. But his reactions were quick and he backed up, taking whoever was a step behind with him.

The door shut with an alarming slam.

Alice swallowed. She was going to be sick, she was sure of it. The ice cream and wine was all going to show itself again any second.

But she didn't move. Instead she sat there, swinging her stilettoe from the end of her foot. There were voices outside, but it was impossible to hear what was being said.

Eventually, after what felt like a lifetime but was probably only a few seconds, the door opened. Julian stepped in, his navy suit and silvery tie as pristine as when he'd stepped out that morning, and shut the door. He leaned back against it and glanced around the room. "I…er…sorry about that. I didn't expect you to be…" He gestured to her then ran his hand through his hair so it stuck up messily.

Alice thought the ruffled look suited him.

"You didn't expect me to be what?" She tipped her head.

"I…er…half dressed." He nodded at her.

"I'm perfectly clothed." She stood and smoothed the negligee over her waist and hips. "For you, but not for your work friends."

"Jose is from—"

"Shh…" She walked across the room, sashaying as she

went. "I'm not interested in Jose." A thrill went through her when his attention slipped from her face and down her body. "In fact, I couldn't be less interested in Jose, so what you need to do is get rid of him." She stopped a foot from him.

"But...I told him he could join us for dinner."

"Oh no." She shook her head and raised her eyebrows. "There will be no one joining us tonight. I'm refusing to share my boyfriend this evening." She paused for effect and lowered her voice to a sexy drawl. "Tonight you're all mine."

He swallowed, his Adam's apple bobbing against the collar of his white shirt. He had a sprinkle of dark stubble around his jaw and over his top lip, and his dark eyes were tired, the usual crease nestled between them. But also, she noticed, there was a sparkle in the depths of his irises. It was only small, admittedly, but she had his attention, of that she was confident. Perhaps she could tempt that spark to grow into a fully-fledged flame.

"All mine," she repeated. "To do with as I please."

"Alice, I—"

She pressed her index finger over his warm lips. "Get rid of him...now. I don't care what you say as long as you do it."

He stared into her eyes.

"Tell him your girlfriend wants her wicked way with your body if that helps?"

He wrapped his fingers around her wrist and moved her finger. Swept his tongue over his bottom lip and then bit on it.

"The sooner the better," she said, nerves dancing in her belly. Damn it, what if he refused? What if he wasn't going to play her game?

He pulled in a breath; it held a slight edge to it, as if his emotions were pinging around inside of him.

Alice smiled as seductively as she could manage, then turned and walked to the dressing table. She retrieved her glass of wine then went to stand at the window, giving him a good look at her ass, only just covered by black silk, and her legs elongated by her sexy heels.

She stared out at the sea and willed her hand not to shake.

There was a click, the curtain moved a fraction, then the door shut.

She blew out a breath. He'd gone to speak to Jose. The only question was what would he say?

It took effort to push a negative thought from her mind about him heading out to dinner with his colleague and leaving her there. She didn't want to entertain the possibility. It would knock her confidence, and their relationship, to Timbuktu.

The wine was mellow and a little warm, but she sipped it, letting the melon and peach undertones spread on her tongue.

Just when she feared tears might spring to her eyes, the hotel room door opened again.

Thank goodness.

Turning, she rubbed her hand over her waist, showing him what he could have now he'd got rid of Jose, and set the glass aside.

Julian leaned his back against the door and studied her.

"Lock it," she said, nodding at his right hand resting by the handle. "We won't want to be disturbed."

He did as instructed.

She smiled and moved towards him, enjoying the way the

air drifted over her flesh, and her hips rolled. When she reached him she took hold of his tie and began to loosen it.

"Alice, if you'd wanted to go to a different restaurant, just the two of us, that would have been fine."

"No." She pulled the tie free and slipped it from his neck. With a flourish she tossed it to the floor. "It wasn't the restaurant that was the problem, or even Jose."

"So what is it?" He frowned.

"It's our lack of quality time together." She undid the top button on his white shirt, then the next one.

"But you're here, with me, in Blackpool."

"I might be physically with you." She swept her lips over his in a teasing, light kiss. "But I don't have your attention." She released two more buttons then pulled the shirt from his trousers so it hung loosely.

"You do now." He dropped his gaze to her chest.

Her breasts were rising and falling with each breath, her nipples hard points pressing against the negligee.

"Good." She stepped back, enjoying the way he looked all dishevelled now, a far cry from his usual pristine appearance, and how his pupils had dilated. "Go take a shower, Julian."

"What?"

"You heard. Shower, now."

"But?"

"I want you fresh and relaxed." She took a small can of coke from the mini bar then poured it into a tumbler. "Here, drink some of this."

She held it out to him and he took it, his eyes never leaving hers. It was as if he were seeing her anew and she was glad. That was what she'd wanted. Excitement, passion and surprise would put colour back into their sex life.

Julian drank several mouthfuls of Coke, then once again Alice reached into the minibar. This time she stooped in such a way Julian would be in no doubt she wasn't wearing knickers.

He cleared his throat and she stood holding a miniature bottle of Teacher's whiskey. After unscrewing the top, she tipped it into the Coke until the fizzing surface was a fraction away from the rim of the glass. "Have a whiskey with it," she said, setting the empty bottle on the dresser. "It'll do you good."

"It's a little early, don't you think?" He studied the drink then her.

"No, I don't think. And what's more, you're going to need it."

"For what?"

"For what I have planned." She gestured towards the bathroom. "Now go and shower, Julian, and take your drink with you. When you've finished, our evening will begin."

Alice watched as Julian went into the ensuite. He pulled the door closed and that suited her. She had things to do.

After dashing to the bags on the floor by the bed, she rummaged through the one from the souvenir shop. She pulled out a Blackpool pencil that had a long red feather on its tip, along with a straw hat. Circling the hat was a length of purple silk that had *Kiss Me Quick* written on the front. It was held in place with a small blob of clear glue and only took a second to release.

Alice set the items on the bedside locker.

The shower was on and Alice guessed Julian would be quick. She wondered if he had a hard on. If he was keen for the action to start.

Nipping to the mini bar, she poured a sparkling water and drank it in one go. She'd never done anything like this before —gone all stern matron and dominatrix. But she'd give it a good go. Their relationship was worth the effort, worth the time and the risk. They were good together, in love, and she certainly saw a future with Julian.

If she could inject some colour back into it, that was.

The bathroom door opened suddenly and Julian stepped out amidst a swirl of steam. He had a white towel fastened around his waist and his hair appeared roughly dried. He held the empty glass.

Alice tensed and a tug pulled between her legs. Damn she was a lucky girl to have such a fine specimen to play with. Her doctor boyfriend was hot. Broad shoulders, a wide chest with a sprinkle of dark body hair, defined abs and long, lean legs.

She could hardly wait.

"You drank your whiskey?"

"Yes."

She took the glass from him and hooked her fingers into his towel. "How do you feel?"

"Curious."

"Curious? Why?" She tipped her head and raised her eyebrows.

"I'm wondering what you have planned."

She nodded slowly and loosened the towel almost to the point where it came undone. "That's for me to know and for you to find out."

"I can hardly wait." His mouth twitched into a smile and he glanced at the bed. The sun was dipping lower in the sky and fingers of light stretched over the white sheets.

"Is that right?" She tugged the towel and it fell away, drifted to the floor and pooled at Julian's feet. "Mmm. I guess you *are* looking forward to it."

His cock was fully erect and standing proud, the tip shiny, his pubic hair still damp from the shower.

He reached for her waist but she batted his hand away. "Oh no. Tonight is on my terms?"

"It is?" He frowned.

"Oh yes." She linked her fingers with his and led him to the bed. "You don't have to worry about a thing, except pleasure, that is."

"Well I'm not going to complain about that."

She smiled as she reached for the length of silk. So far so good. Julian certainly seemed up for her evening of fun…in more ways than one.

With a snap she flexed the material and held it up.

"Kiss me quick?" Julian said.

"I might, in a minute." She pressed the silk over his eyes then shimmied around him, being sure to let her body brush against his arm. Once behind him she pressed her breasts to his back and tightened the silk. "Close your eyes."

He didn't reply. Instead he hitched in a breath as she tied a double knot and made sure it was secure.

"Very good." She set her fingertip at his nape and slowly ran it down his spine to the cleft of his buttocks. "With the blindfold on you don't need to worry about what you can see. I want you to clear your mind and just feel."

"I want *you*." His voice had a dark, husky tone to it.

It was a timbre she hadn't heard for a while, and she smiled broadly as her body reacted to it—a shiver of want spreading over her skin and a dampness forming between her legs. "I know you do." She slid her fingertip around his waist to his navel and dipped in. "Now lie on the bed, Julian."

He appeared to hesitate, but then did as she'd asked. He stretched out supine, his head on the soft pillow and the sunlight caressing his olive skin. His cock angled upright, and as he settled down he wrapped his fist around it and rubbed gently.

For a moment Alice indulged herself in the sight of him. He was like some kind of Greek god lying there bathed in twilight, unashamedly working his hard cock. She could look at him forever…

But she didn't. Instead she reached for the feathered pencil, kicked off her shoes, and crawled onto the bed next to him. "Allow me," she said, unfurling his fingers from his shaft.

"Alice," he murmured, canting his hips as if seeking her touch.

But she didn't give it with her fingers; instead she set the feather at the hollow of his throat and tickled very gently.

"What?"

"Shh, just feel. Relax, Julian, it's all good."

He blew out a breath, his chest sinking and a groan tagging onto the end of it, before pulling in a deep inhalation.

Alice smiled and ran the feather to his left nipple. She circled it with tantalisingly light strokes.

He shifted his head from left to right. She knew damn well he wanted more.

Moving the feather tip to the right nipple, she repeated

the action. His nipples were always tight little buds so the only way she knew he was enjoying it was by the way his belly was trembling.

Drawn to the quivering muscles, she tickled the feather down his abdomen, and at the same time, she flicked each of his nipples with her tongue.

He moaned and shifted on the bed.

"Keep still," she whispered, knowing her breath would be heating his damp skin. "Keep still and just feel. I'm in charge here."

He didn't reply.

The feather created a filigree shadow on his flesh as she edged nearer his cock. Finally she reached the tip and circled his slit with the end.

He hissed in air between his teeth.

She smiled and enjoyed feasting her gaze on him as he lay there blindfolded and submissive. The feather was a surprisingly effective tool, and as she stroked down the length of his shaft, over a long vein that bulged at the surface, she was pleased with her choice. He trembled and moaned, his cock twitched and his belly tensed and relaxed. On and on she went, flicking it over his tip and stroking it down to his balls.

"Alice…" he groaned.

A satisfied smile stretched her lips. He wasn't thinking about work now. Not even a lingering memory of clinic and conferences. Now all that existed was her and a red feather tickling his cock.

She leaned forward and began to pepper kisses down his abdomen, enjoying the soapy scent that mixed with his unique Julian smell.

When she reached his cock, she discarded her toy and ran her fingers up and down his length, mimicking the actions of the soft feather.

He was breathing fast, with his knees pulled up. She wondered if she should have tied him to the bed.

Maybe next time.

Smiling, she flicked her tongue over his cockhead.

"Ah fuck…" he groaned.

"Not yet," she whispered, then stretched her lips wide and took his glans into her mouth.

He stuttered out a breath and slotted his fingers into her hair.

She sat and shook them away. "No. If you want it, it's on my terms." He didn't have to be in control all the time. This was the whole point of the evening. Him surrendering his need to always be in charge of everything in his life.

"But—" He reached for her again.

"Julian, I will walk away."

"Don't do that." He raised his arms over his head and gripped the slatted headboard. His knuckles whitened and he pressed the crown of his head into the pillow. "Please, don't do that. My hands are here…look."

"Good. Now behave." She wondered when anyone had last spoken to him the way she was now. Usually everyone rushed to obey his commands, fussed over details for him, hung onto his every word.

Well *she* wasn't everyone. She was his girlfriend which made her different.

Satisfied he'd lie quietly, she flicked her tongue over his cock again, then took it into her mouth.

He moaned and jerked his hips, but he didn't grab her

this time. So she went lower, hugging him with her tongue, then lower still. He tasted divine, and the solidity of his shaft in her mouth was something she'd missed.

Her internal muscles tensed. Damn she'd missed his cock in her pussy, too.

She pulled up and gripped his root as she did so. Then sank again. Soon she had a steady rhythm going and he was gasping and groaning, clearly lost to sensation.

Her arousal was growing, and when she tasted pre-cum she knew he was getting close.

But rather than speeding up her ministrations, working him to climax, she pulled back and stared down at his shiny, engorged cock.

"Oh God, you're killing me," he said, releasing the slats above the headboard.

"Get your hands back up there," she said in the sternest voice she could muster. "Now."

He gritted his teeth and clenched his jaw but did as he'd been told.

With one hand, Alice plucked her right nipple through her nightie, and with the other she gently scratched her fingernails up his inner thigh and over his balls.

The groan that vibrated from his throat was low and feral. She had him teetering on the edge. A flick of her tongue, one more stroke, one thrust into her pussy and he'd lose it.

But she didn't want that yet. She wanted some pre-fucking fun for herself. She wanted some oral attention.

It wasn't a position they'd done before, but Alice was in the mood for new experiences. So she moved up the bed and straddled Julian's face, one bent knee either side of his head.

He moved his arms and gripped her buttocks. She

decided not to reprimand him, she liked his touch. "Stick out your tongue."

His cheeks were flushed, the blindfold hadn't moved. He poked out his tongue, offering the flat, wet tip.

To see him like that, with her pussy hovering over his face, and his expression eager, thrilled her utterly.

"Are you ready?" she asked, her heart pounding.

He nodded and held her tighter, raised his head to meet her pussy.

She tipped her head back and moaned as he flicked over her clitoris. The headboard was a great height to grip and she held on tight. Julian was busy with his tongue, swiping it over her pussy, prodding at her entrance. The scent of her arousal drifted up and she shifted her hips, offering him her clitoris again.

Damn that felt good.

He was good.

Her belly tightened as he built up the pressure. She tensed, her knuckles aching as she rode against him, making sure he was hitting the right spot. It felt so rude, so primitive to be bucking against his face, but she couldn't help her wriggling hips. Her orgasm was beckoning.

Holding her breath, she was aware of her pulse loud in her ears. The delicious need for release was almost there...almost.

But no. She wanted them to come together. To be as one.

It took every bit of willpower she had to slide to the right of the bed.

"Alice, fuck, come here and let me finish you off. You taste amazing, I want—"

"No." She was panting. "No, when I say...together."

She stood on shaking legs. She had to stay in control. Tease him for longer, and stretch out the moment.

Wiping her brow, she stared out at the sea. Twilight had turned its surface to bronze and it shimmered like a roughly dented shield. Moisture had made her thighs slick, and her breasts were heavy.

Suddenly two thick arms wrapped around her.

"Enough," Julian growled against her ear. "You've made your point."

She wanted to be angry with him for disobeying her, but right now, she couldn't feel anything other than love and longing.

She turned within his arms and his cock pressed against her belly.

His eyes were wild, the sea reflecting in them, and speckles of perspiration sat on his brow.

"What point?" she asked breathlessly as she gripped his biceps.

"That we're not having enough bedroom fun together."

She nodded.

"That too often I'm distracted with work." The crease between his eyes appeared.

Reaching up, she rubbed it away. "I know you're busy."

He shook his head. "But never too busy to make love to the woman of my dreams."

She smiled.

He didn't. "Forgive me," he said, stepping back slightly and running his hands down her collarbones to the top of her negligee.

"For what?"

"For being neglectful lately, and...for this." He yanked.

Hard. The material split apart, the ripping sound blasting around the room. "I'll buy you another, heck, ten more in every colour they come in. You looked fucking amazing when I stepped into this room earlier."

Alice went to reply but he stooped and pulled her right nipple into his mouth and tweaked the left with his finger and thumb.

She slid her fingers into his hair and sighed. Being in control had been fun, but if Julian wanted to run the show now he could, so long as an orgasm headed her way soon.

Straightening, he captured her mouth in a ravenous kiss and pulled her to him. His flesh was hot against hers, and his arms around her so wide and strong. He tasted of her, and Coke and whiskey. She sagged against him, giving in to it. He was her everything, nothing else existed.

He bent slightly, and the next thing she knew she was in the air.

"What…?"

"You've really started something," he said, tipping her onto the bed. "You know that?"

He landed over her and she was quick to wrap her legs around his waist. "Good, that was what I'd intended." She cupped his face. "I love you. I understand you. But I have to have special time with you."

"I know. And from now on, we'll have so much special time. I promise. I'll never wear those blinkers again or get too wrapped up in work." He curled his hips under, gaining the first few inches of entry. "You're my priority, baby."

She gasped as he stretched her, but kept looking into his eyes. She saw love and passion and also a shard of regret. He knew he'd been pre-occupied, and not the best boyfriend going. But that was going to change and she believed him.

He pushed in further, grazing over her G-spot and taking a smooth ride to full depth. His balls pressed up against her and his body ground over her clit.

Alice struggled to stop her eyes from fluttering shut. That was it. Just there…

"I love you," he said. "I love you so much."

"I love…you too." And she did. With everything that she was.

He groaned and pulled back a fraction before easing in again. "Marry me."

"What?" She opened her eyes wide and stilled.

"Marry me. I can't live without you and…fuck…God knows, you're the only one who can handle me."

"Julian." She ran her thumbs over his cheeks and locked her ankles in his back. Had she heard him right?

"It's not a proposal we can tell our kids about in the future, but damn it, you're the one for me. I can't imagine life without you. I had to say it…and I have to hear you say yes." He pulled back and thrust in again. Then repeated the action, circling over her clit.

"Yes, oh yes…" Her orgasm was there, bright and beautiful, and holding all the colours of the rainbow.

"Yes, you'll marry me?" He was breathless, his cock so hard inside her. "Or yes I'm hitting the spot?"

"Yes, yes, I'll marry you…oh fuck I'm coming."

"Me too." He kissed her as he thrust in and out and filled her with his pleasure.

She spasmed around him, surrendering to her climax as it ravished her. It seemed to go on and on, taking her on a spiral of ecstasy. Julian rode it through, kissing her, holding her, being a part of her.

And now it had happened. They'd gone from being a dull, staid, bored, couple to Technicolor lovers who knew what they wanted and weren't afraid to take it. Never again would she let that dull fog descend. In the years to come, she'd take her share of responsibility for keeping the pyrotechnics alive in the bedroom, and the fireworks coming.

THE MAN IN THE MASK

LADY DIVINE

S hhh. We have to do this quick," Miguel says, reaching around the body of the man standing in front of him to undo the buttons of his shirt. "My husband is going to come looking for me soon."

"O-okay," the man acquiesces. "Well, then, do you think I can at least look at you while we…?"

Miguel stops unbuttoning and clamps a hand over the man's mouth before he can say another word.

"No talking!" he snaps. "I don't know you, you don't know me, and it's going to stay that way. Got it?"

"Is that what you want?" the man asks in a softer voice, hoping Miguel won't object.

"What if it is?" Miguel replies, his accompanying chuckle cruel. He's indifferent to the man's feelings because tonight, he's not a man. He's a puppet. A toy. An instrument for Miguel's use…for his *pleasure*. "It's what you must want, too, yes? Otherwise, why do you come here wearing that mask?"

The half-mask the man has on *is* an odd sort of accessory.

114

It's lavishly decorated, almost gaudily so—blood red around the eyes and trimmed in gold sequins, swirling filigree designs, and accented in gold dust and rubies—a dramatic shield obscuring a face of pale skin, meticulously styled brown hair, and stunning green eyes.

"Because I was t-told…" The man stutters to a stop when Miguel's fingers brush his skin, playing through the hairs on his chest. He begins again, wishing he had taken one last shot of the whiskey they'd been serving downstairs. It might have strengthened his voice. "I was told that if I wore it, I would meet the man of my dreams."

"So, you admit to coming here of your own free will?" Miguel asks. Consent is essential to him. Without it, he'll dismiss this man now, no exceptions.

It would be a shame not to get the chance to have him, but there are others willing to take his place.

"Yes," the man replies.

"Say it," Miguel demands. "Word for word. Say you are here of your own free will."

"I am here of my own free will."

"Even though you know what I might do to you?" Miguel has to wonder if this man truly knows anything about his unconventional *tastes,* his unusual cravings. "Even though you know what a night with me might entail?"

"Yes," the man answers without hesitation. "I know, and I consent."

"And you know what to say to make it stop? Sí or no?"

"Yes. I've been told the safeword."

"Excelente." Miguel grins. "And you will call me *Sir* for as long as you are here." He runs his nose along the man's shoulders up to the nape of his neck, capturing a whiff of his spicy cologne. It's masculine, robust but sensual here on his clothes. Miguel can't wait to see what it smells like on this man's skin. He pulls the tuxedo jacket from the man's shoulders and sets it aside, followed by his dress shirt, then his undershirt, stripping him methodically, taking apart his armor piece by piece. "Do you think you were told correct? That I am the man of your dreams?"

"I'm having a difficult time convincing myself that I'm awake, Sir," the man confesses. "So I'd have to say yes, you are the man of my dreams."

Miguel presses his lips against the man's bare shoulder and smiles. Then he kisses him where his smile has left its mark.

"I guess I can live with that." His fingers crawl down the man's abs, reaching for his pants.

"S-sir? How would you like…?"

Miguel shushes the man as he undoes his belt and works his fly open, then shoves his pants and boxers down around his ankles. The man shivers at Miguel's brusqueness. He's nervous, and it's cute, because if this is who Miguel thinks it is, he's spent the last hour downstairs flirting shamelessly, drinking indiscriminately, and making obscene jokes loudly to ensure all eyes on him. But here, in Miguel's domain, with his identity concealed, he is no one. He doesn't have a face, doesn't have a name, and his antics will fail to impress.

There's only one thing Miguel wants, and he's not waiting for the man to give it to him.

Miguel is ready to *take* it.

"*I* give," Miguel explains. "*You* take. *I* use. *You* stay quiet and look pretty. And if you behave like a good little whore, I *might* let you enjoy it. Comprendes?"

"Yes, Sir," the man says evenly, trying not to betray his uneasiness. "I understand."

Miguel doesn't bother undressing too much himself. He doesn't need to. The man standing before him, shirtless, with his pants around his ankles, and that masquerade mask covering half of his face, is simply an object. A present left where someone knew Miguel would find it. Miguel doesn't need to seduce him. The man in the mask does not need to see Miguel's tan skin, his toned chest, or his defined abs for Miguel to fuck him. He doesn't need to gaze into Miguel's bourbon-colored eyes, doesn't need to kiss his plush, full lips.

After all, it's not like they'll be making love.

Miguel doesn't have the inclination nor the time.

"Now, you're going to bend over, you're going to spread your ass for me, and I'm going to fuck you." Miguel can't help that he's hard already. He's about to turn this handsome, athletic creature into nothing.

The man swallows his anxiety like it's the whiskey shot he should have taken. "I don't…I don't usually…bottom, Sir."

"Well, tonight you do." Miguel pushes the man into position. "And you are going to *love* it."

"Y-yes, Sir."

Bent at the waist, the man spreads his legs as far as his pants will allow. He reaches behind, grabs his ass cheeks, and pulls them apart, presenting himself for Miguel's approval.

"Mmm, very nice," Miguel hums, slowly undoing his own belt and fly. He *is* on the clock, so to speak, and should be rushing, but he can't seem to make himself go much faster with this splendor in front of him—strong back and muscular limbs contorted to get into this awkward position, with his legs trembling to keep it. Long fingers pull apart taut flesh, exposing his tight entrance, begging for Miguel to violate it.

Miguel pushes his own pants to his knees. With lube he carries in his pocket for just such an occasion, he slicks his fingers to dripping. He circles the man's hole with his fingertips, then dips his index finger gently inside. He takes more time than he has prepping this man, doing as thorough a job as possible opening him up. Miguel doesn't particularly care whether or not he hurts him. This man came here of his own volition, aware of the consequences. He must find pleasure in pain, feeds off it the way Miguel does. There would be no reason for this man to be here otherwise. But Miguel needs him relaxed and easy to enter.

Again…clock ticking.

To be honest, Miguel would *love* to hear this man scream his name. Out of pleasure is preferable, but he'll take pain if that's what he gets.

He also has to remember that they're not alone in this house. There are about two hundred people downstairs celebrating his birthday—friends, family, and business associates, all including a dozen or so children. It probably wouldn't be prudent to indoctrinate them into the world of his depraved sexual fetishes while they're guests in his house.

Miguel adds a second finger. It slips in on the first go, but the ring of muscle stretching around him is still fairly difficult to manipulate. The man, mewling with every thrust, has become rubbery at the knees, but his cock is only half hard.

"Such a beautiful body," Miguel murmurs. "So sculpted. So sexy. So *hot*. You're not entirely ready for me, but I don't have that kind of time."

"S-sir…?"

"Silencio!" Miguel hisses. He pinches the man's ass, leaving a mark that will certainly bruise. "Just take a few deep breaths." He lines himself up with the man's hole and pushes, but his cock doesn't slide in as smoothly as he'd like. "Try to relax, for fuck's sake!"

"I...I'm trying, Sir," the man rambles, strain tightening his voice. "I want you so much. I swear! I want you to...mmm..."

Miguel is sure the man had more to say, but his cock finally slipping into the man's body shuts him up. Well, not entirely. As Miguel slides deeper, the man's mewls turn into moans, ones of unadulterated pleasure, and Miguel amends his original thinking.

He doesn't want to hear this man screaming his name in pain. Ecstasy. That's what he desires. Pure ecstasy.

"How's that?" Miguel asks, snapping his hips, too eager to wait until he bottoms out to start fucking this man. "Is that better, baby?"

"Yes." The man gasps, short of breath from bending over, his fingers fumbling with his slippery ass cheeks to keep them spread. "Much...*mmm*...better...Sir."

Miguel loves this position. He loves watching his cock plow in and out of this man's body, his hole forming a tight sheath around him. Once Miguel is inside him completely, he feels no resistance, but there's a matter of angling. Miguel wants to slam this man hard, but they keep falling forward, his partner struggling to stay upright and offer the kind of resistance that will allow Miguel the opportunity. Besides, Miguel has found this man's prostate, and every time he hits it, his little puppet lets out a glorious moan. But his knees are beginning to buckle. Miguel doesn't need the two of them falling to the floor and breaking anything important.

"Knees," Miguel commands. "I said *knees!*" he repeats, annoyed when the man doesn't automatically comply. He slaps the man's cock, forcing his body to obey. "On your knees! *Ya!*"

"Yes, Sir! Sorry, Sir!" The man slides off of Miguel's cock and drops to his knees. He nearly trips forward, thrown off-balance by the trousers pooled around his ankles. Miguel kneels behind him, grabs his hips and slides back into him without additional preparation. At this better angle, with no need to constantly fight for balance, Miguel fucks him as hard as he wants, hoping he can make those sinfully pathetic mewls return.

"So," Miguel grunts, "how do you like this? Hmm? Seeing as this is something you *don't normally do.*"

"I...I like it, Sir," the man answers, but he doesn't sound too convincing.

"Do you?" Miguel smacks the man's ass, leaving an angry red handprint. "Don't lie to me!"

"I'm...I'm not lying, Sir! I like it! I swear!"

"Do you want *more?*"

"Yes, Sir," the man whines.

"Do you want *harder?*"

"Yes, Sir!" The man pounds back to prove it. "*Please*, Sir! *Harder*, Sir!"

"Cojeme! I like you calling me '*Sir*,'" Miguel moans, grabbing the man's hips with more nails than fingers and pounding away. "I like it...*very...much.*"

Miguel decides that he wants this man lower, that he needs him beneath him as far he can get him. He plants the knuckles of his fist into the knob of the man's spine and pushes till his arms slide forward, the carpet underneath them burning his forearms with the friction, not stopping until his chin is plastered to the floor.

The man groans, the bend in his spine demanding, but in this position, Miguel fills him so exquisitely, he can't think to complain. His back muscles burn, his legs cramp, he's open, vulnerable, a single nerve being rubbed raw...and he only wants more. "Oh, yes, Sir! Like that, Sir! J-just like that!"

"Ay! Dios mio, I'm cumming," Miguel mumbles, his body giving over to the sensation before the words even come out of his mouth. "Ay! Dios, yes! Ay...Dios..."

As Miguel's hips start to fail him, the man's body convulses, shooting cum over the carpet. But Miguel is unconcerned about that, about him. He's fascinated instead by how hard he just came, and how much, watching as it drips from the man's ass when he pulls out.

"Look at that." Miguel sticks three fingers into the man's gaping hole, slick with his cum. He nonchalantly rubs the man's sensitive prostate, making him cry out. "Look at how gorgeous you are, covered in my semen, aching from my touch. How sweet is it that I get to touch you, hmm? That I get you to play with."

"Please," the man whimpers, head lolling on the floor. "Please, touch me, Sir."

"Oh, I will touch you," Miguel promises. "I will make you..."

Bang bang bang!

A sharp knock interrupts him. "Hey! Hey, Miguel!" a slightly slurred voice calls through the seam of the locked door. "Are you...are you in there, Miguel?"

Miguel could just keep quiet until the intruder goes away, but with his luck, he won't. His assistant Aaron is a very persistent man. He knows that this is Miguel's bedroom. He probably saw Miguel leave the party. And seeing as Miguel has been gone for about an hour, Aaron knows that this is probably the only place he could be.

What Aaron *doesn't* know is how to take a hint, or how to leave well enough alone.

"Sí, Aaron." Miguel sighs, teeming with frustration. "I am here."

"I've been looking all over for you! It's your birthday, man! You're s'posed to be mingling! People are waiting to see you!"

"I know." Miguel doesn't remove his fingers from the man bowing before him. He adds a fourth, pumping them steadily in and out. The man on his knees arches his spine, legs shaking. Miguel picks up speed, and the man bites his lower lip to keep quiet. "Perdón, Aaron. I was opening one of my presents and I lost track of time."

"That reminds me"—Aaron hiccups—"where's your man? It's about…it's about time for the cake!"

Miguel rolls his eyes. "Do not worry about him, mijo…" Miguel sees the man on the floor try to rise to his hands and knees. He makes a fist and shoves it unceremoniously in the man's ass. The man muffles a scream and collapses to the floor. "I'm sure he's around here *somewhere*. Did you check one of the other bedrooms?"

"Uh…n-no," Aaron says, rather uncomfortably. "No, I haven't."

"Then you should get on that." Miguel fondles the man's

balls as he edges him toward another—less fulfilling—orgasm. "I wouldn't want him to miss the rest of the party."

"Oh…uh…okay." Aaron sounds suddenly much more sober. "I'll do that."

"A-ha," Miguel murmurs dismissively, returning focus back to the man he's tormenting, fisting in and out of his hole till his bit lip can no longer contain his moans.

"Oh, *nngh*…oh…oh *fuck*…" The man rakes his fingers down the carpet, slapping with the flat of one hand when Miguel fists him deeper. "Yes, Sir! Yes, Sir! Yes, oh God…!"

"Are you all dried up?" Miguel teases. "Because I want to see you cum for me again, and I'm good to do this *all night*."

"I…I don't know, Sir. I don't think so, Sir, I…God…" The man tries to come up with a suitable answer to Miguel's question, but he has no clue what to say. The buildup of Miguel's fist torturing spots that usually give him pleasure feels intense. He wants to cum, he wants to show Miguel his appreciation, but he doesn't know if he physically can.

"Oh, come on, sweetheart." Miguel moves from the man's balls to his cock, which is trying to grow beyond flaccid. "I have faith in you."

"I…I'm trying." The man stammers like a virgin teenager struggling to find the right words to make Miguel think he's more experienced than he is. But for all of his swagger, he's just a submissive fool, writhing half-naked while Miguel plays him like a violin. The man's shoulders tense; his ass clenches. He fucks Miguel's fist as Miguel strokes his cock, not necessarily because it feels good, but because he wants to please Miguel.

But Miguel has a party to get back to, so he needs to

speed things along before more than just Aaron comes looking for him.

"What if I...?" Miguel leans down and licks the outer rim of the man's asshole stretched around his wrist, and the man's voice shoots up a few notes.

"Oh, *fuck*! Oh, fuck, oh, fuck, oh, *fuck*!"

He's nowhere near hard when he starts to cum, and it's not all that much, but it's enough to satisfy Miguel, make him grin ear to ear that he compelled it out of him. That he owned his body and his will. That he made him perform. Miguel pushes him to the point where he can't prop himself up any longer. As much as he tries, he can do nothing more than lay on the floor, a quivering mass with a throbbing cock. Drained of energy, he is Miguel's for the taking.

Miguel could stay in this room all night and use him. That would be a dream come true. But there are other things to attend to.

Societal conventions.

A party.

Guests.

His husband.

Miguel removes his hands and pulls away from this body —without a face and without a name so long as he's wearing that mask.

"So"—Miguel breathes—"what...what did you think?"

The man, cheek pressed to the itchy carpet, still catching his breath, asks, "Are we...done, Sir?"

"We are done," Miguel says, "for *now*."

"Then I think..." The man removes his mask and sets it carefully on the floor. Thoroughly exhausted and with a sore ass, he does his best to sit upright. Then he turns to face his husband "...we have to do that more often, Miguel, mi amor."

"Really?" Miguel smiles shyly. He had hoped that's what Caleb would say. "What did you like most about it?"

A dozen things swamp Caleb's mind—how demanding his usually nurturing husband was, how much like the Miguel he first met and dated before they settled down and adopted three kids. How he wasn't afraid to speak his mind or tell Caleb what he wanted. How he wasn't timid about *taking* it. It took quite a while for them to get to this point, create these personas, and build up Miguel's confidence enough to use them. And now that they're here, Caleb wouldn't trade it for anything. They'd spent the last three months coming up with this scene, and it played out perfectly.

The only downside is that now Miguel owes poor Aaron an explanation in the morning. Caleb hopes he can convince Miguel to secretly dial him in when he does so he can listen. He's not sure whose discomfort he'll be more amused to hear —his straight-laced husband's, or his straight-laced husband's straighter-laced assistant's.

"I love that I get to have a husband, a lover, *and* a Master, all rolled up in one incredible person."

"Is that all?" Miguel asks. He's bashful when he does, and Caleb loves that, too. Caleb reaches for his husband, and Miguel crawls into his arms.

"Above all else," Caleb says, hugging Miguel tight, "I love that the man I fell for so hard the first time we met that I knew then and there that I wanted to spend my life with him will always be the man of my dreams."

TAKING IT

GAIL WILLIAMS

Chair-leg—Him—Beat—to—Death.
Don't.
Want to.
Grow up. Stop being all caveman.
Cave*woman!*

Okay, it's an odd conversation, but internal duologues tend to be. I know what I mean. Others wouldn't necessarily, but they aren't listening. Besides, I'm the only one in the office this early and I'm seething because I'm reading an email of sheer arrogance, total annoyance and utter brilliance.

He never listens, even when I'm at my most articulate. Which isn't often around him. I just clench up because, though I hate to admit it, he is brilliant. I try, but when I look at him I can't hide my feelings, I can never keep emotion from my eyes. He'd see it anyway. He misses nothing with those eagle eyes.

Beautiful eyes.
Shut up.

Well they are.

I reject that. Just like I reject the fact that I'm thinking about him even when he's not here. His eyes are not beautiful just because they are the most delicious chocolate brown flecked with purest gold. They do not make him handsome. No. Not at all. Not handsome.

Just gorgeous.

Shut up.

The other annoying thing about duologues is that both sides know your secrets. All your shameful secrets.

Like wanting to jump the guy's bones.

Shut UP! Oh my God, can't a girl seethe in peace?

You do think he's gorgeous, though.

Do not.

Do too.

Okay, yes, I think Fletcher is gorgeous. Not Hollywood gorgeous. He's not even that good looking. His brows knit so often his forehead is lined. His nose is even longer than mine, though more aquiline. His lips could be full and generous, but they are usually pursed or thinned as he prepares to argue with me.

Worst thing is, we don't actually argue. He barks and I fold faster than a house of cards in a hurricane. See the thing I always find so truly attractive about him is his smarts. His brain.

The brain you want to moosh with a chair-leg?

Yes. Shut up.

He's always right. He's the smartest man I've ever met; makes me feel like a complete imbecile. He's an actual genius. Especially with people. Other people. I swear, five minutes in that man's presence and I feel about as capable as one of those monkeys who can't be taught even rudimentary sign language.

I try to appreciate that he's good at his job. But it was supposed to be my job. The last owner was preparing me to take over; I'd even started stepping up. Which is when things went sour. I found hidden costs. Accounting that was creative…well, fraudulent. The closer I looked, the worse things got. I took the details to the boss, then had to fetch tissues when he burst into tears, the true horrors pouring out.

Next morning, I came in to find Fletcher in his place. Fletcher announced that he'd bought the business and was taking over. A frantic phone call rang to nothing. I tried again only to have Fletcher snatch my phone.

"He won't answer," he'd growled before shoving papers in my hand and walking away.

The purchase papers proved everything he'd said, and were dated a month earlier. Everybody lies. That was two months ago. And while Fletcher has already turned the company around, my future is gone.

Doesn't mean you give up on the present.

"Shut up!"

"I di—"

My surprised squeal, and near falling off the chair at finding him behind me, stops Fletcher in his tracks.

"How the hell did you get in without me hearing?" The door has a terrible squeak, which come to think of it I didn't notice when I came in.

"I had maintenance change the hinges."

Even his well-bred tone gets on my nerves.

Only because it melts your bones first.

I close my eyes and clench my jaw as I struggle to push the voice down.

"My office, Miss Smith. Now."

His long legs were already striding past and I really wish he wasn't wearing that jacket. Without it I'd get a great view of his—

Shut up!

Desperately trying to control myself, I stomp after him. I am always at my worst around him. His being perfect brings out my imperfections. And I've got plenty of those.

"Close the door."

He's putting his briefcase on his desk as I close the door. Turning, I come to a dizzying stop to find I've strode too far —he's in front of his desk not behind. Sitting on the edge brings his head more level with mine—being about seven inches shorter than him, it's the only way to even us. And I'm a lot more up close and personal than expected. My instant reaction is to move back, but I need to find my backbone; if he doesn't like this, he can move.

He's not moving.

"I understand you don't like your position here."

"Hope you didn't pay a psychic to tell you that."

"I hardly need to. Your sour expression tells me every morning."

I flush with embarrassment, but the truth is, I've already lost this game. Nothing left to lose. "I'm sure it's more eloquent than I am."

"Usually."

My hands ball into fists. I imagine picking up the chair next to me and bashing his head in. He is as impassive as ever. His eyes roam over me, but I doubt he's impressed with supermarket chic or flat brogues. His eyes stop at my chest. Perhaps something impresses him. A small frown wrinkles his brow.

"Are you wearing a corset?"

"Well there's no law against it." He's still frowning as he stands up. Way too close. "The dress code says smart casu—"

"Take the jacket off."

The command stops me just as much as the interruption. He didn't really say that. *Did he?*

Now he's leaning in, his nose millimetres from my face, his dark eyes dilated, boring into mine.

"Take the jacket off."

The words are ground through gritted teeth. I taste the mintiness of his morning tooth brushing. I hate myself for it, but I fold and take the jacket off. Standing with that upright posture, chin high, he looks down his nose at me. I shiver though the room isn't cold and hold the jacket before me, gripping it tightly as he deliberately circles and assesses. Suddenly my mouth is dry and there isn't enough air in the room.

He stops right behind me.

I don't remember a time when I have ever felt this uncomfortable. Overall the outfit is demure. Calf-length straight skirt, jacket over the top. Most people don't even notice that I wear corsets a fair amount of the time, but now the jacket is off, there's no getting away from the fact that my arms and shoulders are bare and that I am not wearing a bra. I can feel the heat rolling off his body as he moves even closer.

"Hmm." He's leaning over my shoulder.

I stare dead ahead.

"You hate being here, but you can't afford to leave, can you?"

"No, sir." I try for sarcasm with that title, but a very different tension is skidding through me in waves of—well—frustration.

"Good."

Suddenly his hand is on my shoulder. I only ever pin the front of my hair up, so his other hand comes up and moves the long curls out of his way. He's able to see easily down the rigid circle of my corset. I don't know what to do, so I do nothing. Nothing but enjoy the attention and his burning touch, his hot breath on my neck.

"This isn't the way I like things arranged."

There isn't time to figure what he means before his free hand reaches down. I suck in air, but his grip on my hair tightens, gently pulling back my head as the strong digits of his right hand slip beneath the corset to cup my left breast. My eyes close. I should protest, but my head is now back against his chest and all I can do is revel in the attention. Carefully, caressingly, he moves the swollen flesh of my breast up, those talented fingers offering a tantalising squeeze to my erect nipple before they move to the right side and reposition that mound too.

"Better."

The word shivers down my flesh as he peruses the heightened cleavage. His hand moves from my hair and I pick up my head and look forward. There is an inch or two between us now. Blood is pumping far too hard and heavy in my ears. I really should complain. I'm sure there are laws against this. But my mind and body scream in protest at the thought.

Suddenly I feel hands behind me. Fletcher is pulling at the cords tied at my waist. I try to speak, but as I draw in breath, he shushes me. I try another breath.

"The plaything will submit and be quiet."

I shouldn't like that idea. In fact I should argue tooth and nail, fight to be seen as something more. But the temptation is too great. Besides, if he undoes the cords back there I'll struggle to do them up should anyone walk in suddenly. My loins tighten surprisingly at that idea.

He leans in and whispers in my ear.

"You will submit, won't you, Plaything?"

Suddenly I realised I have a choice. He is still and awaiting my answer.

"Yes, Master."

I feel his smile and the small dark laugh he gives.

"Oh!"

I hadn't meant the sound to escape me, and I clamp my jaws as he pulls the corset ever tighter. And tighter. I have to resist, the corset requires it, but the tighter it grows, the hotter I get. I'm panting as he finally ties the lacings.

I've never worn a corset tighter. I look down. *Wow!* My breasts never looked that good before.

He leans over and inspects the display. "Much better." But that is his normal voice, and as he moves back, he pulls my jacket from my hands and slips it up my arms onto my shoulders. He spins me to face him, then does up the single jacket button.

When his eyes meet mine, I am pinned by that dark gaze.

"No release until I decree it. Understand, Plaything?"

Unable to separate my tongue from the dry roof of my

132

mouth, I am overly aware of another body part that is far from dry. I simply nod.

"Get out."

He is already moving to his chair. I don't think he's forgotten me, but he has other things to do and so do I. Annoyingly I can't tell if he is as affected by the experience as I am. I leave quickly.

How the hell am I supposed to think now? Luckily I don't have to fake it for long. There's a meeting in the boardroom; yet another update after the takeover. I choose to stand near the back, arms crossed as women in heels and men with too much ego take the chairs around the table. It is an old fashioned boardroom, all dark walls and build-in cupboards, and a proper wooden table.

All the senior staff have assembled by the time Fletcher decides to grace us with his presence. He looks so damn calm and cool. I'm still thinking about his long fingers and the way they felt tweaking my breasts. His eyes glance toward me, but do not linger. I doubt he's even notice that I've had to put on a scarf to hide the cleavage he enhanced.

"Calm down."

I look up at Barry Craven as he twists around to speak under his breath.

"I am calm."

"Then stop huffing like you just ran the Epsom Derby."

As Fletcher thanks everyone for coming, I stand there resenting him and wondering about Craven. Craven has been with the company as long as me, twelve years. We have both worked hard to move into senior positions from junior admin assistants. He has a flare for organisation and change, which was how he'd ended up in HR, but my talent is more analytically related. Numbers make more sense to me than humans do. And they're less likely to stab you in the back.

My eyes go to Fletcher. He'd stab you in the front. I have to swallow the thought quickly—I know exactly what I want him to stab me with and where. I try to catch my breath, but the restrictions of the corset prevent me and I feel I might faint. Instead I grab the back of the chair nearest me.

"Is there a problem, Miss Smith?"

"She said Salvador."

I blink up at Craven. *Salvador?* Oh, Salvador! That was a project we'd worked on together. Time to show some backbone. It turns out while I was thinking about other things I had actually heard what he'd said.

"Project Salvador," I say and move through the crowd towards Fletcher. "It's basically what you were outlining." I stand right in front of him. He is sitting on the low level cupboards, trying not to be overly formal. It's his manner and I actually quite admire it—I'm just not going to tell anyone that, especially not him.

The closer I get, the deeper his frown gets. "What do you want, Miss Smith?"

Chilly tone. I'd freeze, but the memory of this morning still warms me.

"For you to step aside."

His lips purse and the whole room is holding its breath.

"Left or right, I don't care which." I swing my hands indicating the directions. "I just need you to move from that cupboard."

He moves to his right, but the scowl doesn't ease.

"That cupboard doesn't open."

I offer up a saccharine smile. "That's only because you

don't know how things work around here." Jamming my foot under the nearest door I lift it. The hinges come free, but the double doors are held tight by their lock and open as one on the hinge of the other door. Bending in a corset isn't easy normally, but when tied extra tight, it's virtually impossible. I have to squat to go down, which puts me eye-level with his groin. *Don't think about it.* Face forward determinedly, I retrieve a large white A4 binder and dump it in his hands.

"Project Salvador. A fully detailed, programmed and costed plan for the upgrade of all the company's IT systems. The only thing that will need updating now are the costs. Given we are now part of Fletcher Incorporated, and other sections already have Dynamics, that means you can negotiate a better licensing deal than we could when we looked at this last year. But that," I tap the folder, "should save you about fourteen months of investigation and planning because Craven and I already did it."

Another sour look and I turn away. Back behind Craven I turn and dare Fletcher to complain. The meeting wound up fairly quickly after that.

It's lunchtime and I am pretty much ready to pass out. I really need to loosen this corset, but I don't dare without his decree. He is still in his office with Lockheed, head of IT. It's ten past twelve when Lookheed leaves. I let him walk past, before I stand and head for the lion's den.

I can feel I am being watched. Word of what happened in the boardroom has spread like wild fire and everyone's waiting on the inevitable explosion. I knock Fletcher's door and wait until I get his permission to enter.

Hating the weakness in my knees, I open the door and see he is on the phone. I raise a hand in apology and turn to leave, but he waves me in anyway. He finishes the call and studies me; I already feel half naked and wish I really was.

"What do you want, Smith?"

Clearly I haven't caught him at a good moment. I'm not sure how to change that. I'm not even sure how to tell him what I want, because it is rapidly becoming what I need just to breathe.

"Master, I—"

He stopped me with one raised hand. His eyes graze over me again. I am terrified of what he is going to say or do, but when his eyes return to mine, they are full of a fire that had nothing to do with anger.

"Come here, Plaything."

His voice has taken on that dangerous edge, the one I heard earlier, the one that sends shivers down my spine and other things down there. He indicates the side of his chair and I instantly go to him. As I do he swivels to face me. Light headed with facetted need, I stop before him.

"I need your release."

"No."

I swallow. This is a turn on, but I really need to take a deep breath. "Please."

He doesn't react.

"Please, Master?"

"Beg."

The rumble of his voice shivers through me. My nipples

are hard and my juices are flowing. Obediently I go down on my knees in the traditional posture of subjugation.

"Please," I say. "Please release me."

"Why should I?"

His legs are parted and I see the involuntary twitch in his groin. My eyes on his as I put my hands on his inner thighs, just above the knee. His brow twitches, his lips part and show a small upward curve. I run my hands higher, slowly and carefully pull them back to his knees, run them up again. I can see the change in his breathing, the bulge of his increasing erection.

The knock on his door makes us both jump, and there's little choice as the handle turns; he moves his chair back under the desk, effectively hiding his arousal. With no time to stand, I turn to the desk and reach for the mouse, awakening the screen to the spreadsheet I'd spotted just as Lockheed walks back in.

"Fletch—"

He's obviously surprised to see me here like this. I look at him, another challenge. "Well who do you call when the monthly reports don't work?" I look back at the spreadsheet and point to what I can instantly see is wrong with the report. "That's supposed to be a lookup field, but someone's overwritten it so the rest, which relies on that lookup, has stopped working." I amend the formula before struggling to stand and leaving the room. I really need out of this damn corset.

A couple of minutes later Fletcher and Lockheed leave the office. Fletcher is carrying his jacket in front of him, hiding the obvious. Good to know I can affect him too. I smile at the idea of his erection; it was still contained when I saw it and it seemed big then. That leaves me with a problem. Well two. The inability to breath and the need to complete this report within an hour and a half. Three if you include the desperate need for an orgasm.

I'm staring at the computer screen, trying to focus, when my mobile whistles. A text.

Top services door. Five minutes, Plaything.

A grin appears on my face before I can contain it and I check the office to see if anyone has noticed, but thankfully they are all as busy as I am. Five minutes. Not long. Yet it feels like a lifetime before I'll be with him. *Released by him.*

Dear God when did I turn submissive?

The second that man touched me is when, but it won't last.

Fletcher will play with me for a while, but like all boys, he'll grow bored of his toy and discard it, discard me. That idea should hurt, but my need right now overwhelms my concerns for the future, and I give up trying to hide the smile as I start up the deserted stairwell. At the top, I find the door is locked, but I don't have long to wait.

Slow measured steps echo through the concrete space. My pulse runs a sprint. He'll be here any second. I close my eyes and draw my bottom lip between my teeth. The footfalls stop and I know he's standing in front of me. I can't see him, but I know. I recognise his scent—spice and musk—Him. I keep my eyes closed, but I feel the heat as he steps closer. He doesn't speak.

His fingertips brush the skin of my throat then travel down to grip the scarf and pull it away. Next the button of my jacket is freed before the material is brushed aside. I push forward, only my head against the door, to allow him to ease the jacket from my shoulders and down my arms.

His hands touch my neck, his fingertips drawing patterns across the back of my scalp, and my lip comes from between my teeth as I draw in a breath. His thumbs move around my throat and he squeezes gently. My eyes spring open; I don't speak as he shushes me. His eyes are dark, his own breathing laboured. The pressure tightens, but not painfully.

"Like?"

His word is just a whisper. Knowing that sound travels far on these stairs, I answer with a small nod. He smiles triumphantly. For a moment the hold becomes painful, but only a moment. His hands move down, kneading my breasts, before moving again and circling my waist. Then he crunches over as he grabs my bottom. Suddenly I'm pulled up off my feet, his body pressing against mine, pushing me into the door, squashing me in the most delicious way. The closeness assures me of his arousal, hard and hot at my Mount of Venus. There are too many clothes between us.

I wriggle, panting as I look at him. His face is so close. I really want to kiss him. Well I want him to kiss me; I'm his plaything, he has to make the play. He grinds his groin into mine.

I bury my head into the angle between his neck and his shoulder as a small whimper escapes me.

"Want?"

It's little more than a breath. I nod again, and feel his silent chuckle. He rocks against me, picking up pace as I cling to him. I'm light headed with need and can take no more, clamping my jaw to hold in a moan as the climax overtakes me.

Suddenly I am on my feet again, and he's spinning me around. With one hand on the top of my spine, he presses me forward into the door. The pressure disappears, but I don't move. Then I feel the pulls on the lacing of my corset as he loosens the vice.

Breathing becomes easier, more comfortable. Until I feel his hands on my bum again. God, I've never known a man with such hot hands—or maybe I just burn when he touches me. The heat moves to my hips, my thighs.

Then the heat is all over as he presses the length of his body against me. I can't resist, and waggle my bottom against his groin.

I'm rewarded with a gasp of need.

"Bad Plaything." His lips are next to my lobe, whispering in my ear. "Tomorrow wear stockings."

"Can't."

His hand is in my hair, pulling my head back painfully.

"I'm off to the Carlisle office this afternoon," I explain quickly and quietly. "Won't be back in till Monday."

The pull on my hair disappears and so does he. Have I upset him? I take a moment to regain my breath, my composure. My coat and scarf are on the door handle, and I grab them and pull them carefully back on. My legs are jelly as I return to the office.

The drive to Carlisle takes twice the time it should thanks to road works everywhere and a crash on the M6 that closes all three lanes. With very little sleep, I find the training day for new starters particularly difficult, and as I return to the hotel I am surprised when the receptionist calls me over and says a package has arrived for me.

Wondering what this is all about, I go to my room, drop my bag, kick off my shoes, and flop onto the bed to look at the box. No identifying marks. Not even a label.

It doesn't make sense. Only the office knows I'm here. Uncertain what it is, I put the box aside, stand up and undress. As much as I want to know its contents, getting into something more comfortable and finding a place to eat are more of a priority. I am down to my underwear when my mobile rings. Caller ID just says unrecognised. Probably another marketing call; I answer anyway.

"Hello?"

"Plaything."

Heat washes through me, steals my breath and weakens my knees. I ease myself down on the edge of the bed.

"Master."

It feels both weird and exciting to say that.

"Well?"

For a moment I frown. "A well's no good without water?"

"Five."

The frown grows deeper. I hadn't expected him to enjoy the sarcasm, but I don't understand the number. "What can I do for you, Master?"

"Say thank you."

"Thank you?" My eyes fall on the box. "Oh! It's from you!" Actually that would have been obvious if I didn't feel brain dead from the day.

He laughs. "Didn't the contents tell you that?"

"I haven't opened it yet."

"Why?"

"Because I only just got in and I wanted to change before I did."

"What are you wearing?"

I look down at myself. I can't remember the last time I did that and liked what I saw; except yesterday when he rearranged me.

"A balcony bra in royal blue satin finished off with black lace and trim. I can see my nipples jutting forward just because you're on the phone." His chuckle does odd things to my stomach, and my tight nipples push through the lace of the cups. "My briefs are narrow boy shorts, royal blue but all lace."

I hear his drawn in breath.

"Are you shaved or *au naturel*?"

I smile, glad that to relax last night I had treated myself to a bath and a pamper. "Shaped."

This time it was a growl. "Open the box, Plaything."

It takes some scrapping to lift the end of the tape, but then it comes off easily. Layers of brown packaging give way to pink tissue paper, which moves easily aside. My breath catches this time. I can hardly believe my eyes. A black waister, fishnet hold-up stockings, and a pair of very high heels. I pick up the waister. Leather with steel boning. Beautiful. Then underneath I see a paddle, also leather, a pair of handcuffs, and a box marked Vibrating Tongue.

My smile just can't be stopped. "What would Master like me to do first?"

"Dress. You can keep what you already have on. I'll call back. Be ready."

Since he disconnected without giving a time frame, I guess I have no time to waste. I tear open the stockings and stretch them over my legs. The shoes go to the floor as I pull the waister around me. It clips together easily enough, and I tighten it as much as I can, but I can't tie it as well as Fletcher would if he were here. I barely have it fastened when the phone rings.

"Hello?"

"Tighter."

I swallow. "It's as tight as I can get it." It really is, and I never knew how erotic this restriction could be. It never had been before—maybe Fletcher was the difference.

"Sit back on the bed, with the box at hand."

"Yes, Master." I push the box towards the pillows on the wide double bed and scoot up until I am sitting in the middle, my legs stretched out in front of me. The black fishnets and heels are accentuated by the white duvet.

"Plaything want to play?" he asks while I'm still getting comfortable.

"Yes, Master."

"Open the smaller box."

"Yes, Master." Swallowing, I reach in and pick up the vibrating tongue, and clamping the phone between my shoulder and ear I open the box. A pink triangle comes out. "What am I supposed to do with it?"

That dark chuckle is so thrilling. "Put it on your middle finger."

"Yes, Master."

"Switch it on."

"Yes, Master." It takes a moment to figure out how to and the tip of the triangle starts to vibrate.

"Touch it to your clit, Plaything."

I hold the phone to my ear and reach down. The

vibrations stimulate my most sensitive flesh. I've used a dildo before, but never a vibrator and my eyes roll back as the tremors shake every fibre through my core. The vibration titillates, my juices brim.

"Oh Master, this is so good."

His breathing is getting rougher. Moving the lace aside I touch the vibrator directly to my clit and groan with pleasure. The vision of his head between my thighs intensifies the feeling. If this were his tongue, I'd be in danger of drowning him I'm so wet. I remember the heat of his thighs when I was kneeling before him, the way he rocked against me on the stairs. The idea of what his erection would look and taste like is a thought that parts my lips. "I wish I was sucking you right now, Master."

My heart is pumping so hard, my breath rushing.

"Stop."

The instruction is irrational. "I'm so close."

"Ten."

I'm groaning in mindless pleasure, can barely sit still. I am so ready to orgasm.

"Stop now!"

His voice is harsh and cuts through my buzz.

I groan in displeasure as I obey. "Yes, Master."

His chuckle fizzles through me. "Don't worry, Plaything, you'll get what you want. There are other things to play with yet."

Looking in the box, I'm a little confused. "The rest kind of needs two people."

"You'd better open the door then."

For a moment I stay where I am, eyes wide.

"Plaything," his voice is low, rumbling down the phone line to tighten my vagina. "Open the door."

My legs are trembling as I swing them off the bed and totter to the door. The handle is cold and I turn it slowly, opening it only a crack. I nearly drop the phone when I realise that Fletcher is actually here.

"Good Plaything."

The voice comes in stereo and slightly out of sync.

"Now let me in." He moves the phone from his ear and I mirror the action as I step back and open the door wider.

He clamps one hand around my wrist as he moves in, allowing the door to close naturally behind him. The grip around my wrist gets tighter, and suddenly he yanks my arm up, pulls me forward, and I stumble in the stupidly high heels and barrel into his chest. He pulls my arm higher, keeping me against him as his other hand reaches down and clamps over my mound, pushing between my legs and feeling how soaked my panties are.

"Oh you have been a bad Plaything," he says. "Having fun without me. That's fifteen."

I start to realise that the count probably has something to do with the paddle in the box, and for the first time in my life the idea of a good spanking seems like the best reward in the world. But he gives me little time to enjoy the idea, shoving me away from him towards the bed, spinning me so my back is to him as he forces me to bend over. As I lean my elbows on the mattress, his hands are on my back, undoing the lacing again. This time he is standing right behind me, his erection hot and hard against my bottom; my stance has spread my ass and I can feel the ridge of his penis pressing my anus. He yanks hard and I cry out as the waister cuts across my middle.

"Better now?"

I'm not sure. It hurts, but in a good way, and all I care about is the feel of his cock and how much I want it stuffed inside of me. "Yes, Master."

"Stay put."

Bereft and cold in his absence, I mewl in grief. He looks back at me in conquest before reaching into the box and lifting up the paddle. My throat goes dry.

He's going to spank me and I can't wait!

Stopping at my side, his hand smooths the rounded muscles there, branding me with his touch. Then the heat moves away. The paddle is lifted. I bite my lip and tense, not sure what to expect or how much pain I can take.

Wap!

"One."

Actually it doesn't hurt that much, and he rubs the paddle over the site of the hit, caressing any pain away.

Wap!

"Two."

Breathing isn't easy with the waister so tight, but at least my ribs can move. The gentle soothing of the paddle turns me on as much as the impact.

"Three."

Oww, I am really quite liking this.

"Four."

I flinch in surprise as he slaps the other cheek.

"Get back here, Plaything. Keep taking it."

With these high heels on, even with the bed being higher than most, I am almost doubled over as I rest on my elbows and move back, thrusting my bottom higher, more ready for him. I hear the catch of his breath and know that he can see every part of me.

"Five."

I take a breath; this slap was slightly harder than the others. Now the thick leather is rubbing over my left cheek, and I can feel my legs starting to quake.

"Six."

Whapp!

"Ouch!"

He leans over towards me. "Too hard?" Even as he says it his hand roams over my bottom.

"Who cares?" All I care about right now is the need to have him inside me. Seven. Sharp but less stinging. My buttocks must be glowing. Eight. Oh yes. Nine.

"Yes."

Ten.

"Master!" I can't even see straight any more.

The paddle is thrown back into the box. His fingers are moving under the lace of my panties, jerking them down till they fall to the floor. I shift, but he pushes me back down. His hands move to my hips and forward, then his fingers are in my pubic hair, foraging. One digit touches my clit with the most delicious zing. He rubs for a moment and my breathing catches. I am so close to coming, I'm actually quaking.

He moves away.

"Please, Master. Don't stop."

That chuckle flows over me. "I do what I want. Plaything will succumb or suffer."

Even as he's speaking, I can hear his zip unfastening. Putting my head down, I can see between my breasts that his trousers are down, and then I feel the heat as he come closer.

The brand of his penis moves between my legs. It's as delectable as I'd hoped.

"God, you're so big!" He really is. Suddenly I'm not sure about this. "I—"

"You'll take it."

The order worries me but his hands move around me, and all fear is forgotten as those practised fingers find my wet labia and part them. His penis presses against my exposed opening, then the tip pushes in, already stretching me.

I groan. "Please, Master, please."

For a second he starts to pull away, and then he thrusts hard.

"Yes!"

The shout is his; I'm too inarticulate with conflicting, wonderful sensation.

My vagina is stretched by the thick throbbing length of his penis. My God it's like someone just shoved a red hot poker into me. Only this feels so good. The initial shock is just that, no pain. He fills me perfectly like no other man ever has.

He rocks gently and I can feel every vein on his perfect penis. Another thrust. His hands on my hips, those long strong fingers imprisoning me as his movements start in earnest. Each forward motion massaging every point of sensation. We groan in unison.

"Yes."

Close eyed, I listen to his sounds, my juices slurping as he pulls out and plunges in. I've never liked that before, but today it's audio stimulation. I can feel his fingers, his cleanly manicured nails digging into my hips. The fire moves inside my belly, poking deeper than anything ever before. His balls slap my clit. My legs quake. Sound is retreating as my heart booms in my ears. The pulse in my vagina is like thunder. My world narrows to that commotion.

Whimpering as my pleasure intensifies, I can feel the swollen demand of his fucking, his harsh breathing against my skin. I want to hold on for him, only I can't. I cry out, the cascade of my contractions gripping his cock inside me and I feel his pumping start, his celestial call matching mine. With one last thrust he ejaculates into me.

Every bone in my body seems liquid. His grip is still strong. Suddenly he picks me up, withdraws, and throws me onto the bed. I'm too exhausted to complain, but I feel empty without him inside me. As my breathing calms, I know my smile is a mile wide and I don't even try to hide it. I want his body next to mine, but it doesn't appear. My heart rate is slowing and I can hear again, but the room is almost silent. A frown flickers and I open my eyes. Just in time to see the door closing. Fletcher has left.

After crying myself to sleep, I wake up bruised and bereft. Dressed in demure suits, I finish the training days and drive home alone, the box of his gifts sitting accusingly in the boot of my car beside my suitcase. I take it in with me—too embarrassed to leave it in the car, too hopeful to bin it.

Monday morning sneaks up quicker than I want, and with my nerves screaming, I decide that high heels and stockings would be too obvious, opting instead for trousers and a bustier under a long line jacket. I pin my hair up and put on green base and colour control foundation to hide the guaranteed blush when I see Fletcher.

When I get to the office, I know Fletcher is already there as his office door is open and I can hear two voices. Lockheed appears in the doorway as I put my bag in the drawer.

"Can you step inside, Miss Smith?"

Dreading what I might be walking into, I take a reassuring breath. It feels like that is the last breath I'll get to take as Fletcher and Lockheed quiz me over everything in the Salvador file and we work on renewing the proposal. All day. No breaks.

Lockheed's watch interrupts us at 17:20. I'm surprised it's so late. He says he has to go pick his kids up, so he leaves, carefully closing the door. I finish the notes I am working on, then look up at Fletcher. He's sitting behind his desk again.

"We done?" I figure he's had his fun so we must be. There's been no indication of interest, not even one darkly promising hint of a look.

"If you want."

His expression is utterly unrevealing.

"If I don't?"

He's watching me now. A wicked grin spreads slowly across his face and heat spreads through my stomach. I can't believe how much I want him.

"Plaything, heel."

Again he's pointing to the floor beside his desk. My knees tremble as I move to his side. I remember the way I knelt before him on Wednesday, the scent of him. The scent of him on me after that incredible fucking Thursday evening.

He doesn't turn though. Instead he reaches into the

bottom drawer of his desk and pulled out an anonymous box file. He offers it to me.

"You open this tomorrow morning. You will wear everything in here. And only what is in here."

I frown and take the file, unsure if my curiosity can last twelve hours. Besides, tomorrow is a meeting with the IT supplier.

"Understand your instructions, Plaything?"

I look from the file to him. I can't help the smile. "What about tonight, Master? Now?"

His brows rise. He doesn't look impressed. "Turn around."

Putting the file on the corner of his desk, I turn my back to him.

Wap!

"Eleven."

Every fibre in my body screams out. I bet there's a hand mark over the bruises. I desperately want more, but without instruction, I daren't speak. Four more spanks follow. I am so ready I could orgasm to a single touch. He must know because he's laughing again.

"That's all you get. I make the decisions, understand?"

Disappointed, I turn back to him. Those chocolate eyes are dark with arousal. Whatever he might say, he wants it too, so I lean over to kiss him.

Two fingers over my lips stop me.

"I kiss lovers, not playthings."

Ice washes all pleasure away. I straighten, turn, and stride away without glancing back. Back at my desk, I yank open my bottom drawer and grab my bag, turn to—

"Argh!"

I slap Fletcher's arm.

"Don't creep up on me!"

He's scowling, and all he does is thrust the box file at me. "Be ready tomorrow." Then he stalks away.

The following morning, after an alcohol-induced sleep, I crawl out of bed and quickly shower. As I return to the bedroom to dress, I remember the box file. It would serve him right if I were to just ignore his instructions.

Maybe he'll fine you more spanks.

Shut up.

You'd love it.

Damn right I would. But now he knows that, it's more likely his punishment would be to refuse to spank me. I drag the towel over my damp skin and decide not to be his plaything anymore. Now I'm dry, I open my underwear drawer.

He'll get mad.

He probably is mad.

You any better?

Apparently not. I empty the box file on the bed. A three quarter sleeve white shirt, another waister, grey satin this time, and a wide black skirt in crushed silk. The balcony bra is featureless white, as are the thong panties. But they fit perfectly. After dressing I look in the hidden mirror in my wardrobe and like what I see. The shirt is thin enough to show the bra—it's so sexy. A note sits at the bottom of the file.

Use the stockings and shoes I bought.

I don't really want to. In fact, I really don't want to. I've encountered the consultant we're meeting with before and he's an utter letch. I pull on plain stockings—hold ups—and two inch heels. But I'm not entirely stupid; I take the shoes and fishnets just in case Fletcher says anything.

At seven precisely, I hear the car horn honk once outside my front door. Fletcher. I am not rushing to see him I tell myself as I walk much faster than usual.

He's silent as I greet him and slip into the front seat. His car is fabulous. Leather seats, so comfortable I could fall asleep in them. Mind you, that might be because I didn't sleep much. So as he drives I sit back and close my eyes.

I wake with a surprise when he breaks suddenly.

He's parked under the bypass out of the way, off the beaten track.

I face him; he's scowling.

"You disobeyed me."

"You don't know Davies—"

"You disobeyed me!"

I shrink back. He's really annoyed. "I…" I have to swallow the squeak. "I have the others in my bag. I'll put them on for you, but—"

"Now."

I open my mouth to—

"Now."

He didn't need to shout. I kick off my shoes, pull up the front of my skirt, and roll down the tops of my stockings. Well aware that he's watching my thighs more than anything, I find the replacements in my bag and smooth them up my legs. His hand runs up my thigh, circling the bruises he left.

"You're marked as mine now."

Silently I beg for his hand to shift between my legs, for him to finger me, but he doesn't, so I finish his demand and slip into the shoes.

"Better?"

"Yes." His hand moves away. "I was going to fuck you here. But you've been bad. So you can suck me off instead."

I really should tell him to get stuffed, but all I want is for him to stuff his erection into me. So, I reach out and move his jacket aside, watching his erection grow as I find his zipper and lower it.

Once freed, I run my fingers up his length and then take it in my my fist. He is sitting back, already breathing hard, and I leaned forward, stretch out my tongue, and run it gently over the dome of his tip. I am rewarding with a growl of need. But it isn't enough. I kiss the tip first, lick around it, then stretch my lips wide and take him into my mouth, sucking rhythmically. Matching my hand movement to the sucking, I work on him. His hand is in my hair, clenching, pulling, holding me down. Accidently, I slurp as I suck, and the way he moans in desire tells me he enjoys the noise. He pushes his hips up and my head down. That fabulous length fills my mouth. I rear up and slurp again.

"Yes."

The sound definitely excites him.

"Deeper."

I shake my head as I suck.

"Take it."

His grip on my hair is painful and he pushes me down further, the tip of his penis touching the very back of my throat. Thankfully I have little in the way of a gag reflex. My breathing is ragged, little air making its way passed his helmet as I suck and play. My other hand goes inside his trousers to caress and softly squeeze his testicles.

He cries out, holds my head in place, and ejaculates so heavily into my throat I risk choking as I struggle to swallow it all. I continue sucking until he stops pumping before licking the last drop of cum off his tip, easing up his underwear and carefully zipping him closed. Finally, I take a last deep breath of that special sexual scent of him, sit up and settle into my seat.

"Insert these."

I frown at him and then look down at his hand. There are two balls in his palm.

"In?" I ask as I take them.

"In your wet pussy." He says it as if he's talking about the weather. "I want to watch."

Slowly I pull up the front of my skirt and slump down in the seat. I spread my legs, bringing my knee up over the handbrake to tip my hips towards him. He's watching every movement as I pull the crotch of my panties aside and use my fingers to spread my labia. I'm glistening with want. The first ball slips easily inside me and his growl assures me he's enjoying the view. The second one, I press to the top of my opening, and hold it there. His eyes are fixed on what I'm doing. As slowly as I possibly can, I push it deeper, and move my fingers up to touch my clit.

His hand snakes out and grabs my wrist.

"Bad Plaything. You don't deserve relief."

He pushes my hand away and starts the car. Adjusting my clothing I sit straight and belt up, trying not to let my frustration show on my face.

"They stay in until I decree otherwise. Understand?"

"Yes, Master."

The meeting is every bit as uncomfortable as I expected. It gets even more uncomfortable when I discover midsentence that the jiggle balls are remote control vibrators and Fletcher has the control. I do everything I can to minimise my reaction, but I need to breathe and I can see Davies watching me like I'm his next meal. I excuse myself and virtually run for the ladies as Fletcher increases the strength of the vibrations. Even before I've locked the cubical door, the tremors of orgasm quake through me, and I collapse on the toilet and let my body do what it must.

I am surprised when I finally step out of the ladies to find Fletcher waiting for me. Looking furious, he grabs my arm and frog marches me out.

We are halfway to the office when I pluck up the courage to ask what I did wrong.

"Nothing." He grinds the word out.

"Bu—"

"He said he wanted to fuck you. I had the bastard fired."

I can only stare at him. He had a man sacked for wanting to do what he is doing? Jealousy is good, right?

Over the following months we work together to find another supplier and prepare the new system. He keeps the jiggle balls and I put them in whenever he tells me to. He has a gift for getting me excited when it's most inconvenient, he turns up at my door whenever it suits him, and he sends me messages to meet him in strange places. Missionary; doggy style; fellatio; cunilingus; bondage; with or without toys; anal — always his decision. Just no mouth to mouth kissing.

I really miss kissing.

But when in company, he is always so calm and cool. No one would know he's interested in me. But several colleagues' comments made it clear I can't hide my attraction. I am such a fool to want that man. The truth is, I can't take any more of Fletcher not giving a damn about me. I love the fucking—hell I love the man—but he's only interested in his ejaculation.

And your orgasm.

True. He can be a generous lover, but he still only comes to me for sex. Never dinner or a date. Never out. He wants me to himself, he says. A year and still not a single, actual, mouth to mouth kiss.

I never expected tears or upset, but I thought Fletcher might give some reaction to my leaving the job. As Project Salvador finally comes to fruition, he accepts my resignation calmly and never mentions it as I work my notice. Not that my notice makes any difference to the way he works me. If anything he has become even more demanding. He's increased his use of bondage, and when he can't bind me, he crushes me. Hidden behind me or under a desk, his hand will grip mine, or his fingers will create a vice across my knee, or his foot will bear down on my toes. And because it's him I am instantly flooded with desire by every ounce of pain. I have no complaints, he never hurts me beyond my tolerance, and he soothes every bruise, takes fantastic care of me and my trust.

And I do trust him. Completely and utterly. I couldn't let him do the things—those glorious things—he does to me otherwise.

Which is kind of the problem. He has me turned into an absolute sex maniac. Some people need coffee to wake up, I need sex. I can't start the day properly without my first orgasm. It's affecting my professionalism. I am nowhere near as efficient as I used to be and it bothers me. I am not a mindless being and I don't want to act like one, which is why I have to leave.

After placing my personal belongings in a box, I scan the office, but there is no sign of Fletcher. I had hoped for a personal goodbye at the very least, just one more glimpse of him, and my chest aches as I realise that he isn't going to give me that final piece of closure. I guess 'plaything' is all I was to him after all. Just a bit of fun to be discarded without a second thought. I hesitate at the door and give one final look back before making my way out of the building and heading towards my car.

"Face forward."

His voice takes me by surprise, and my heart dances. So I am worth a personal goodbye after all.

"Put the box on the floor."

I do as instructed, and fabric flashes in front of my eyes, blinding me.

It stretches around my throat, tight but not strangling, and I am pushed against the side of the car. My hands are pulled behind my back, bound one above the other with a zip tie. His weight presses against me, and his foot moves between mine, kicking my ankles apart as he pulls up my skirt.

Oh my God! We're in the company car park—anyone could see us—but I'm too turned on to care. My breathing comes in ragged gasps as his hand pulls my panties down and I feel the heat of his erection against my bottom. I tilt my hips, parting my thighs, desperate to be one with him. He bends his knees, and with practiced ease he is inside me. With my hands secured behind me, my corset regulation tight, and the bag or whatever this is over my head and around my throat, I am utterly helpless, pressed against the unyielding cold of metal and glass. I am his to command, and if he wants to fuck me in public, he can. The idea of the whole office watching us suddenly springs to mind and humiliation tightens around me, enslaving me. I am his plaything and he can show that to the world, let them all know. I stifle a cry as I quiver around him and he explodes into me.

Then he withdraws, moves away, and a sudden rush of cold air hitting my over-heated skin chills the wetness between my legs.

A sob escapes me as I realise that all he has to do now is release me, and it's over.

But he doesn't.

His footsteps echo off the cement walls as he paces back and forth. I wish I could see his face, one last glimpse. That's a point. What if he just walks away and leaves me here? No he wouldn't. He's more discrete than that. Besides his footfalls are growing closer. I know he's near, I can smell that wonderful scent of him.

"Please let me go," I whisper, the space between us hurting more with each passing moment.

"I...can't" he replies, suddenly pressing against me once more.

159

"My hands are numb. You need to let me—"

Before I can finish, he snaps the tie, and the bag is undone and removed. I blink my sight clear and revel in the warmth and weight of his body still pressed against mine. His head nuzzling at my neck, biting. God I love that!

He spins me around to face him but I'm given no more room to move.

"I can't let you go." His mouth moves over my ear, my jaw, my chin, before moving up and claiming my lips. I can't deny him. As he plunders my mouth I open up and let him in. I shouldn't love him but I can't help it. I'd do anything for him. Finally he breaks the contact so we can breathe. He's looking down at me and I blink back tears.

"You've never kissed me before," I say. "I'm just a plaything, remember?"

His fingers are stroking my face. "Oh, Annie, you're so much more to me than that. You're everything. I can't let you go. Not now. Not ever."

For a moment I look up at him. Is he saying what I think he's saying? "Fletch, I'm leaving the job, not you. Not if you still want me."

Smiling at me the way he is now is new. My belly tightens and I return the smile, stretch up, and *I* kiss *him* this time. Slow and deep, breathing him into me as my heart screams with joy.

"My master," I whisper into his mouth, my hands wrapping themselves through his hair. "Now and always."

ON SELKIE BEACH

SAMANTHA MACLEOD

I s this your first trip to the Western Isles?" I glanced up. The man standing next to me was disturbingly handsome, with a deeply tanned face and a strong build. His eyes were the same color as the ocean, a dark and moody blue. How had I not noticed him earlier? This was a small ferry, and he wasn't exactly the kind of man who blended in with a crowd.

"Excuse me?" I stammered.

"Your first trip," he said in a lilting Scottish accent. "No offense, but you don't exactly look like a local."

I smiled in spite of myself. I was certainly the only one wearing a Burberry raincoat. In fact, I was the only person on deck wearing a raincoat at all; the Scots seemed to keep their raincoats for when it was actively raining, not just broodingly overcast.

"I'm Bridget," I said, offering him my hand. "From Boston."

"Ah. You know there's a legend about Bridget around here?"

"You know the legend?" I was honestly surprised. No one ever knows the legend of Bridget the Celtic hero. My own mother didn't even know it when she picked the name.

"We know plenty a legends around here." His eyes sparkled, and his lips curved into a smile. "I'm Muir."

My body responded to those lips with a sudden flush of heat, and I chided myself. *He's just being friendly.*

"Look over there," Muir said, pointing at the rapidly approaching shore. We'd been travelling for almost two hours, and the Outer Hebrides had gone from a low, dark line on the horizon to verdant green hills rolling above the sea. "That's the selkie beach."

I could just see a glimmer of gold between the black rocks and emerald grass.

"The what?"

He laughed. "You're named after a legend, and ye don't know the selkies?"

I flushed as I met his eyes. "That's not exactly my field."

"Well, allow me to enlighten ye then. Perhaps over dinner?"

I blinked. *Did he just ask me on a date?* At that exact moment, the boat shuddered, and I stumbled forward, crashing into his chest.

"You okay?" His arms wrapped around mine, steadying me.

My cheeks burned as I stepped away, trying to salvage some of my dignity. "Sorry about that. I haven't spent much time on boats."

"They're slowing the engines as we approach port," he said. "It can be a bit of a jolt. No need to apologise."

The sun broke through the low clouds and the world

flooded with light. The ocean around us was a bright, translucent blue, so vivid it looked like a painting. Muir's eyes swam with specks of light, echoing the sun-tipped waves.

"So…dinner?" he asked again.

I nodded. The feel of his strong chest under my fingertips was burning in my mind, and I didn't quite trust myself to speak.

"You're staying in town?"

I nodded again.

"There's a little pub called Codrum's right near the water. You can't miss it," he said. "I'll see you there, what? Around eight?"

"Uh, yeah. Eight sounds great."

He gave me another wide smile, turning my insides to water. Before I could catch my breath, he was off, his blond curls disappearing down the protected metal stairway. The ferry shuddered again, leaving a great frothing trail of bubbles in its wake.

I was used to travelling alone. In the past decade, as my job moved me from one six-month stint to another, I'd practically made it an art form. But I usually went out of my way to avoid conversations like this, and I'd never once been invited to dinner by a random stranger.

An incredibly handsome random stranger.

"Get a hold of yourself," I growled under my breath.

I walked across the trembling upper deck of the ferry, trying to think of a rational explanation for his behaviour. Why would the world's most handsome Scotsman strike up a conversation with a middle-aged financial consultant traveling alone?

I stopped in my tracks, two steps from the stairway. The

explanation was so obvious I could've hit myself in the forehead. His handsome, tanned face. His strong chest. He must work outside, and if he wasn't a fisherman or a farmer, then he was probably some sort of guide.

A hiking guide. *He's going to meet me for drinks and ply me with brochures about hiking the Isles.*

I sighed. *There's that mystery solved.*

Still, I couldn't help but feel a twinge of disappointment.

Codrum's Pub was indeed easy to find.

It was hushed and cosy when I entered, with a small fire burning on the hearth and bottles lining the darkened mirror opposite the front door. I glanced around the small room but didn't see my handsome hiking guide.

"Bridget the hero," Muir said.

I turned. Muir leaned against the door frame, looking even more handsome in the dim light. "Join me," he said, gesturing to a tiny booth tucked in the corner. "I've a treat for you."

The booth was so small I had to almost touch him to sit down. My body surged with heat when our legs made contact under the table, and then again when he didn't move away.

"Share a drink?" he asked. Two glasses sat on the table between us, filled with amber liquid.

"What is it?"

"Only the best single malt whisky in the universe," he said. "Brewed right here, of course."

He picked up a glass and offered it to me. Our fingers touched as I took it, sending a scattering of sparks across my hand and up my arm. *Oh, God. I am so going to sign up for his hiking tour.*

He raised his own glass and tilted an eyebrow toward me. I'm not a big drinker, and I've never had much of a taste for scotch, so I took a small, hesitant sip. My surprise must have shown on my face, because he laughed.

"Not what ye expected, then?"

"It's…actually pretty good," I said.

His grin widened. "And now, Bridget from Boston, is it true ye know nothing about selkies?"

"Last call!" The heavy brogue cut through the smoky air.

I shook my head. "Last call? It can't possibly be—"

Muir brought his hand to my chin, tilting my head to meet his eyes. "Bridget, do ye still want to see the beach?"

I blinked. Was this it, finally? After that meal, and the drinks, and hours of laughing together, was he finally going to give me the damn tour guide pitch?

"The…beach?" I stammered.

Muir stood, offering me his hand. "Aye. The selkie beach. The one I showed ye on the ferry. It's but a short walk."

"Oh," I took his hand, coming to my feet. "Yes. Yes, I'd like that."

He pushed open the door for me, gesturing into the darkness. "And have ye learned about the selkies, then?"

"I think so," I said as I shivered against his arm. The night had grown colder than I expected.

"Tell me," he said. It sounded like he was smiling.

"Are you testing me?"

163

"Perhaps."

I turned to him, but it was too dark to read his expression. "Well, selkies are seals in the ocean and human on the shore, right?"

He didn't respond, so I continued. "They turn into seals when they put on their seal skin. Or humans when they take the seal skin off."

Muir's chest vibrated with a hum of agreement.

"And they intermarried, in the legends," I said. "You told me they had babies who were good fishermen. Or just good with the sea."

I paused, certain I was forgetting something. The road took a dramatic curve up a hill, and Muir veered away from the pavement, leading me through a gap in the low stone wall beside the road.

"This way," he said. He stepped down, holding a hand out to me. His eyes sparkled in the starlight, and the wind tossed his blond curls.

I took his hand and stepped down. Muir pulled me to his chest, crushing us together. I gasped and his lips were on mine, fierce and hungry, tasting like the wild, smoky scotch we'd shared. My body responded before my mind could register what was happening, my mouth opening for him, my arms wrapping around his broad shoulders. He kissed me for a long time, our tongues embracing, dancing. When he let me go, my heartbeat thundered through my body and every nerve was on edge.

"Bridget," he rasped, his voice thick.

My body trembled, hungry for his touch. Desperate for another kiss.

"Follow me," he said, turning toward the vast darkness of the ocean.

I followed. Perhaps I shouldn't have, but I did.

He kissed me again when we reached the beach, a wild, hungry kiss that took my breath away. His warm hands lifted my shirt, caressing my skin, and I moaned into his mouth. His lips left mine, although his hands tightened around my waist.

"The selkie can only come ashore once every seven years," he whispered into my neck. His breath sent shivers through my body. "Do ye know how he picks a woman?"

My body was so bright with desire and longing I could hardly find my voice. "No," I whispered.

Muir laughed. "He looks for the most beautiful woman on the island, of course."

His hand travelled up my shirt, squeezing my nipple, and I moaned again. He grinned as he unbuttoned the top of my shirt, kissing the skin he revealed. My nipples were hard and sensitive, pushing against the thin fabric of my bra.

He didn't even bother unfastening it. He just shoved the fabric down, under the swell of my breast, and then took my nipple in his mouth. I gasped as his lips closed, his teeth gently caressing the sensitive flesh. I was panting and trembling when his lips moved to my stomach, following his fingers as they deftly unbuttoned the rest of my shirt.

The wind gusted, pulling my top back from my overheated body. He paused, his lips just above the top button of my jeans. I was shivering again, although now it wasn't with cold.

"Lie back," he whispered.

I sank onto the beach, watching the stars dance above us. The soft, cool sand against my bare back send a slow undulation through my abdomen, prickling my skin. He bent above me, grinning as he unfastened my jeans, slid them down my legs, and tossed them to the side.

"You okay?" he asked.

"Y-Yeah," I stuttered. My body trembled with arousal; heat poured off me in waves, slicking my thighs. I couldn't remember the last time I'd been this desperately turned on.

"Good," he murmured, bending over my body to kiss the curve of my stomach, his tongue tracing a slow line from my belly button while his hands moved across my thighs.

I gasped as his touch surged through me, drowning out all thought. The world narrowed and shrank until the only thing that mattered was our two bodies and the space between them, space that quivered and burned with every breath.

His hands moved higher, tracing the outline of my panties. I arched my back, digging my shoulders into the sand and pressing my hips against his palm, pleading for his touch. His fingers moved against my soaked panties, slowly, almost delicately, as if he had no plans to do anything but caress me through the thin silk. He pressed harder—slowly, almost imperceptibly. The world was spinning now, and my breath came in short little bursts.

"Oh, please," I whispered. "Please, oh please, oh…"

He laughed softly as his hands moved faster. His fingers slipped inside the wet fabric of my panties, his thumb circling my clit. My hips rocked against his hand and my body shook under his touch. He leaned over me, kissing my neck, nibbling on my ear—

I came like an explosion, burning and gasping in the night, the fire of my orgasm eclipsing even the stars above.

"Oh," I cried, breathless. "Oh, God!"

Muir's face swam above me, smiling against the black sky. And then he dropped, vanishing from my sight.

"Muir?" I asked, propping myself up on the sand.

He lay between my open legs, a rapt expression on his face. Our eyes met long enough for him to wink at me before he buried his face between my thighs. I opened my mouth to protest that it was too soon; I couldn't possibly come again. But as he pulled off my panties and pressed his lips to my clit, all I could manage was a whimper.

His tongue moved inside me, rippling across my labia. My hips started to sway against him. When he groaned with bliss, his voice reverberated through my entire body. He grabbed my ass and pulled me closer, devouring me, his lips and tongue pressing deeper and harder, demanding more and more. I panted his name and my fingers grabbed at the sand beneath me as swells of euphoria tore through me, moving faster and faster.

I came again, harder and longer than I'd thought possible. This orgasm crashed over me like a wave, flooding my body as I cried out, my back and legs stiffening under his touch. It ebbed slowly, leaving me limp and dizzy in its wake.

When I finally opened my eyes, Muir was sitting between my spread legs, his erection huge and heavy. He bent over my naked body; the delicate rasp of his chest hair against my nipples made my breath catch in my throat.

"Do ye want me?" he whispered, his voice rough against my cheek.

"Oh, yes," I cried, surprised by my own honesty. I'd just come twice, hard, and I was still nowhere near satisfied.

He moaned and my body responded with another rush of heat, my hips rising to meet his. The hard, hot head of his cock pressed against my entrance and I whimpered. I wanted him so badly it almost hurt, a deep, intractable ache.

"Ah, Bridget," he muttered thickly.

He entered me slowly, delicately, filling me inch by agonisingly sweet inch. I gasped and writhed under him, wanting more, begging him for more.

And then we were joined.

He threw his head back and cried out, a quick, harsh bark. My body shook, enveloped by waves of pleasure radiating from the spot where our bodies came together. Muir entered me again and again, moving slowly and carefully, his lower lip pulled back against his teeth. He carried me along, my body matching his deliberate rhythm, moving together in a dance I didn't realise I knew. Our climax built slowly, so slowly I didn't see he was leading me back to the obliteration of another orgasm.

Once I realised what was happening I tried to slow down, to extend our lovemaking just a little longer. But we were too far gone for that, and my body failed to respond to my commands. My body was no longer my own; it was his, it was Muir's, and he could do what he liked with it. His hips rolled faster against mine and I cried out, rocked with ecstasy. He moved faster still. Sweat covered our bodies, pouring from our skin onto the cold sand. I could feel the climax coming, I could feel it, I could—

Muir gasped above me and my body filled with his pleasure, thrusting me into my own oblivion. My muscles tightened around him as I felt his cock spasm deep inside of me, red heat blotting out the entire world, leaving only the two of us, wrapped around each other.

For a while we were still, panting in unison, our foreheads pressed together as his cock softened inside me. Then Muir shifted above me, turning to press his chest against my back. He kissed my neck and pulled something soft and warm over both our bodies.

"Ye'll be okay, then," Muir whispered.

I sighed. My exhausted body melted against his chest, safe and warm in the circle of his arms.

"Course I will," I murmured as sleep took me.

I woke some time later to a hiss and a rustle.

I blinked, opening my eyes. The beach was still dark, although the sky was now a dim grey and the stars seemed to be fading. Muir was on his feet, walking toward the ocean. I held very still, suddenly certain I was not supposed to be seeing this.

He knelt before a large, gnarled piece of driftwood and pulled something dark from the sand. Something as long as his tall, muscular body. He wrapped it around his shoulders and kept walking. My vision blurred with tears as his feet hit the ocean. He walked until the water was up to his knees, then up to his thighs.

When the ocean reached his waist, he leaned down. His blond head vanished beneath an incoming wave.

He did not reappear.

I closed my eyes and let sleep reclaim me.

The high, lonely cry of seagulls woke me. I sat up, wiping the sleep from my eyes. Thick, golden sunlight was just beginning to drop from the tops of the cliffs, lighting the white-tipped crests of the breakers. I yawned and stretched, noticing my neatly folded clothes next to the blanket.

Once I'd dressed, I sat on a piece of driftwood and watched the waves for a long time, the dark blanket I'd shared with Muir bunched over my stomach. *I'll need to make some adjustments. Request a permanent position within the company. Find somewhere to settle down. Buy a house.* I sighed.

A child who is comfortable with the ocean. Yes, that would suit me just fine, I believe.

A child who loves the water would like this beach.

"I'll see you in seven years," I whispered to the sun-dappled waves.

LAZY SUNDAY

TONY FYLER

A clotted cream spring clean duvet on a Sunday morning. There's nothing better in the world.

That first breath in that wakes, translates, orientates you in the world of all that's good, and then, if you're the luckiest of men, you realise you're wrong. There's something better in the world. There's Her, your American beauty, right there with you in among the folds of cream and sunlight on a British Sunday morning, there because you once had courage, and you dared to ask, and she found a something in your eyes that made her stay.

Soft back skin, shoulders like a freckled statue. Hair that smells of shampoo, sleep and something else that you just know as Her.

A kiss, a simple not-resisting thank you for the years of still being here, on that shoulder, and the stirring of her body underneath your lips.

She yawns a Snoopy yawn and arches back to find you,

pressing against a thought you haven't even had, a promise of pleasure, a kiss of her own…

———

Carrie moves against me, stretches like a napping cat on waking, and then collapses down again, all Sleeping Beauty hair and grin.

The thing they never tell you when you're young is that as you go on together, life gets better. Life gets easier, and hotter, and more fun if you dare to let it.

We've been together fifteen years now, this napping cat and I. I know what works. I know what can't be, never is, resisted.

Some women love the hands-on type, a taker who can bring them with him where he leads. Some love to love a listener, who lets them breathe the heat in through their skin with the rarity of choice. Some love a man who'll talk them down in deep degrees of flaming words, like warm wax down their spine to make them burn with not-in-daylight fire. Some love their white knight, bringing breakfast and a simple grin, the kind to woo a princess.

With Carrie it's:

"A new day, love, awaits our lovers' twist,

The sun is up, and he is not alone."

She groans at my Richard Burton, burnt cork rumble at her shoulder. It'll never win any awards, but the simple act of poetry, made up just for her and given a Welsh burr, is Carrie's special weakness.

"No fair," she whines, but the giggle breaks through too.

"So who are we mere mortals to resist,

The myriad delights we may be shown."

"Unff," she grunts, not at the immortal quality of the verse, but at its soft and rhythmic growl, that fifteen years lets me know is snaking in through her ears and shivering down her spine, landing somewhere down beneath the duvet, whispering to her like a serpent in the garden.

She rolls beneath the clotted cream and flings it off her back. Four simple lines have earned me the warmth of her back to kiss.

I put my hands on her, like tiny wing-prints either side of her spine, and think hot thoughts, feeling my palms warm, feeling her softness beneath my fingers, and already the touch of her, the stroke of her sends its own serpent through my mind, stretching into me, pulling the skin taut in places I won't think of yet. If I focus on her being here, on her being here and soft and naked beneath my hands, the moment will have come and gone and lost its power in a heartbeat, and I'm not going to let it do that.

I bend and kiss her shoulders, the nape of her neck, breathing the sleep-smell of my lover in from the crease there, growling out my next lines.

"Though lovers may consent to knotted be,

And never know the sun upon their back…"

She sighs softly, and I kiss my way across her shoulders, down her spine, still chaste because it drives her mad. My hands slide, firm, so's not to tickle, down each side of her, to the waist she swears she hasn't got, till I'm talking, rhapsodising to the first curve of her hip, the first duvet-hidden promise of what she calls her butt.

"The sun himself will weep for those who see,

But never know what pleasures they may lack."

She kicks out roughly, shoves at the covering till it falls off her, slides down her legs like every teenage yes ever whispered.

I take her bottom in my hands like a prayer, squeezing soft, kissing down to the dip at the base of her spine, the dimple there. Warm as she is, the first goosebumps flush on the peach-flesh under my hands, and I slide off the end of the bed, standing in the pooled clotted cream, looking up the length of this woman I love. This woman I've steadied on drunken, laughing up the wall nights. This woman who's woken me at 2 a.m. to share the wonder of a full moon. This woman who brings me coffee when she knows I need it, but am working too hard to *realise* I need it. This woman who stops to take pictures of tourist couples, so their memories are of being together.

This woman whose every inch I know, who knows me inside, outside, up and down, who I've seen shudder, and cum, and cry, who's shared that with me all these years, and who, lying here bathed in kisses and poetry, is more beautiful to me now than she was when we were young and dumb and wonderfully certain of ourselves.

This woman who knows what I can see, and what I can't, and parts her legs for me just a little, to give me just that little more. I gaze at her, the pink and brown and promise of her pussy still obscured from me by tufts of cloudy hair that work like lingerie, enflaming by what they hide and what they promise. Stepping forward, I put my hands on her ass again, the words in my brain growing coarser as the ache of stiffness in my cock becomes a force unto itself. I bend to kiss her goosebumps—

There's a vibration. For a moment, I'm not sure if I've missed a beat in my raptures on my woman, but no.

Her phone.

"Aaargh," she whines, picking it up off the nightstand. "Oh, fuck."

Insert your own smart-alec comment. They run through my mind, but I'm still close to a beautiful view. It would be churlish to make them.

"It's Elaine."

Ahhhh, Elaine. Part of me wants to put a stake through Elaine's heart the next time we meet, but again—churlish.

"I'm so sorry, honey, I'd better take it. You know what she's been like since Marcus…"

Marcus is a dick. To be fair to him, he's been a dick as long as I've known him, but now he's an extra special dick with a nineteen-year-old cherry on top. I step back towards the bedroom door, gather up the duvet and crumple it back on the bed for her as she scurries to turn over, sit up and swipe her phone, to talk Elaine through another moment of probably-genuine crisis.

Carrie pulls the duvet up over her ice-block feet, her right leg pulled up and dangling off the bed. It's unconscious, I'm sure, but it gives me a line of view all the way up her left leg to her—

The head of my cock flares involuntarily, sending messages up to my brain. The messages are clear. As the years go by, the messages tell me, there are times when you should allow an 'Elaine call' to disrupt your plans…

And then there are times when you shouldn't.

I grin, stepping back again, pushing the door closed. This is our world, this room. Our world for giggles, for snores and cuddles and gibberish…and for this.

For a moment, I don't take my eyes off her left leg, but

then I let my gaze deliberately drift up to the tuft of shrouding fur.

"Hey Laney. What's up, hon?"

I stare at Carrie's pussy, the distance between me and it maddening, and as Elaine begins to pour her latest woes into her ear, I reach down and slide a fist around my cock, my mind giving me images of times when the distance wasn't there:

The first time we fucked, in her single student bed, when I was trying to be Mr Sensitive, and all she wanted was the heat, the friction, the definite push and presence of my cock inside her, the oblivion of fucking almost like scratching an infinite itch. I'd been…honoured. Even as I felt it, I knew it sounded odd, but that's what it was—an honour, that of all the guys who wanted her, she had chosen me, found enough in me to be the man she took to bed.

The second time, half an hour later, all about her, the grind of her hips, and rubbing her clit as she rode me, and came with me inside her—the first time I'd ever felt that with a woman. The third, fourth, fifth times—each different, each learning, each making me want her more, making me want to never be without her.

The time I first discovered her poetry weakness, outside, in the park, with my back against a tree. Reading French poetry, being desperately pretentious. She was doing the sun dress thing that Summer, and she looked like something from a watercolour in the yellow dress with strawberries on, and a broad straw hat. As I read, she closed her eyes, her breathing getting heavier.

"Seul, inconnu, le dos courbé, les mains croisées,

Triste, et le jour pour moi sera comme la nuit.

Je ne regarderai ni l'or du soir qui tombe," I read.

She reached over, letting her hand lie, as if testing a theory, in my lap.

I looked down, surprised but thrilled, and flared a welcome to her. She took off the sun hat, then unzipped me, pulling out my cock and covering her hand with the hat. "Keep reading," she said, the Summer thick in her voice.

I did, the words, the intonations rising and falling along with her fist on me. I'd just started "La vie est une fleur dont l'amour est le miel" when she squeezed the base of my cock, I thought to make me stop.

"Le miel," she repeated, seeming content and yet frowning.

"Life is the flower, and love is the honey," I translated. She nodded, as if to say she wasn't an imbecile.

"Oui," she said, releasing me from her grip and letting the hat cover my modesty. "It's no good," she decided, her voice quavering. "Was gonna wait till I got you home, but that can't happen now." She reached quickly up both sides of the sun dress and drew her panties down, letting the dress fall quickly back into place and handing me the sodden scrap of fabric. That was it, that was the word, it was absolutely sodden, like you read about in stories and don't believe until you experience it for yourself and realise you underestimate a woman at your peril.

"One day, my darling," she said, her voice raw and thick as she pulled the hat away, exposing me to the breeze and any wandering eyes, "I'm going to sink down your body while you read me this stuff, and I am going to suck your cock and blow your tiny mind to the sound of the French poets."

I looked around nervously as the light summer breeze

played over the flesh of my cock. I needn't have worried—she had no intention of leaving me high and dry. She put the hat back on her head and straddled me, the sun dress a floaty convenience that disguised nothing of what we were doing, should anyone walk by.

"But for now," she said, taking my shaft in her hand underneath the long skirt, "don't you stop. Don't you fucking stop, my darling man." And with that, she sat back on me, and it was like nothing I'd ever known, barely a form around me at all, more like some living, pulsing, demanding part of her was taking what it needed, like it needed to be earthed, through my body, through the tree, through the grass and ground itself, like the poetry was taking her up and she needed the vicious thrust all the way back down on me, her nails digging into my shoulders. The heat of her pussy, the slick hot barely-friction of her movement was like an engine on my cock, like it was turning her into something else, some expression of everything urgent in the world, like Summer and life, like sap and beework, like—

"Andy!" she yelped, her pace not slackening. "I'm gonna...Oh God, Andy, come with me! Come in me! Come home!"

I read a few more lines, my eyes blurring with the sweat of Summer and her heat. I saw the scarlet flush along her neck and in her cheeks, and she flung one hand from my shoulder and dug it into her groin through the fabric of the dress.

"A—"

And then there was no sound; no birds in the trees. Just the bellowing of heartbeats as her muscles clamped, as my flesh could stand it no more and surged in shuddering pulses inside her. Eventually, I knew that she'd put both her arms around me again, holding me, cradling. I was deaf, dumb, numb, not really me, and the first sound I could make out when I came back from the soundless somehow purely white world was her soft, soft sobbing into my neck. The first sensation not sexual, but her fingers, stroking my cheek, her kisses on my face.

"I love you," she cooed, over and over, as though reassuring me that she was still herself. We'd said it many times already by then, but this…this was different. Special. Real.

"Je vous adore," I said, pulling her lips to mine for a soft, grounding, reconnecting kiss. "Je vous adore…"

I'm looking at her now, remembering her cumming, remembering time after time of us anchoring, earthing, flying together.

She gives me an odd sideways look, raises her eyebrows. I grin at her, moving my hand back and forth along my shaft. Yes, the grin says. This is what you're doing to me. I nod at her. She gives me innocent eyes, puts a hand on her chest, as if to say 'Whhhhhat?'

"Mm-hmm," she says into the phone. "Well, clearly he's an idiot, honey."

I nod at her again, then bring both hands up, miming at her, an old turn-handled cine camera.

She grins. Hesitates. Lets her other leg fall sideways, giving me a better view, a clichéd, centrefold view. I keep turning the imaginary handle. I know she has a fantasy of being filmed. Not in the modern age of harsh lights and instant uploads, but back in the day of real cameras, noisy things, with jerky footage, intense and black and white and breathless. Somehow that trips something over in her mind. She gives me another sideways look.

"Tiramisu," I whisper to her, and she explodes in silent giggles, then seems to make up her mind that I am serious. Nods, slowly. Puts two fingers in her mouth, then draws them down through the thatch of hair at her groin. Begins to stroke herself, softly, gently, outside and barely even any kind of show. This is Carrie starting out, building from the distraction of the phone call.

She smiles across at me as her fingers briefly part, a wishbone over her clitoris, her lips a little sticky from what we'd started. She pokes her tongue out at me in defiance, and I remember what it means…

She'd been as good as her word under the tree. In fact, she'd been better than her word many times, but it's Rome that comes shuddering back to me as she pokes her tongue out in defiance. Rome, where we went on our honeymoon.

Naturally, I picked up a book of Italian love poems in a bookstore on the Via della Lungaretta, and on our third night, I brought it to dinner at La Pergola. The rooftop restaurant had spectacular views all across the city, caramel tablecloths and ivory roses on the tables, with smaller bowls of humbler daisies for a less imposing feel. The room was finished in polished toffee-coloured wood and a Moorish fretwork pattern that, like the daisies, stopped it being too grand. The views belonged to Caesars and Popes, and you could believe you'd conquered the world as you stared across the night and the unsleeping city. It took the waiters some time to drag us from the windows to our seats. After three ridiculous, exquisite courses of the kind of food that underscored the views and made you feel like, if you absolutely had to, you could die happy now, I pulled out the book and started reading in a sotto voce growl.

"Andy!" She tried to be stern.

"Si, Senora?" I asked, all innocence and eyebrows, before carrying on.

"Era il giorno ch'al sol si scoloraro

per la pietà del suo factore i rai,

quando ì fui preso, et non me ne guardai,

chè i bè vostr'occhi, donna, mi legaro."

She gasped. Swallowed. "Andrew James Jenkins, you stop that this minute!" She went to a whisper herself. "I'm gonna wet my chair!"

I grinned. "Si, Senora," I said again.

She poked her tongue out in defiance. Then she knitted her eyebrows together and picked up a fork. "Oh dearie me," she said, the sarcasm flashing in her voice as she brushed her hair back off her face, "I seem to have dropped my fork. Must be under the table somewhere. I'll just go and get it, shall I?" She theatrically dropped the fork. "If they ask, tell them I'll have the tiramisu," she said. "You should feel free to keep reading while I'm gone, dear."

I couldn't believe she'd—I mean, not here, not now. In the park close to home, things had been comical somehow—getting caught there, we could have laughed it off as young love. Here, in Rome, we might get thrown out of the—

I felt hot breath misting through my trousers. The weight

of her hair against my thigh. I tried to distract myself, tried reading from the book. Felt her hands on me, through the fabric, stroking gently, but with impish purpose. Felt myself twitch and grow beneath her fingers, then the moment I almost dreaded—the slow, slow pull of a zip. She was taking her time, deliberately teasing me with second after second of heart-attack fear that we'd be discovered, deliberately teasing me with the hot breath that made me anticipate. I wanted to push, to reach out, grab her head and pull her onto me, but the tablecloth was her only shield. It was like being handcuffed to my chair, and she'd taken control of the situation, the pace, the pleasure. I was helpless. When she reached in and pulled me out, it was terrifying, thrilling, like going on stage without knowing the lines. Still, for moments, there was nothing but the tease of her breath, the tickle of her hair around me. Then her mouth covered the head of my cock, just the head, and there was no urgency, no stroking, no sense of getting to a destination, just warmth and wetness and a soft sucking kiss. I knew that about her by then—she enjoyed my body just for itself, not as a means to an end. If I tried to force a pace on her right now, she wouldn't stop, but there'd be something spoiled. I looked around at other diners, at waiters, turned my head to see the shades of blue and gold and white of the Roman nightscape, tried to read some more. Yes, I decided. I'd give her some poetry to deal with. And that was the key. The words, rumbled quietly as if to an empty chair, made her move her head, sink slowly down on me, inch by agonising, warm, succulent inch, then back towards the head, and down again. I poured Italian words down on her, speeding up as she began to find a rhythm that she liked, swirling her tongue, lapping with it, reaching down towards the base of me in longer and longer dives, like she was testing herself, moment by moment. She came back up to softly suck the very tip of me, and—

"Senora?"

I froze. Had we been found out? I looked around frantically, saw the well-groomed waiter at my side. He had question marks in his eyes. Oh…Oh, thank god, he was asking where she was.

"Oh, er…bagno?" I tried. "Bagno." Yes. Yes, of course, she was in the bathroom, not kneeling on the floor with my cock in her mouth as this handsome young man asked me questions about her.

"Ah," he said. "Si, si, bagno." He nodded, then opened his palm to me. "Dolce?"

Dolce? I made a mental note next time we came to this city to buy a bigger phrasebook and less poetry. Then, out of nowhere, Carrie almost threw herself down on my dick, sliding sharply all the way down till I could feel the back of her throat on the edge of my flesh.

I gulped, yelped, squirmed as little as I could.

"Signor?" The poor boy looked worried for me, and I tried to cover.

"Dolce?" I pleaded.

"Si signor. Antipasti, primi, secondi…dolce."

Oh, dolce! Dessert. Carrie was determined to seize her moment, and she moved her head rapidly now, bringing her hands to me for the first time, stroking me up and down into her mouth.

I squirmed to hold in a groan as I felt myself rise—my heartbeat going to a war charge, the tingles starting in my hands, my feet, my neck and everywhere, the message duly sent—we're past the point, there's no going back now, this is happening whether you want it or not.

"Duo tirameeeeeesu," I told him, the smile on my face barely more than a rictus, a look of knowing that the boy had done nothing wrong, but an urgent need for him to go the fuck away right now.

"Ah, si signor. Duo tiramisu, Bueno. Grazi."

And he left me just as my eyes closed, the hoofbeat heartbeats overpowered me and I felt Carrie's hands work me, work me, her soft, warm mouth still on me. I'd have told her what was coming but I couldn't and she knew it anyway. Knew it and wanted it, exactly where she was.

When I came, I thumped the side of the chair, arched my back against its unfussy beigeness, accidentally slammed a fist down on the table. My own fork went flying, and I had to make conciliatory gestures to everyone.

She stayed down there till the desserts arrived, and our poor befuddled waiter-boy looked concerned at the length of time she'd been in the 'bagno.'

I tried to allay his concerns, and all the while she was licking the last rivulets of cum off my deflating dick, and sliding me back into my trousers, doing me up.

The explanation came to me as she patted me fondly. I mimed taking a drag on a cigarette. "Il fumo," I said. "Il fumo."

Again, at this monstrous subterfuge, he seemed entirely satisfied, like he'd solved the riddle of the ages. "Il fumo..." I sighed again to his disappearing back. She was smoking. Damn straight she was.

When she popped back up from under the table, she sat triumphantly back in her chair, a grin in her eyes. "Are we clear, darling?" she asked, sliding her recovered fork through the tiramisu in front of her. "Don't mess with me, Poetry-Boy, I have skills too, y'know?"

That was her message. I wasn't going to have it all my own way, just because she had a weakness for poetry. That's the message now, too. She's moving her hand faster over her pussy, and settled back against the pillows, allowing her to dip her fingers inside herself from time to time, more for my benefit than hers, I know, but mostly, she's keeping herself on a low simmer, circling her clit with steady movements. Her lips have grown fuller, pinker, and there's a shine of slickness there as she moves her hand around and around, her nails never exactly focusing on the nerve-bomb, but brushing it as if in passing, to send sparks through her body, but never to build to something she can't control.

I smirk at her. It's what I'm doing too—staying hard but never pushing the strokes to the point where my cock needs to explode. I can feel the tightness in my balls though, just waiting for the signal.

No, I decide. Sometimes you can wait till you get home. Sometimes you have to have it, right there in the open under a tree. This is one of those times. Besides, there's always room for a little Roman revenge.

I move, advancing on the bed, crawling on all fours slowly up the length of it, between her open knees. I pull her body to me and hold it tight, her phone hand round my back suddenly, and swoop, kissing her mouth to give her the gift of my hunger, to let her know. She clings on to me, pressing her breasts against my chest and meeting my tongue with her own. The kiss tastes of hope, and need, and poetry, and Sunday morning niceness to her friend, but when I pull my mouth from hers, I don't stop. I kiss her face, her throat, her collarbone, the nape of her neck, moving my hands up her body while she clamps her knees together and presses her pussy against my leg. It's warm and damp, the hair feeling fresh-from-the-shower as she moves, rocks against me, and puts a knuckle in her mouth to stifle a squeal. She desperately lifts her phone to her ear, to catch up, takes the moment to throw an "Mm-hmm" in to Elaine's monologue of misery.

My hands squeeze her breasts, softly. She shakes her head just briefly, and I turn up the intensity, taking her nipples and pinching them, making her grunt in her throat. I dip my head to her left breast and take the nipple in my mouth, sucking, swirling, clenching it gently with my teeth—clearly the nice-girl stage has gone by while she was touching herself, and now her reactions need sharper stimuli.

The grunt comes again, longer, wilder.

She speaks into the phone. Her voice has turned thick, and if Elaine doesn't know the signs, I do. "Sorry hon," she explains. "Something in my throat." She keeps the phone to her ear longer this time, as I suck, flick, nibble, while pushing a hand down the length of her belly.

"Mmm-hmmmoah!" she agrees, the last a loss of control as my big hand slides between my leg and the satin-slick flesh of her pussy, cupping it, rubbing it like a prize. I judge she's ready, and push a finger in between the folds, feeling the true heat inside her.

She flings the phone as far away from her mouth as possible, to whisper to me that I'm an unprincipled bastard.

"Si, Senora," I agree, grinning up at her.

"What…about…Elaaaaaine?" she almost pleads.

I give it a moment's thought, then shrug.

"Bastard!" she says again.

I withdraw, tangling my arms in her legs as I step off the edge of the bed, dragging her with me. I lift her legs straight in the air, exposing the whole profile of her pussy and ass, then push a little further, her hot flesh seeming to peel itself open like a flower to the Summer sun.

Then I kneel, dipping my tongue into the dent of her ass —flashbacks of Greece come to me, where she'd announced quite calmly on the plane that it was time for something new, and that she was going to 'be my hoplite' on this trip, so if I wanted to fuck her, and she believed I would, it would be 'in the Greek style or not at all.' I draw my tongue, my whole mouth up to her pussy, lapping languid as a cat at her, hearing an occasional, increasingly raw 'A-ha' directed at the phone. I slide a finger back inside her, watching her body part around it, then seeing her muscles tighten, gripping it, milking it as I move it in and out of her, while sucking on the shiny, musky, hair-tufted flesh all around and sending a spear-lick now and then up to her clit.

I know she's close, that the situation had gotten out of her hands even before I properly got to her clit, but I love her body just for the sake of it, for all of its quirks and kinks and wonders. I close my mouth over her clit like a cave and breathe, feeling her thighs tighten, like a bow being strung to fire.

"Honey," she says, "can I call you back. Something's just come up. Bit of an emergency. I'll call you back, OK, promise."

Even before she ends the call, I've begun to lick, sliding a second finger inside with the first at the same moment.

She growls at me, and I use both fingers in the way you can with two where one won't do, to curve, and stroke, the rhythm inside and the rhythm of my tongue outside synchronising to a cause. Different motions, but the beat is the same, the beat of a river rising to drums, the beat of sunshine and creation, of all the thousand things a woman is, brought to a moment of miracle, of perfect flesh and wonder.

And then she's there, and over, arching, jerking, roaring at me, wordless, soundless, primal. She is many things, this woman—proud and kind and happy and wicked-grin mischievous. But right now, she is reduced, enhanced, immortalised in a moment of this physical thing, this lightning-bolt of love and lust and power. I take my mouth off her eventually, slow the stroking as her muscles clamp and clench and slowly, slowly let me go. Then I slide up the length of her body, to cover her with warmth and hold her close, as the shivers ripple through her and she clings, as she often does, on the verge of tears for moments, minutes, till the hush and the heartbeat come back down in her.

"So…what do you want to do with your Sunday, baby?" I ask, smiling at her sweaty-headed Meg Ryan like-I-give-a-fuck-right-now grin. Usually she's famished and I'll nip out and bring her McDonalds while she naps.

"Oh no you don't, Mister," she tells me, rolling me onto my back. "You are one evil bastard, Andrew Jenkins, and no mistake."

"Guilty as charged," I agree, chuckling. She pushes herself up to straddle my belly, finds my dick already hard for her and simply sits back, the heat of her pussy engulfing me in what feels like sleep, so warm and dark and wonderful. She reaches for my hands to use as supports, and our fingers clench together.

"What do *you* want to do today?" she demands, rising barely an inch or two on my cock, in no hurry whatsoever.

"Buy poetry," I tell her. "Walk hand in hand down by the river, and visit the second-hand book market, and buy lots and lots of poetry."

She drives down on me and I gasp, feeling her lips either side of the base of me, still sticky from her cum.

"Weapons of my destruction," she says, mock-scandalised and pouting.

"And you love it," I tell her.

"Well, this is true. Go on, what else?"

"Eat ice cream, the Mr Whippy kind, in big long licks, and give you my Flake."

She rises and falls on my cock again, using her legs more than my hands to power her now.

"Cheesy, but sweet."

"Dance with you in the rain, to music only we can hear," I say, sliding my hands to her thighs, to her hips, and up to hold her breasts, more gently now than before, the urgency of need in her abated.

"Typical Brit, say they want to get you wet and then you realise—"

She moves again, the rhythm of her hips, of her swallowing me into the heat of her body, intensifying. I could hold out a little while yet, but the first notes of crisis sound around my body, little neuronic emails that say 'She's doing the thing again.'

I brush my thumbs over her nipples as she rises and falls,

rocking and giving occasional jerks to wake me up from the rhythm.

"Maybe go see a play by someone we've never heard of, something we won't understand. Grab a lunch in a surprising little backstreet bistro somewhere."

"What…bistro?" she demands, panting as she keeps up the pace. "Everything in this godforsaken country…closes on Sundays. People…sleep, I swear it."

"Watch it, Yankee," I laugh, reaching up and rolling her over, pulling out and pinning her wrists playfully by the side of her head.

"Then what?" she demands.

"Then find an old camera," I say, kissing her hard. "Turn your dreams into reality, capture you on film forever, lost in your moment, hmm? Would you like that?"

She arches her hips up at me. "Mmmmaybe."

"Maybe tie you to the bed, like this, hmm?" I say, drawing on a darker fantasy she shared with me years ago. "Invite people round to see you here, spread open, writhing. Have them watch while I fuck you?"

She pushes up, trying to recapture me inside her, but I pull back, despite my own growing need to be inside her, to be fucking her, to be one with her again.

"Mmmyeah."

"Maybe even, if the price is right, let *them* fuck you, and I'll do the watching, hmm? How would that be, Yankee Girl? All-comers, like the Romans used to do, hmm?"

"Fuck me, Andrew."

"Say please."

Her eyes gleam as she thrusts her pussy up to me, trying to paint me with its heat again. "Shan't."

"Spoiled brat." I grin down at her. "Well, you've had your ration for today. No more for you unless you ask me very nicely."

"You want it. I know you do. I can see you do. You need it."

"Not as much as you do, sweetheart. Say please."

She giggles, pouts underneath my grip. "Pleeeeease," she mocks.

"Tell me what you want."

"What I really, really want?" She smirks up at me. "Don't play hard to get, Brit-Boy. I know you want me. I know you do. Fuck me."

"Again," I demand. "Say it again."

"Fuck me, Andrew."

I bring my cock to her, run it up and over her clit, getting it wet and hot and slippery with her juices again. She shudders.

"One more time. Shout it for me. Tell me what you want!"

"Fuck me!" she yells. "Fuck me now!"

I sink straight into her, the heat shared between us now. She brings her feet up to lock me in, and we ride the wave of each other, me pulling her hips on to my stiff, thick shaft, her riding it, demanding it, milking it with every thrust. As we speed up, I hunch over her body, tight against her pussy and pushing, trying to stretch every inch of need out of my cock, out of my body, and she holds me as tight as she can as the rhythm rises, the endless drumming of our hearts, our thrusts pushing us on to the edge of the universe and over into the black or white or nothing that's there.

"Oh god, Carrie. Oh god!"

"I got you, baby. You're mine, I got you…"

And she does. It's like confessional, and therapy, and love, and marriage, and a hundred other things besides to be able to be there with this woman, this woman who knows me upside down and inside out, to be able to open to her, with her, in her, feeling the spasm of need and the hold of love and the shared, impossible joy of her and me together. It's a thousand angels singing, with the devils on bass. It's everything I know, and every smile she has, and as she wraps her arms around my back and pulls me in and holds me, it's everything I ever knew was right.

By the time my heart comes back to nearly normal, she is shushing me down to earth like she would a child. And when she's sure I'm nearly back to myself, she kisses me softly on the lips.

"So…what do you wanna do first, honey? The walking by the river? Or the book-shopping? Or the dancing in the rain? Or the ice cream?"

My mind's gone blank. She could be speaking Swahili. I nod.

She chuckles, reaches out to the bedside cabinet, picks up a leaflet. Grins at me. "Or shall I call for pizza?"

MISS BLUE HAIR

ELLIE BARKER

The first thing that attracted me to her was the bright blue, almost luminous hair. It's not often that you see a young woman with that particular shade of dye, and when you add chocolate skin, it makes a rather arresting combination.

She was with another woman; tall with long blonde hair, pale skin and dark eyes. She was pretty, sure, but fairly generic. I'd just come back from a stint in a place where beauty was in the unusual, and found that I'd gotten bored with standard looks. It takes something different to catch my eye, which Miss Blue-Hair provided. The hair drew my attention…and the rest of her kept it. Shorter than me—but then at over six foot, most people are. A slim body, from what I could see beneath her leather jacket. A tight ass beneath jeans that had holes in both knees. An effortless walk and a quick glance from dark eyes that took in every shadow and detail without seeming to.

We were in a bar, and I admit I assumed she was there to

do what everyone else was there to do—drink, flirt and forget about work. But as her friend found a likely target and homed in with a well-practised flick of her hair, Miss Blue-Hair just found a table and pulled out her phone. Interesting.

Well, I can't say I'm averse to a challenge. I strolled over to Miss Blue-Hair, and her eyes flicked up to me as soon as I got within range. Maybe she was on the pull after all. I met her eyes and smiled, gesturing to the seat opposite her. "May I?"

She gave me an assessing look, and I wondered what she thought of me. Six-foot-something with dark hair tied into a ponytail, bright blue eyes and a lean face, mostly consisting of planes and angles. As her eyes scanned down my body and back up, I resisted the urge to smirk. Nice muscles covered by jeans and a black t-shirt that had short enough arms to show off those muscles; I say it myself, but I look good. Obviously she approved, because she nodded towards the empty space. "Of course."

I slid into the seat and grinned. "I would ask what a nice girl like you is doing in a place like this, but…"

"I'm not a nice girl." I saw the glint in her eyes, and then a real smile curved her mouth as she saw that I got the joke. She had a faint accent, and to my ear it was hella sexy. "What's your name?"

"Nikolas. Yours?" I prompted when all I got was a faint frown.

"Sky."

That took a moment to sink in. "Fucking hell, *the* Sky?"

She rolled her eyes and leaned back. "Which stories have you heard?"

"The thief."

"You've still got all of your valuables, right?"

"So far."

"You've been here for a few seconds. You're safe."

"I wouldn't say that." I smirked at her.

That made her grin and lean forward again. "All right. You want to fuck me?"

I couldn't help the laugh. I liked her. "It had crossed my mind."

"Do you like gay sex?"

It took me a moment to catch on, I admit, and I think my eyebrows went up. She was slim, sure, and now that I noticed, there wasn't any bust beneath that leather jacket. But she'd moved like a dancer, and I'd sure as hell not have suspected anything.

She was waiting for me to react, but hey, I've lived with surprises for long enough that nothing really phases me. I grinned. "I'm a bit out of practise, but I've always got time for re-learning."

She—he?—returned the grin, eyes flashing with amusement. "All right. Drink?"

"Water."

That made…let's go with 'her'…eyebrows go up. "Just once or is that a habit?"

"Habit."

She shrugged. "Come and loom over the bar, then. You'll get noticed."

I took advantage of the pause as we were leaning there, waiting for drinks. "All right, so just to get this straight…" No one can accuse me of being subtle. "Are you a man or a woman?"

"Male genitals, but female pronouns." She'd obviously

been asked enough times, and she had a steely glint in her eye. "Good enough?"

I can't resist an opening like that. "I dunno, you haven't proved that yet."

She had the dirtiest laugh that I've heard for a while, and that was the point I decided I was taking her home. If any woman laughs like that to one of my bad jokes, then I'm doing everything in my power to get her into bed. It's a policy that's earned me most of my best nights.

We had a few drinks and then she made sure her friend was set, slung her jacket back on and gave me the most come-hither look I've seen in a long time. I took her back to mine, trading insults the entire way and getting quite a few more laughs. She made me laugh too, which was a pleasure. I didn't get a lot of answers out of her, but then to be fair, I didn't really answer any questions either. We reached a mutual understanding—the first of several that evening, I admit.

She declined a drink and poked around my flat briefly, and then I steered her into the bedroom. That was when I got my second surprise of the evening.

She'd undressed, and I was admiring her from behind, enjoying the faint curve of the hips and the definitely gropeable buttocks...I might have tested that on the way home. But it was as she stepped back and raised her arms above her head, lifting her bright blue hair, that I realised I'd seen her before.

She'd had shorter hair then, as black as night. She'd been dressed in practical trousers and a t-shirt, and carrying a bag full of tools; an electrician's apprentice, fixing lights in an office building. They'd been in and out before anyone had realised some rather valuable documents had been copied and somehow removed from the building despite the security.

I'd idly wondered if the maintenance crew I'd walked past had been involved. After all, it wasn't a dissimilar cover to one that I'd occasionally employed for similar jobs…

Sky. Thief, seductress, gambler and heartbreaker. This slim, dark-eyed thing in my bed was that legend.

Well, I can't refuse a chance to fuck a legend. I'd just have to discuss her previous activities with her when we'd finished this business.

That train of thought came to a very nice conclusion as she turned to me, lifting her arms and stretching, taking my open mouth and caught breath as appreciation. "Lost for words?"

I managed a smile. "I've never been one for talking when I could express my appreciation in…other ways."

She fitted perfectly across my hips, her strong legs pressing on my thighs. I felt her cock slide against my stomach, leaving a wet trail in contrast to the warmth of the smooth skin. Her mouth pressed onto mine as I pulled her closer, and we spent a while like that, chests pushed together and skin sliding as my hands explored her body and her tongue teased mine, her long fingers winding into my hair.

"All right, enough," I said when it got too distracting, forcing my mouth off hers and pushing her shoulders back a little to get some distance. "I want in you."

Her mouth twitched into a smile. "Condom?"

"Always to hand." I put my hand behind my back and pulled one from under the pillow. "You or me?"

"As you asked so nicely, I figure I should let you fuck me."

Sky has a certain turn of phrase, and in that case, it was turn-on phrase. I was hard already but that just put the edge on it.

The condom was cool against my hot skin and as Sky stayed where she was, it meant I was touching us both as I rolled it on. She seemed to like my hands against her, and I took a moment to stroke up her cock where it rested against my stomach.

"C'mon," she told me, her voice wavering into a groan for a moment. "Lube?"

I found that under the pillow, too, much to her amusement.

"What else you got under there?" she asked.

"Hang around and you might find out." I liked the way her mouth twitched when she was amused, and took a minute to kiss it as I smeared lube on my cock.

We were still mouth-to-mouth as I tipped her backwards onto the bed, her legs still against my thighs and my arms around her back. It put my lubed cock in the perfect spot to slide down between her ass cheeks and press against her.

"Do it…" the husky voice said into my hair, and I felt her yield as I pushed against her tight circle. Slowly, that was the way, gentle and slow even though what I really wanted to do was bury myself inside her…

She was good, I'll give her that. A few strokes and she was relaxing around me, and then her legs shifted to wrap around my back and she'd pulled me to her in one swift, unexpected movement. My hands tightened on her shoulders and I swore into her neck as she took my length, still so tight that I could feel her ring gripping at the base of my cock. It was probably the most intense thing I'd ever experienced, and I nearly came right then.

She kept me for a moment, legs tight around my back. I slid my hands up to her bright hair and pulled her head back a little, biting at her neck, trying to make her twitch. When she did, I could feel the movement all the way down her body.

"Bastard," she murmured to me, and I felt her legs loosen a little. "You feel good."

"So...do...you..." I told her, matching the words to slow strokes and seeing her eyes start to unfocus, her hands grasping my shoulders. I pushed myself up a little and stopped for a moment.

"You...ok?" she asked, refocusing on me.

"Just adding something." I reached back for the lube and got a handful, and then pushed myself onto my knees so I could reach her cock.

I was rewarded with a convulsive spasm and a low moan as I ran my hand down the length and then up again. "Oh, fuck..."

"Absolutely." I snagged one of her hands and wrapped her fingers around her own cock, and then slid both of my hands down her slim body, admiring her slender chest. There was barely any change of shape between her ribs and stomach and hips, the bones all protruding ever-so-slightly under the muscle. My hands stopped at the top of her legs and then I was moving again, shifting my hips backward and forward, pushing into her. I was rewarded with a moan and her legs tightening around me, and her hand started to move.

She matched her strokes to mine and I felt her entire body open to me as I increased my speed. My own pleasure was taking over and I don't think I could have slowed down, wanting the next thrust and the next and next—

She moved her thumb up to the head of her shaft and a moment later was twitching, gasping, and everything tensed around me as a stream of white shot across her stomach and chest. That was enough to push me over the edge—well, I'd been close for a while. I left bruises on her thighs from my hands as I came, and I probably swore. I try to mind my language a little, but that was intense.

When I opened my eyes, I was looking down at her face, framed with that bright blue hair. Her eyes opened a moment later, lazily, and then focused on me as a smile twitched at her lips. "Nice."

"Agreed." I felt my thigh muscles protest as I shifted back and then started to withdraw. She released her legs from around my back and looked around for a tissue as I pulled my condom off.

"Here," I told her, and snagged the box from the side of the bed. Hey, I like to be prepared.

We both cleaned ourselves up, and then looked at each other, sat on the edge of the bed. I think that set the tone; neither of us are particularly cuddly people. But I ran my hand down a strand of that hair and then across her wet lips, and got a smile. "So," I said conversationally. "Gonna tell me what you did with the documents you stole?"

I'll give her credit; she didn't flinch. I was expecting her to try to run, but she just gave me a thoughtful look, tinged with a certain amount of amusement. This was a game, and she was playing. "You'll have to be more specific, Nikolas."

I liked the way she pronounced my name; she gave it the correct harshness of the *k* and some length on the *a*. "You were being an electrician, and then just after you'd vanished some documents were also found to have vanished." My fingers returned to her hair and wove into the bright strands. "You were dark then."

And before she could answer, before she could lie to me, I tightened my grip on her hair and dipped my head to her exposed neck.

"And don't think," I added, feeling my lips move against her skin, "of lying."

"But if I lie," Sky's breathy voice said from somewhere by my ear, "you'd just have to get the truth out of me, wouldn't you?"

"How would I do that?" I let my teeth enclose a bite of skin, with enough pressure to tell her that I could make a mark if I wanted to.

"You don't know how to?"

My teeth did leave a mark, white on her dark skin, and she groaned. I felt one of her hands come around my back and the other trail up my leg, towards my now-stiffening cock.

"But the problem with this," I said, and left another mark on her neck, "is that you like it."

"If you're nice to me—" Another groan as my teeth bit in again. "Maybe I'll tell you the truth."

I trailed my tongue down her neck, keeping my hand entwined in her hair. Her hands were now doing interesting things to my shoulders and back. "How nice would I have to be?" I asked when I'd finished with that patch of skin.

"Very."

With one movement I pulled her onto my lap, one hand still wound in her hair and her buttocks lying across my thighs. And I brought my free hand down sharply.

Sky groaned, and I felt her cock twitch against my leg. "That's not nice."

"No." I punctuated the word with another slap. "It's not." Another slap.

She was gasping and I felt her thrust her hips against me as I spanked her again. She wasn't even trying to fight; one hand was wound under my legs and the other pushed against my calf, and she was almost rock-hard now. I was, too; the way she moved on my lap was infuriating.

I spanked her until she was moaning under me, begging me to stop and please just fuck her again. But I slid my hand across her burning skin and smiled as she panted. "You were going to tell me some secrets."

"Fuck me."

"And you'll tell me?"

"Yes."

I unwound my hand from her hair and pulled her upright, back to where she had been sitting, and then promptly pushed her back onto the rumpled sheets. She went back onto her elbows, wincing as the fabric moved under her sore buttocks. "What now?"

I found a condom and rolled it on to her cock, and then shifted myself to kneel between her thighs and pulled her forward by her hips, sliding my cool hands under her ass.

"I'm going to be nice to you. And you're going to talk."

Her dark eyes were watching me as I lowered my head and gently licked the tip of her cock. The way she shuddered told me she was just as turned on as I was. Not that the rock-hard cock in front of me was disagreeing with that summary.

"I am an electrician. We did the work."

I slid my tongue down her shaft and back up, and felt her shudder again as I flicked the top.

"I knew of the documents."

Her cock fitted into my mouth, but I made the descent slow, tantalising.

"I…didn't…steal…them…"

Back up and down again, swirling my tongue around the head as I came up, feeling it jerk in my mouth.

"I carried…. I carried them. We were there…and could take them out."

I was moving faster, letting her hips move in my hands, pushing her up towards me as my mouth slid down her cock.

"I knew they…were important. But I didn't…steal. Not that time."

She was still lubed from earlier, and I freed a thumb to slide into her asshole. The thrust of pleasure nearly made me choke. Good thing I'm still ok at deep-throating.

I pulled out and teased the tip of her cock with my lips, raising my eyes to see the desperate face framed by bright blue hair, body tense with desire and need.

"That's all. I swear. I swear—"

And she did swear for real as I lowered my head again, plunging my thumb in and out of her ass as I let my mouth do the work. It was only a few seconds before her body jerked and tensed under me, and she made the most adorable deep groan as she came.

As she relaxed, I slid my hands out, and gave the tip of her cock a flick with my tongue that made her twitch.

"You," she told me, opening her eyes, "are very good at that."

"I'll start advertising as a professional torturer."

That got a smile, and then abruptly she pushed herself up. "You. On the bed."

I wasn't going to disobey. "What do I have to tell you?"

"Why were you there?" She knelt between my legs and grabbed the lube. As her hands stroked up and down my cock, I wondered how the hell she'd even been able to talk while I was blowing her. I was *so* turned on.

"Business. Same kind. You nicked the documents before I could."

She laughed, and then I swore and lost track of time for a bit. When I came back from that intense burst of pleasure, she was still there, kneeling naked between my thighs. "Who wanted them?"

"The highest bidder," I managed.

She snorted and climbed off. "Big shots with too much money."

"Who did you give them to?"

She gave me a long look, and then a smile. "The Queen."

I admit I was surprised that she'd told me, but hey, don't look a gift horse in the cock. I leaned myself up on one elbow and smiled at her. "So, now we've got that little confessional out the way…wanna come back sometime?"

She made a face, but her eyes were glinting in amusement. "Leave the money on the dresser?"

"You know it." I grinned at her. "I'm just gonna pee, so back in a minute."

That was when I learned something about Sky. I didn't take long to pee, but when I came out, she'd gone. Clothes gone, jacket off the hook, front door shut; and she'd done it absolutely silently.

I had opened my mouth to swear when I spotted

something. A white card, left on the hall table that's probably the closest thing I have to a dresser. Written on it was a mobile number, and the message, "Call me." And then a scrawled, "S".

I held the card between two fingers, smiling down at it. That was one intriguing woman, and the sex…well, it was good. Possibly even great.

Yeah, I called her. But that's another story.

THE BUTTERFLY WALTZ

LISA MCCARTHY

The silver Prius pulled into the driveway, coming to a halt next to a swathe of lilac bushes. Amy slid her hand down the side of the seat, releasing the belt. As the door opened, the car was filled with a sweet heavenly scent, and she sat in silence, breathing deeply. It calmed her, ready for the day ahead. Chances were that Michael, having finally taken a few days off work, was still in bed; at least she hoped he was as she needed time to get her thoughts in order before confronting him. She shuffled from the driver's seat, gravel crunching beneath her feet as she stood, the sound repeating with every long step as she made her way around to the front of the house. A sharp rasping came from the garden next door. "Good morning, Mrs Reed," she called, not bothering to wait for an answer. It wouldn't come anyway; it never did. Amy let out a sigh and twisted the keys in her hand, preferring to face the loneliness beyond the door to that outside.

Greeted by silence, she made her way through the large

empty hallway, passing doors that never opened and pausing briefly at the bottom of the staircase before deciding not to check on him. She carried on to the back of the house, her mood lifting slightly as she entered the kitchen. Colouring books lay scattered on the floor in the corner, and the table was covered with the remnants of breakfast. It was the only room that felt lived in; like home. Gathering the plates together, she scraped the leftover eggs and bacon into the waste-disposal and propped them one behind the other in the dishwasher. Once the drawer was full she turned and flicked the switch on the kettle, its low hissing filling the room as she spooned dark granules into a mug.

A splash of red by the window caught her eye, and she stood motionless as a pair of butterflies performed their courtship dance on the other side of the glass, swirling and swooping around each other before flitting out of sight. She held herself, arms wrapped tightly around her stomach as a single tear sauntered down her cheek.

When Michael first started his business, it was with the dream of spending more time together. She'd known the first few months would be tough; new staff, building a client base, and everything else involved in the start-up process, but it had gone surprisingly smoothly and profits had skyrocketed. What she hadn't expected was that he'd become so wrapped up in his work that she and the children would become nothing more than a distraction. They use to dance like the butterflies. Now, they hardly ever touched. Steam rose from the spout of the kettle and she poured the boiling water over the coffee. It sizzled as it hit, sending clouds of bitter-sweetness into the air, evaporating like their marriage. She couldn't go on with things the way they were, that much was certain. Today, she'd sit down with him and lay it out. Either he wanted her or he didn't; at least she'd know.

The milk jug was empty and she turned to open the fridge, catching Claudia's sun painting with her arm. It tore free from the magnetic strips, taking the rest of the door decorations with it on its journey to the floor. Amy knelt, her hands pulling pieces of paper from all directions. The fridge was a safe-haven for all those things that had no place, and rather than sorting them out occasionally, it was easier just to place new on top of old. There were receipts, drawings and a letter about a trip for Bethany. "Shit," she mumbled, looking at the date, chiding herself for being so absent minded when it came to school activities. A Christmas card from Mum and a photo from their holiday to Spain last year completed the collection. Once they were gathered into a pile, she lifted them up and placed them on the table.

A sound drifted in from the back room. Originally designed as a dining room, Michael had taken one look at it and decided it made the perfect office. He was supposed to be taking a break so there shouldn't have been any sound, unless.... Amy leant her ear against the door. Muffled conversation seeped through the wood. She turned back to the kitchen and slumped into one of the chairs. "You bastard," she said, her fingers kneading her temples, "You promised."

Her handbag hung from the back of the chair and she dug through it, searching for her phone. She could take the girls to Mum's, leave straight from school. Her hand shook as she scrolled down the list of numbers, pressing the call button when she found the right one. The sound drilled into her brain, loud and harsh, over and over, silencing itself after the twentieth ring. Where the hell was Mum when she needed her.

Sliding the pile of papers across the varnished oak, she leafed through them, looking for the photograph. It was taken by the pool about a week into their holiday, and his parents had taken the girls home by that time so it was just the two of them. From the glossy paper, Michael stared back at her, his deep brown eyes alight with passion. She traced his smile with her finger. He'd kissed her with those lips just after the picture was taken, then he'd grabbed her, tickling her until she gave up the camera, and thrown her down onto the sun lounger. His kiss had started at her ankles, slowly working its way up her body until their tongues were locked in a tango. The memory caused her breath to catch in her throat. They'd lived in each other's skin that week, wrapped up in a world of oneness. That kiss had lasted until evening when he'd pulled her into the pool and made love to her under the fire of the setting sun. Amy's heart thumped against her chest.

What on earth are you thinking, my girl?

"Mum, I need you, where are you?" Amy's voice echoed in the empty kitchen.

You don't need me. You know what you have to do.

"But I've done everything I can. It's over."

Don't you dare quit, you hear me? You are a fighter, always have been. You've just forgotten how strong you are. He's a man, Amy. They don't always see what's right in front of them. Make him see.

"But, what if I can't?"

And who are you again? My daughter would never think that way. You can do anything you put your mind to. You just need to want it bad enough. Do you want him?

Amy pushed herself away from the table. Even when absent, her mother knew exactly what buttons to push. Yes, she wanted him, and she was damn well going to get him back.

The dressing room was the only redeeming feature of the house—a space that belonged to her alone. Rooting through the chest of drawers, she threw day-to-day underwear to one side, hunting for one set in particular. Most of her sexy stuff had made its way to the back through months of neglect, and this set, bought for Valentine's Day, had never been worn. The collection on the floor was starting to cover her feet as the warm feel of cotton on her hands was replaced with the roughness of lace and the cold touch of satin. She pulled the remains of the drawer forward, sorting through pale pinks and whites. A flash of red appeared from the bottom of the pile, contrasting sharply with the rest of the fabric. Amy smiled.

The crimson silk clung to her body like a second skin as she stood in front of the mirror, her even tan enhancing the colour. Turning from side to side, she admired the reflection. Even after two children, her body remained in good shape, something she was very grateful for. Weekly swimming sessions had toned her muscles, and luck had played a big part in the lack of stretch-marks. The curve of her hips was in perfect harmony with the rounded swell of her breasts, the impact of which was all the more noticeable against the flatness of her stomach. Amy grabbed a lipstick from the dressing table and applied the deep red to her full lips. From housewife to siren in two simple steps, she mused. Try and resist this, Michael. Still, it wasn't enough. Turning to the clothes rail, she flicked through the array of outfits and picked out a crisp white blouse and short black skirt. Role playing wasn't something they'd tried before so it would definitely have an element of surprise to it. She pinned her hair up into a simple bun and grabbed a pair of dark-rimmed glasses. "And what would my secretarial duties be today, Mr Swanson? A massage? Certainly, Sir." Giggling to herself, she slipped on a pair of stilettos and headed downstairs.

Michael paced through the office, phone glued to his ear; the computer in the corner spitting out angry blasts of light as he thumped his fingers down on the keys. "Damn it, Rob, I told you to keep me informed every step of the way. Have you removed the multi-linking protocol? And it still won't connect? Try again, maybe you messed it up the first time." He ran his free hand across his chin and slumped into the leather chair, his face taking on a green hue as he leaned forward, staring at the screen. Rows of text mirrored themselves on his cheeks as his fingers moved with speed and precision across the keyboard. "Ok, I've sent you something to try…. No, keep me on the line." Amy watched from the doorway, trying to gauge the right time to interrupt. "Ok, well keep trying, and get the company on the phone. We may need to do this from their end…I don't care…I'll double check everything again from this end. Call me back when you get hold of them." The phone slammed down on the table and Michael leant his head back, massaging his nasal bones.

Amy walked behind him and placed her hand on his shoulder. He took hold of her slender fingers in his and squeezed. "I'm sorry, Amy, you know how it is. No rest for the wicked, as they say."

"Actually I don't know, Mr Swanson. I'm simply here to tell you that your next appointment is waiting." She swivelled the chair around, forcing him away from the computer. "It's your wife, and she misses you." She undid the buttons on her blouse, letting it fall open.

"Wow, you look amazing." Michael's eyes widened as they scanned her body. He reached out, yanking the blouse back, and ran his hand across her breasts, down around her stomach, and pulled her towards him. "It's not a special occasion, is it? Don't tell me I've forgotten something?"

Amy ran a hand through his soft dark hair and leant forward, her lips level with his ear. "You've forgotten a lot recently and we need to do something about it." He kissed the top of her breasts and she gasped sharply as pleasurable shivers spread from his touch. Moving back, she grazed her lips against his cheek, searching for his mouth. He grabbed her, drawing her onto his lap, his lips pressing into hers with an intensity she'd almost forgotten existed. She thrust his mouth open with her tongue, feeling him, tasting him. A fire ignited within her stomach, spreading downwards, and she felt her own wetness seeping through her panties. Michael slipped a hand under the back of her blouse and ran his nails gently down her spine. She arched her back into him, pulling the clip from her hair, shaking the long blond strands free. "I want you, Michael, right here, right now," she whispered into his parted lips. He moaned, filling her with his breath, and she inhaled, taking him deep into her lungs.

"I—"

The phone rang and Michael's muscles tensed. He stared into her pleading eyes for a moment, his hand hovering over the piece of plastic. "I'm really sorry, honey. I need to take this." He pushed her off his lap and scooped the phone from the table, placing it to his ear. "Rob, talk to me."

Amy stood, unmoving apart from the clenching and unclenching of her fists. Getting out of bed to work on the day he'd promised to her was bad enough, but to push her away as if she meant nothing.... What to do? Her mind spiralled. Earlier she'd been capable of walking away, but now she'd had a taste of what was missing and it tore into her heart like a dagger. She took a step back, reaching for the door handle, her eyes never leaving the back of his head.

You're not seriously giving up are you?

Her hand faltered on the cold metal.

Who is more important, you or them?

I am, she told herself. He's not going to do this. Come on, girl, you love a challenge. Amy moved around the chair into Michael's line of sight. He placed a hand in the air, fingers splayed. No, five minutes wouldn't do anymore. From now on, if Amy wanted attention, Amy would damn well get it.

Ignoring the hand gesture, she knelt in front of him, her hands deftly undoing his jeans. He stared down at her, eyes wide, his lips mouthing the word 'no' as she moved from button to button. He was hard already. His erection pushed against the faded denim and she rubbed her hand against him, letting her nails grate over the top of the taut fabric. A hissing sound escaped from his mouth and he scrunched his eyes closed at her touch. Placing a hand over the receiver, Michael whispered, "Please, don't."

"Stop? I wasn't going to," she replied, a smile playing across her face as she slid her fingers through the opening in the jeans and wrapped them around his shaft. The tinny sound of Rob's voice played on in the background as she pulled him free. "This was supposed to be my time, remember? So, you carry on with your call, and I'll amuse myself instead." She leant forward, holding him in a firm but gentle grip, and ran her tongue around the tip of his swollen cock. Small beads of pre-cum appeared in appreciation and she licked them off with a swirling motion, savouring them. God, she'd forgotten just how good he tasted, and this little appetiser had made her hungry for more. Opening her mouth, she slowly pushed onto him, her lips sliding down, pulling his entire length deep into her throat. His work became the last thing on her mind as her senses were overloaded with his smell, taste and feel. It was their world again and nothing outside of it existed as she explored him; nothing except the giving and receiving of pleasure.

Somewhere far away she heard the words "Can I put you on hold for a moment?" and she twisted her head slightly, looking up at him. Michael's hand was no longer glued to his ear; instead it fell to the side, the phone held between whitening knuckles. Amy followed the contours of his arm with her eyes.

His face was still, eyes closed, mouth open. He looked as if he'd simply fallen asleep, but his quick, shallow breathing told a different story, and the sound of it sent a surge of tingles through her abdomen. She lightly bit the tip of his cock with her teeth, soft enough not to hurt yet hard enough for the feeling to register, before tracing the same path with her tongue. He gasped, hands now at his side, gripping the arms of the chair. She let her tongue wander down the whole length of his shaft, soaking him with saliva. He pulsed against her as she gently blew onto his skin, cooling it, before taking him once again into the heat of her mouth. His breathing was heavier now, intermingled with sighs and groans. She loved the sounds he made, or that she produced from him, and she matched the pace of his breath, drawing him into her, sliding him out, feeling every inch of him moving over her lips and her tongue.

He grabbed the back of her head, tangling his fingers into her hair and pushed her downward, himself deeper into her. She took him hungrily, feeding off his growing need, her hands grasping at his shirt as she sucked and licked him. His hands tightened around her head, fingers painfully twisting through her hair. She didn't care. The power she held over him was better than any painkiller, and it meant that he was close. Amy increased the pace, sucking harder with every thrust until he exploded into her mouth. She swallowed, taking him down, not wanting to waste a drop. Every living cell he'd just ejaculated was a part of him and she urgently needed to make them a part of her also. He softened slightly, losing rigidity in her mouth. Tenderly, she took him in her hand, licking the last remaining cum from his head. Michael's grip on her hair loosened and he stroked her scalp with his thumbs. After tucking him back into his jeans, she stood. Running a hand through his hair, she planted a ghost of a kiss on his still lips. He raised his arms to her, the phone still in his hand. He looked at it, then back at her. Crap.

"Rob, sorry about that...yeah...he is? Put him through then...Daniel, good morning..."

Michael listened intently to the voice on the phone, his spare hand fiddling with his jeans. Managing to push the last button back through its hole, he patted down the front of his shirt and turned to the computer. Amy pushed the door open as quietly as she could and slipped through the gap, closing it behind her.

Sunlight bounced off water droplets, turning the garden fountain into a cascade of diamonds. Amy placed her hands under the cool flow, letting it slip through her fingers. Inside, she glowed as brightly as the summer sky, and the colourful array of flowers that framed the lawn seemed to nod their agreement. Yes, this was the start of something new and exciting; a chance to fix the past, enjoy the present, and build the future. It was the sense of freedom that hit her most. The chains around her heart had disintegrated and she finally felt able to breath. Grabbing a pair of secateurs from the shed, she wandered around the garden. Birds sang from the bushes, their melodious tunes broken occasionally by a sudden flitting of wings, and Amy hummed along with them as she carefully cut a selection of roses as a centrepiece for the dining table. She ran the blade down each stalk, removing the thorns, before gathering them up and heading back to the house.

The door to the office was still closed. Amy didn't mind. Events had been set in motion and that was all that mattered; besides, she needed a bit of time to organise things for the evening. Michael's parents had already agreed to have the girls overnight, which was a lovely gesture on their part, and her mind was racing with ideas for a romantic night in. Pulling a piece of paper from the drawer, she started a list: fillet steak, baby potatoes, asparagus, strawberries, two bottles of Rioja. She paused, pencil to her mouth. Was there anything else? Ah, yes, chocolate and cream. Chocolate sauce was a must for desert and she bit her lip as she imagined the possibilities. She scribbled down the final items on the list and placed the paper into her bag. Then she picked up the roses and walked over to the sink. Their perfume filled the room as she carefully arranged them in a water filled vase, and closing her eyes, she buried her face in the soft petals, allowing the smell to seep into her skin. A swooshing sound followed by footsteps rang through the kitchen. Any minute, he would walk up behind her and slip his arms around her waist. In her head she could feel his body heat, his hot lips on her neck, the touch of his hands as he ran them over her body. She wanted to hold him, to kiss him, their bodies dancing in unison. Today we become butterflies, she thought, today we finally get our wings. Turning, she placed the vase on the table, positioning it in the centre. "Hey, Sexy, I was just going…"

"Don't 'sexy' me. What the fuck are you playing at?" Michael stormed across the room, stopping within inches of her face. "I mean, is there something wrong with you? Don't you understand how important that call was?" He dragged his white-knuckled hands through his hair. "Daniel is my most important client and we almost fucking lost him thanks to your stunt."

Amy tried to speak. Her mouth moved into the shape of words but they refused to come out, stunned into silence. She turned back to the sink, desperate to avoid eye-contact, her arms wrapped tightly around her chest. Thoughts whipped around in her head like moths to a flame, burning up before she could make sense of them. What the hell was happening? Her wings drooped, singed and crumbling with the heat of his waiting glare. "I'm sorry," she whispered, as all her future hopes disintegrated.

"Sorry? Is that all you have to say? How the fuck could you even think of doing something so selfish?"

A hard ball of anger formed in her chest, growing larger with every intake of air. Selfish? Her? Of all the hypocritical bastards. "You didn't try and stop me," she said, her voice cold and quiet. Its usual power concentrated on keeping the ball in place. She grabbed a dishcloth and started scrubbing the side of the sink.

"What did you say? I can't hear you." He took hold of her arm, twisting her around. "Fucking look at me when you're talking." His touch released the ball of anger, and it swept through her system, extinguishing the flame in her mind. The moths exploded from her mouth in the form of words, and she spat them in his direction.

"I said you didn't stop me. You enjoyed it just as much as I did, and if you want to see selfishness, just look in the fucking mirror." She threw the cloth at the sink, knocking over the utensil pot. "When did you last spend any time with us, huh? When did you so much as kiss me goodnight? It's all fucking work with you these days. I can't even remember what it feels like to make love to you. I'm sick of it, Michael. I'm fucking sick to death of it."

"Do you think I like things the way they are? I'd much rather spend time with the girls or curled up on the sofa with you, but I can't. I have to do this now." He turned and smacked his hand into the wall. "We talked about this. You knew damn well that it wasn't going to be easy, so what the hell do you want from me! You didn't complain when I gave you your perfect fucking house in your perfect fucking street, did you?"

"Oh, I get it," a bitter sounding laugh escaped from her throat as she fought to keep the tears back. "This is all my fault. Well, here's something for you. I never wanted any of this. For you to be your own boss, yes, because it's what you wanted, and I get that it took time to build up, but you did build it, and you have Rob who's more than capable of picking up the slack, but will you use him? No, because you've turned into a fucking control freak, that's why." Amy paused for breath. "And, this house? This lifestyle? This isn't what I wanted. I just wanted you, that's it." Her fists clenched with frustration and she let out a yell, hammering them against his chest. Michael grabbed them, throwing her back.

"Don't you dare hit me."

"All I ever wanted was you. All I'll ever want is you, and you can't even see it." She swung at him again, connecting with more force than last time. His eyes flared and he caught her arm, forcing her backwards until she was trapped between his body and the wall. Amy fought back, struggling to push him away, but he took hold of her other arm, manoeuvring her until both her hands were pinned above her head. His breathing was heavy, laboured, full of anger. She could feel it in the heaving of his chest against hers and the hot blasts on her cheek from between his clenched teeth. She could feel his erection growing, pushing against her, the anger in his face glowing, and his eyes, dilated, were those of a wild animal.

"I want you too," he growled, his mouth closing in on

hers. She sank her teeth around his bottom lip, gasping as he pushed his body harder against her. Pinning both her wrists with one hand, he gripped her throat, squeezing as he ran his teeth across her cheek. "You have no idea just how much I fucking want you."

Stars began to appear in her peripheral vision as she struggled for breath, adrenalin coursing through her brain. It was terrifying yet exhilarating and she ground her hips against him in desperation. He released the pressure on her neck and she gulped air down, her head spinning as every nerve in her body shot to life. His touch seemed to be magnified a thousand times as he ran his fingers down across her breasts, bringing her skin to life with an onslaught of goose-bumps.

She felt his fingers tracing the top of her bra. They slipped inside and tugged sharply, releasing an erect nipple. He took it between his thumb and forefinger, squeezing. The sudden pressure sent a web of heat through her breast and she opened her mouth to cry. His mouth closed over hers, swallowing the sound as he squeezed again, harder, stretching her as his hand continued its downward journey.

She fought to release her hands, wanting to scratch, to bite, anything to push him away, to drag him closer, but he held her fast as his free hand grabbed the wet silk fabric between her legs and ripped it from her skin. It tore into her flesh as it parted, sending her body into meltdown. The fantasy of making love to him was long gone and she begged with what little voice she had left, "Michael, fuck me…please fuck me now."

He pulled back from her face, and she could feel his huge erection digging into her stomach. "Please," she whimpered. A smile spread across his lips as he lifted her panties to his face, breathing deeply. Without a word, he lowered her arms and slipped the blouse from her shoulders. He reached behind and unfastened her bra, dropping the clothes to the floor. Amy grabbed for him, wanting to feel his hard cock in her hand, but he caught her again, spinning her to face the wall.

"I'm the only one who gets to touch," he whispered in her ear, drawing her arms behind her back. Placing his feet against hers, Michael thrust her legs apart. "Do you want me to touch you?" She nodded, throwing her head back onto his shoulder as his hand slid across her ass and between her thighs. He ran his fingers over her swollen lips and thrust them inside her. Her body shuddered as they slid through her wetness. "Is this enough for you or do you want more?" He didn't wait for an answer as he let his thumb glide over her clitoris, stroking it with a circular motion, his fingers pumping into her. Pressure built inside her at the first touch, growing in intensity until she thought she would explode... and she did. Wave after wave of muscle contractions tore through her body, threatening to rip her apart, clamping hard on his fingers as they fucked her. He stopped as her climax subsided, pulling his hand away.

Amy collapsed against the wall, her legs barely holding her weight as aftershocks trickled through her. She wanted to be in his arms now, close, warm, revelling in her post-orgasmic glow, but he held her in place. Something wrapped around her wrists, tightening.

"What are you doing?" she asked, her chest still heaving.

"What you asked me to. Now, be a good girl and shut the fuck up, or do you want me to gag you as well?"

She shook her head, eyes wide. He'd never been forceful

before, never tied her up, and she should have been scared by the sudden change. Instead, it was turning her on in ways she never thought possible. Her body was screaming for him as he dragged her over to the table, sending the glass vase hurtling towards the wall with a swoop of his arm. It shattered, a violent, romantic outburst, sending blood red petals and glistening shards across the kitchen floor.

Amy bit her lip to stifle a moan. Michael's new-found power seemed to seep from his pores, filling the room with his sexuality. Her inner ache deepening as he lay her across the cool wood, face up, arms immobilised beneath her. He stood, his dark eyes running the length of her body. With her wrists tied, she had no choice but to arch her back, thrusting her breasts into the air. He ran his hands across them, barely making contact with her skin. It was as if an electrical current had passed through her, and he watched as she trembled under his touch.

Stepping back, he moved to the end of the table. Amy twisted to keep him in sight but found she couldn't. She felt his hands on her knees, opening them. One of her legs was drawn to the side and something soft wrapped around it. She tried to move and found she couldn't. Then the other leg. This time the restraint was firmer, biting into her skin in places. Hands reached around her waist, dragging her towards him until her ass was hanging over the table edge. She closed her eyes, waiting for him to penetrate her, but there was nothing. No touch, no sound, no anything. Her skin prickled with anticipation.

A sudden chill spread between her legs as he blew on her, and her clitoris pulsed with delirious desperation. Fingers spread her outer lips, pushing down on them from both sides. She was wide open to him now as he ran his thumbs around her juice-soaked opening. The sensation was overwhelming. Every part of her mind focussed on one small part. Then she felt heat. His tongue, pushing inside her, swirling and licking. She clawed at the table as he flattened his tongue, drawing it harshly across her most sensitive part. With every millimetre, the pressure inside her built, pulling her down into a swirling mass of painful pleasure. Fireworks appeared behind her eyelids and she threw her head back as the orgasm surged through her body.

A thousand molecular explosions racked through her brain, only matched in intensity by the animalistic sounds erupting from her throat. Michael placed his hands on her stomach, feeling the rhythmical contractions beneath her skin, before reaching down and releasing her legs. She drew her knees upward, trying to curl into a ball, needing to shut off from the world while her senses recovered, but he moved between them.

Amy let out a mewling sound as he pushed into her, her swollen, aching lips gripping him as he entered, making him feel harder and bigger than ever before. Already, she could feel the tension inside her building again. It was too much. Her mind flailed, trying to grasp at something, but there was only a deep and frenzied wanting. She wrapped her legs around his waist, pulling herself around him, matching his rhythm.

There was a harshness to his breathing now; not quite a voice but more than the movement of air, and it filled her ears with its urgency. Her insides tightened, clinging to him as he thrust forward, filling her completely, his fingers tugging and twisting her breasts. Outside of that feeling there was no time, no life, no world. Her entire existence centred on that one moment and she gave herself to it completely.

Michael stopped thrusting as her pelvic muscles contracted around him, their rhythmical force drawing him deeper into her, bringing him to the point of climax. He roared, filling her with his cum, her muscles pumping him for every last drop. Collapsing onto his elbows, his panting breath flowed across the skin of her stomach, drying the beads of sweat that dropped from his hair. Eventually, he rose, pulled her to a sitting position and untied her hands. She gazed at him with flushed cheeks, still high on endorphins and adrenalin. She hardly felt his hands as he rubbed them down her arms, the sudden increase of circulation sending pins and needles from shoulders to fingertips. Slumping forward, she buried her head into his neck, her back heaving as he gently ran his hand across it.

"I'm so sorry, Amy. Are you ok?" His voice overflowed with love and fear.

She tried to speak, to put into words what had happened and how she felt, but her mind was full of mist. Thoughts twirled around on a carousel, rising up then pirouetting away, just beyond her grasp. It was frustrating yet beautiful—magical almost—and she wanted to share it with him. Her mouth opened and closed, willing the words to come, but all her mind would give was a stream of soundless tears. Amy pulled him closer, letting them flow across his skin, not knowing why, just that they were good tears and he needed to feel them.

Michael took her head in his hands, wiping the wetness away with his thumb. "Shit, I'm sorry. I didn't want to hurt you." He stood, fumbling with the buttons of his jeans. She could see the confusion in his face, wanted to comfort him, but everything seemed to be in slow motion. He picked his shirt up from the floor, and stood, back to her, head lowered. "I didn't mean to…" She watched a droplet of water bounce off the floor between his feet…then he was gone.

The kitchen suddenly seemed very large as she sat on the wooden surface, knees pulled to her chest. The ticking of the clock pounding off the walls sent judders through her skin. She'd heard the click of the front door latch, wanted to run after him, but the bones in her legs felt like jelly. Was this it?

Loneliness surged through her, threatening to bring another bout of tears in its wake. She'd messed everything up, pushed him too far, and now he was gone. Knowing that the pain would keep building if she sat there, Amy struggled to the edge of the table and lowered her feet to the floor. Her knees buckled as she placed her full weight on them, sending her sprawling onto the cold tiles. Gritting her teeth, she crawled over to the door and pulled herself up with the handle. It felt as if her legs were nothing more than a memory, sensations fading in and out as she worked the muscles. Gradually, they took form and she shuffled her way across the expanse of the hallway to the stairs.

The plush brown carpet encompassed her feet as she made her way, one step at a time, to the upstairs hallway. It felt good as it wormed its way between her toes, the warmth of the fibres flowing through her skin. Amy shivered, suddenly aware of how cold she'd become. All she wanted was to crawl under the heat of the duvet and hide from everything. Her eyelids felt heavy as tiredness washed over her. She needed a shower first though, her body salty with sweat, Michael's cum drying on her thighs. Wrapping her arms around her nakedness, she opened the door to the bedroom.

Michael's dressing gown was closest, draped over the corner of the bed, but she bypassed it, not wanting to wrap herself up in his smell. Instead, she made her way through to the bathroom and grabbed a towel from the shelf. It felt soft against her skin as she drew it over her shoulders, and she reached up, turning the shower to hot. It spluttered for a moment, then came to life with a harsh blast.

Stepping back, Amy laid the towel over the radiator, catching sight of herself in the mirror above the sink. She stared at the stranger in the glass. Lipstick smears covered the lower half of the face, but it was the eyes that stood out. They were puffy, blotchy with tears, but bright, the blue shining with a strange new spark. She pulled her hair back, holding it behind her head as she studied herself. Exhaustion, yes, that was apparent, but there was more. Knowledge? Excitement? They were the eyes of someone who'd taken the universe apart and put it back together piece by piece, not quite understanding the complexity of what they'd found, just knowing that they'd found it. They were the eyes of experience, and it frightened her.

Mist covered the glass as she quickly checked out the rest of her body, the red scratch marks on her stomach, bruising on her wrists, wiping the mirror as she went until the wet distortion turned her perfect figure into a monstrosity. She let out a sigh, stepping away from the sink and into the harsh spray of the shower.

Hot water pounded her back, massaging her aching

limbs. It stung at first, contacting with the welts on her skin, and she scrunched her eyes until the sensation passed. Once her body adjusted to the temperature, the pain turned to a warm numbness. She turned slightly, allowing the stream of water to cascade down her breasts. Her nipples were erect, still sore after his insistent tugging, and she ran a soapy hand between her legs, inspecting the rest of the damage. Swollen lips greeted her, tender to the touch, but as her fingers gently ran across their surface a jolt of excitement shot through her veins.

"What's happening to me?" she whispered, the hissing and spluttering of water jets eating her voice. Where was Michael? Would he ever come back? Amy shook her head at the thought. He had to come back, to help her understand what was happening between them; how he could have been a gentle, timid lover all his life then end up like this, and why she loved it, why she suddenly felt more alive than at any other time in their relationship. She closed her eyes, resting her cheek against the cold tiles, her mind scolding her like a naughty child. *Don't overthink, Amy, what good will it do?* The water pelted down on her, leaving redness everywhere it hit, but she stayed in its flow, letting her thoughts drain away.

Coldness swept across her skin, wiping away the days events. She stood, eyes still closed, letting light shivers cleanse her from the inside out. No more thoughts, no more worries, just a freshness of body and mind. The musical tone of the water had ceased to play but she didn't question why, wanting to stay in that place just a little longer.

"Amy?"

Michael's voice bit into the silence. She didn't answer.

"Oh, God, come here."

She felt his presence, heard the rustling, then found herself wrapped in the soft, thick towel. An arm slid behind her legs and she was lifted into the air, being carried towards the bedroom. "Michael?"

"Yes, honey, it's me." He lay her on the bed, dragging the duvet all the way up to her chin. It was heavy, comforting, and she pulled her knees up to her chest. Leaning forward, he brushed a single strand of damp hair from her face and tucked it behind her ear.

"I'll get the bed all wet."

"I don't care. You'll catch your death if you don't warm up."

Gentle, caring Michael, the man she'd fallen in love with all those years ago was back. Amy shifted under the weight of the duvet, curling around to rest her head on his lap. "What's happening to us?" She reached an arm out, resting it softly on his leg. "What was that earlier?"

"I honestly don't know." Taking her hand in his, he stroked each of her fingers in turn. "I never meant to hurt you. The last thing I would ever want to do is hurt you. It's just…"

"It's just what? Talk to me." Her hand wrapped around his, squeezing it tightly. He pulled away.

"I can't."

Amy stared into his eyes, seeing the worry lines around them for the first time. He broke eye contact with her, staring at the clock on the bedside table instead.

"I was going to leave you today." She watched his eyes widen. "You've become more and more distant. I couldn't even talk to you. That's why I did what I did; not through a selfish need for sex, but because I had to make you see what you were throwing away." Reaching forward, she laid a palm on his cheek. "I love you so much, Michael, but I can't go on living like this. I need to feel worth something to you, that we're a team, that you trust me enough to open up to."

"I'm so sorry. I love you too. You mean everything to me. That's why I've been pushing myself. I want you to have the life you deserve." Michael climbed into the bed next to her, pulling the covers over both of them. "Were you really going to leave?"

"Yes."

"And now?" He wrapped his arms around her waist, burying his head in her breasts. "After what I've done today? I don't even know what that was. I look at you now..." he ran a hand lightly over her chest, "and I feel how soft your skin is, and I hate myself for what I did. I was just so frustrated with work, and you came to me looking the sexiest I've ever seen you. Something just snapped. If I could take it back, do it over, I would."

Amy ran her fingers through his hair. The warmth of his body seeped into every strand as they covered the back of her hand, falling back into place as she moved across his scalp. "I don't want you to take it back. Yes, you scared me, but I needed it as much as you did. Seeing you lose control, feeling your anger, it made me a part of your life again. And, I don't know why exactly, but it excited me." His lips brushed against her skin, tender kisses trailing up towards her neck. She moaned, raising her chin as his tongue brushed against it. "Stop," she whispered, fighting the urge to kiss him back. He didn't listen, his teeth grazing the side of her neck. "I mean it, Michael. Stop." She pushed him away, bringing his face level with hers. "I want this too, but it doesn't solve anything. We really need to talk. What is going on with you?"

Michael sighed and rolled onto his back. He rubbed his face, pausing for a moment as if in thought. "The business isn't doing as well as I'd hoped. Yes, it's making money, the bills are getting paid and there's a bit of spare cash, but I have to be on top of it all the time. If I lose just one big client it could all fall apart. We'd lose everything, Amy, and where would that leave you and the girls? I am so stressed right now. I can't sleep, I don't want to eat, and I don't want you to have to deal with all of this."

Amy pulled his hands away from his face. His eyes glowed with vulnerability, and a single tear sauntered down his cheek. Sitting up, she took his chin in her fingers. "Where would it leave us?" she said, kissing the damp tear-track. "With you, that's where. I didn't marry you for your money. As far as I remember, we didn't have any back then." Turning her back to him, she wrapped herself in his arms. "Do you remember the first house we bought, the one in Viewside?"

"With the glorious view of the park for all of two months before the council built that block of flats? Of course," he laughed.

"I still remember the first time I tried to use the washing machine at night and we found out it was attached to the same fuse as the lights."

"Clean clothes and candle night, we'd grab a cheap bottle of wine and pretend to have a romantic night in."

Amy raised his hand to her mouth, kissing across his knuckles. "There was nothing pretend about it. It was romantic. Just you and me, the glow of the candles, and music to drown out the machine. We slow danced for hours, and we could have put the lights back on when the washing was done but we never did."

"It was a death-trap. We were lucky to get out of that place alive."

"Yes, it was," she said, laughing with him for a moment before sighing, "but do you remember how happy we were?"

"Yes, but I also recall how young we were. We didn't know and couldn't afford any better. Now we can."

"Is this better though? More rooms than we know what to do with, extra cleaning, neighbours who look down their noses at us. Really, Michael, can you honestly say that we're better off?" She rolled back to face him, propping her head on the pillow next to his. "I hate this house, I hate not having you around, I hate that the girls are going to grow up with a father that's too busy to spend time with them, and most of all now, I hate that you hate it too."

"It kills me to watch them play through the window and not have time to join them...shit..." Michael clamoured over her, his elbow catching her stomach.

"Ouch, what on earth are you doing?" She sat up, rubbing her side.

He ignored her question as he reached for the bedside table, turning the clock into view. 14:35. "The girls," he said, trying to untangle himself from the bedclothes, "what time does school finish?"

She grabbed him around the waist, easing him back onto the bed. "Your mum is picking them up. I was going to do a romantic meal tonight but things didn't really go to plan."

"Well, in that case," he kissed her gently on the lips, "you relax and I'll sort out dinner. I've got some other things I need to take care of so I'll probably be gone a few hours, but I'll definitely be back and I'm all yours tonight. Can we talk later?"

Amy nodded, "Just as long as we do. I don't want to ignore this, ok? Oh, and there's a shopping list in my bag if you need it."

Michael ran a finger down her cheek and neck, and lifted the covers. A knowing smile spread across his face. "We could do a lot more than talk if you want to."

"I don't know, you've left me kind of sore from earlier." She bit her lip and raised an eyebrow. "I'll have to do a bit of checking myself first and let you know." A wink and a giggle followed him through the door.

———

Sunlight filtered through the cream chiffon curtains, filling the room with a warm hazy light, and Amy pulled the covers from her body, allowing it to illuminate her skin. A bottle of moisturiser sat on the bedside table and she picked it up, twisted the lid off, and poured it into her hand. The scent of vanilla seeped into the air and she breathed in deeply. She loved the smell. It was sweetness, home-baking, and naughty little treats when no-one's looking. Lifting a leg, she ran her hands across her thigh, down towards her ankle and back up, fingers massaging the cream into her skin as she went. The other leg followed, then arms, down onto her palms, then up onto her shoulders. Another squeeze of moisturiser, then her hands smeared it across her chest, rubbing each breast in a circular motion, her thumbs concentrating on her soft, pink nipples. Fingers kneaded across the supple skin of her stomach and down onto her hips, hovering around the sensitive area at the top of her inner thighs, causing her to moan slightly.

The sound of crunching gravel filtered in from outside and Amy stopped mid-stroke, self-consciousness flooding her system. She held her breath, listening, then a clatter in the hallway and more crunching. A giggle escaped from her lips. Why do they always drop leaflets at the most inappropriate times? As the sound faded, her hand resumed its exploration. Tentatively, she ran a finger across her inner lips. The swelling had subsided, leaving them dry and sore, and she winced at the touch. How long would it take to recover from a fuck like that? She figured it would be days; so much for Michael's hopes for the evening. But as the memory of that afternoon played in her head, as her body remembered the sensation of his forceful fucking, it reacted. The deep muscular tingling returned and wetness seeped from inside her, coating her fingertips. Raising them to her mouth, she licked each finger in turn, ingesting the juices. The smell and taste of her own arousal created a desperate need to be satisfied and she lowered her hand once more. Her clitoris stood to attention, waiting, ready for her touch, and she drew her saliva soaked fingers across it.

———————

It was seven o'clock by the time Michael arrived home. Amy was asleep on the sofa and he laid a whisper of a kiss on her head before heading through to the kitchen. She stirred, a contented smile spreading across her face as the metallic sound of pots and pans moving seeped into her ears. He was being good to his word and it filled her with an overwhelming love for him. She sat up and ran her hands through her hair, a yawn escaping from her lips. She had wanted to be perfectly made up when he got home, but it didn't matter. She could run and get dressed while he was cooking, and the most important thing was just being in each other's company. Shuffling into the kitchen, she stopped to take in the view. He was bent over the sink, knife in hand, removing the last remnants of fat from the steak. She wasn't sure if it was the fact that he remembered she didn't like fatty meat, or simply the sight of his firm ass in those jeans that thrilled her more, and she longed to touch him. Tiptoeing across the room, she slid her hands around his waist. He jumped, sending the knife clattering to the floor.

"Jesus, you scared me. I thought you were sleeping," he said, turning to kiss her, his hands raised to avoid smearing her with meat juice.

"I was. I thought I'd had a wonderful dream. Turns out it wasn't a dream…"

Michael's mobile phone rang. He rinsed his hands quickly under the tap and grabbed for his jacket. After checking the caller, he shook his head. "I'm really sorry, I have to take this. It's Rob. I've been trying to get him all afternoon."

The dream spiralled downward, threatening to drag her with it. Why had she thought it would be this easy? It didn't matter how much he promised, the business would always come first. It was his baby, his number one priority, and she was…

"Please trust me," he mouthed, holding eye contact with her before stepping into his office and pulling the door behind him. Trust him? What the hell did that mean? There'd been too many questions, too many possibilities already, and

Amy was tired of them all. What she did know was that there were steaks ready to be cooked and an expensive bottle of Rioja on the table.

The meat hit the pan with a loud sizzle and she opened the cupboard next to the cooker, retrieving a large goblet. Usually, they let the wine breath for a while before drinking, but she poured a glass, knocking it back straight away. Turning the steaks, she filled the glass once more. Michael was still locked away in his sanctuary, and chances were he'd be in there for the night. A few leaves of lettuce, some cucumber and a tomato thrown into a bowl was the most she could be bothered to do for a salad, and she jabbed a fork into the rare meat, transferring it onto the plates. She thought of taking hers, along with the bottle, into the living room, leaving him to eat when he felt like, but something prompted her to knock the office door. He opened it, sniffing the air.

"Glad you agree, Rob. Now I really have to go…yes, I'm sure…I'll have the contract ready for you tomorrow afternoon." He placed the phone on the counter and sauntered over to the table. "Something smells really good, and I'm not talking about the food," he said, kissing the side of her neck.

"Whatever. You'd better eat before it gets cold." Amy picked up the glass and took another mouthful.

"What have I done now? Was it the phone call?"

She shrugged her shoulders, stuffing a forkful of steak into her mouth.

Michael's laugh filled the room. "I can't drop everything without warning, and besides, I'm here now, and so are you. Can we just enjoy a meal together? I'll explain everything later."

Amy scrunched her eyes, trying to scowl at him, but his smile was infectious, and when a slice of cucumber caught her on the side of the face, she broke into laughter with him. It had been a long time since the cheeky little boy inside him had been allowed to play, and she flicked a piece of tomato back in retaliation. "Don't think you can get away with that, Mr Swanson, I do believe we have chocolate sauce for desert."

Michael raised an eyebrow. "And how are you planning on serving it?"

"How? Don't you mean on what?" She rested her little finger against the corner of her mouth, raising her eyebrows back at him.

"Well," he said, laying down his knife and fork, "I think we should leave desert until after we've talked." He ran his foot up her leg. "It will be so much more enjoyable then."

"And why is that?"

"You'll see. Grab your glass and follow me."

He stood and held out a hand. Amy took it, following his lead. In the living room, Michael motioned to the sofa. "Sit here. I'll be right back."

A rustling emanated from the hallway as she sat, arms folded across her lap. Years of mindless shopping trips allowed her to differentiate between the sound of bags from the cheaper outlets and those from the more expensive stores, and it was definitely the latter. All of a sudden she felt guilty. Apart from the phone call, he was making an effort to create a good atmosphere between them, and there she was, hair tousled from sleep, wrapped up in a coffee stained dressing gown, doing nothing but complaining. She scrambled up, grabbed a brush from the mantelpiece, and dragged it through the tangled blonde strands. One side kinked outward where she'd rested on it, and no amount of brushing would straighten it out. She sighed, taking a hairband from the handle and scraping the uneven mess into a ponytail. It wasn't perfect but it was better. In the corner of the mirror, she watched him enter the room.

"I thought I told you to sit," he said, stepping back until all but his head was out of view. "I'm not coming back in until you're sitting down." Amy did as she was told once more, conflicting thoughts running through her head. It was lovely that he'd bought her something, but if it simply came from a guilty conscience then it was worthless. The words 'trust me' echoed in her mind, chastising her for being so negative. She'd sprung this situation on him and the least she could do was wait and see how he dealt with it.

"Are you ready? Close your eyes."

In the darkness, she took a deep breath and slipped into the moment. A delicate scent surrounded her, filling her mind as she inhaled. She opened her eyes. Michael sat next to her, his lap filled with the most beautiful orchids she'd ever seen. Bright colours melted into one another, framed by harsh edges, bleeding towards the erotic fullness of the labellum in their centres.

"I was going to get you roses, and then I saw these," he said, holding them forward. "Roses are beautiful, but orchids capture your power and vibrancy. I remember the first time we met. You were dancing on the beach, and even though there wasn't any music, I heard it anyway. The way you moved, the look of sheer bliss on your face, you were magical back then and that's what I fell in love with." He dropped his eyes, his voice quiet. "I've taken that away from you recently and I'm sorry. I promise you things are going to change from now on."

Amy buried her face in the flowers, desperately wanting to throw them to one side and hug him, but it was his time to talk and he was saying all the right things. His hand disappeared down the side of his leg, reappearing with a black box the size of his palm.

"The orchids will only live a week or two, but this will last forever. I hope you like it."

She took it from him and slid the lid open. Inside was a delicate white gold chain with a butterfly pendant attached. The wings held tiny diamonds that caught the light, giving the illusion of life. This time she did let the orchids drop to the floor as she threw her arms around his neck. "How did you know?" she said, hiding her smile in his cheek.

"The shopping list. You had butterfly wings doodled all over it. It made me think of that first date and how you moved as if you had wings of your own."

"It's…it's perfect." She drew back from his cheek and stared into his eyes. He really meant every word; she could see it in the way they shone. He brushed his lips against hers, and it was like an electrical current passing through them. Wanting more, she pressed her mouth harder against him, feeling his smile.

"There's time for that later," he said, placing the chain around her neck. "There's a few more presents to come yet. Let me just…" The clasp slipped between his fingers and he caught it, trying again. "There. You look so beautiful, Amy.

Now, every time I see you wearing this, I'll remember what an idiot I've been."

"You haven't been an idiot at all. We've both let things get this bad, not just you." She kissed his hand. "And you didn't have to do all this. Just being here would have been enough."

"So you don't want the rest of the gifts then?" A smirk spread across his face. She countered it with a fake pout. "Ok then, but don't get your hopes up. You've already had the expensive ones." Michael walked to the door and retrieved his briefcase. Pulling out a single sheet of paper, he placed it in her hands.

"What's this?" she said, the faint lines on her forehead deepening. It looked official, but paperwork had never been her strong point.

"This is a contract, and it's not really for you, it's for Rob. You were right. I could have been giving him more responsibility, so, first thing tomorrow, he'll be taking over as manager and I get to spend more time with you. I still have to work and we won't have as much spare cash, but it should make things easier all round."

The lines faded away as the reality of his decision hit her. "You'd really do this for me?" At that moment, she was back on the beach in his arms, staring up at the most amazing man she'd ever met.

"It's not for you, it's for us. You really think I want to be head of my own company, raking the cash in, if I don't have you by my side? I'd rather be living in a two bedroom flat somewhere with you than in this house alone…which brings me onto the next part." He dug into the briefcase again and pulled out a large wad of leaflets. "Not quite flats, but these are a few of the four bedroom houses in the area. What do you think?"

Amy took the leaflets, flicking them over slowly, her eyes unable to take in the information. It was overwhelming. The houses in the photographs looked so small compared to their own house, yet so perfect. Her hands shook as she held them up to her chest. Tears welled, sliding down her face and into her open mouth. She wanted to smile, to laugh, but the world around her had come to a stop. A touch to her arm broke the spell and she gasped in a lungful of air.

"If it's not what you want to do then we can work something else out. It's just that you said—" His words were cut short by her mouth, and this time he didn't push her away.

Pulling her closer, Michael wrapped his arms around her shoulders, his tongue circling around hers. He tasted of meat and wine, and she melted into his arms, taking his breath as he exhaled. His lips were soft yet firm, with a magnetic force that held her own lips in place, unreserved in their wanting and attentive to her needs. Her body hummed like a tuning fork as he ran his fingers around her neck, barely touching her skin. "I have one more present for you," he mumbled into her mouth, the vibration of his words creating an exquisite tingling that spread throughout her head. Amy kissed across his cheek and nibbled at the tip of his earlobe, "Is it you?"

Movement caught her eye and she turned her head to see what it was. Michael's arm had removed itself from her shoulder and was hovering in the air with a glossy black bag hanging from his fingers by thin cord straps. She moved to take it but he twisted his arm away.

"No, let me." Michael said, getting to his feet and pulling

her with him. He reached into the bag, withdrew a cobalt blue satin slip and held it against her. She took hold of the fabric and ran her hands over it. It fell through her fingers like water.

"Wow, Michael, this is too much. It's beautiful."

"It will be even more beautiful when you're wearing it. Why don't you put it on and I'll get another bottle of wine." He turned, heading towards the door, stopping her when she tried to follow. "Where are you going? You can get dressed in here."

"No, I can't, unless you're hiding another bag with underwear in it."

He leaned into her and kissed her again. She could feel his smile on her lips. "No, I'm not, and yes, you can."

The grating sound of a drawer opening rang through from the kitchen as the dressing gown dropped from her shoulders and landed on the floor in a heap. She took the soft satin in her hands and raised her arms in the air, letting it float down onto her body. The fabric spilled effortlessly across her skin, clinging to every curve, coming to rest at the top of her thighs. It hadn't looked as short when it was held against her, and her lack of underwear made her feel exposed. With flushed cheeks, she tried to pull the slip lower as Michael entered the room. "You look amazing," he said, topping up the glasses on the table. "Don't try and cover yourself, you have no idea how gorgeous your body is." Amy grabbed one of the glasses and swallowed the contents in one gulp. A warm buzz spread through her chest, trickling down into her arms and legs as he pressed a button on the stereo, filling the air with soft violin tones.

"You really think so?" she said, cocking her head to one side, "it isn't too short?"

"Too short?" he pressed his body against her. "If it was any longer I wouldn't be able to do this." A hand ran up the back of her thigh, coming to rest on the curve of her ass. The corners of his mouth raised as he pulled her into him, moving her in time with the music. Their hips swayed as one to the slow sultry sound, feet gliding over the hardwood floor as the single instrument became many in harmonious perfection. His other hand ran up the back of her neck, guiding her towards his mouth. They kissed, still moving with the music; slow, passionate kisses that set her lips on fire.

Throwing her head back, she presented her neck to him, gasping as his tongue stroked the area just below her ear. He ran his hand down from her head, sliding it underneath her breast, lifting it to his mouth. Her nipple strained against the satin as he pulled it taut, scratching the surface with his teeth.

Pulling away, Michael ran a finger across the dark, saliva-soaked fabric before dropping to his knees. He kissed the front of her thighs, lifting the hem of the slip with his nose. Amy sucked in air as the thrill of the moment soared inside her head. His hands ran across the soft hair between her legs, parting her, and he drew his nose between her outer lips. A high-pitched groan escaped from her mouth as his tongue connected with her, flicking back and forth.

A hand wandered between her thighs, and Amy moved her feet wider apart, opening herself up to him. Her longing to give herself completely to him was countered with the control she needed to stay on her feet, enhancing the sensations that flooded her body and mind. He eased a finger inside her, massaging her inner walls, his tongue delicately playing against her clitoris. The powerful tension she'd felt so often that day began to build again as her muscles raged against his touch.

She fought to keep her balance on shaking legs as the torturous heat of an impending orgasm coursed through her body. Michael seemed to sense this and pulled his hand away, using it to steady her instead as his tongue increasing its speed. It hit her like a nuclear bomb, sending every part of her body into meltdown as she finally came, filling his waiting mouth with her juices.

He caught her as she fell, her body twitching uncontrollably in his arms and a smile spread across her face. "I love you," she whispered as he lay her on the sofa and pulled the slip over her head. She watched him undress, the shirt falling from his toned body, fingers popping buttons open on his jeans. His cock sprang from the fabric as he pushed them to the floor, kicking the denim to one side.

Amy wrapped her hand around his erection, stroking it gently as she parted her legs. He slid in between them, his body resting on hers, and eased himself into her. Every emotion she'd ever felt for him surfaced as he thrust slowly inside her, his weight on her body, his lips around hers. They became one both physically and spiritually, bodies breathing and moving in unison. He grew firmer, and her inner-muscles matched him, tightening with every thrust until they climaxed together, their moans muffled by each others mouths. They lay in silence, sweat-soaked bodies entwined, his head resting against her shoulder. The room shifted around them, fading in and out of focus. Amy watched colours blend in and out of one another with every blink of her eyes.

"I can't believe I forgot how amazing we are together," Michael said, tightening his grip around her waist. "I've forgotten a lot recently, haven't I?"

"More than you think," she gave him a cheeky lop-sided grin.

He pulled himself up onto his elbows, staring at her. "And what exactly do you mean by that?"

She bit her bottom lip suggestively. "Well, the chocolate sauce is still in the fridge."

He laughed and kissed her. "I guess we'll have to start again then."

ABOUT THE AUTHORS

JANINE ASHBLESS

Janine Ashbless is a writer of fantasy erotica and steamy romantic adventure. She likes to write about magic and myth and mystery, dangerous power dynamics, borderline terror, and the not-quite-human. Every so often she'll write something grown-up and contemporary, but then she gets all confused and embarrassed and goes back to the fallen angels.

In Bonds of the Earth, the second of the *Book of the Watchers* trilogy, was published by Sinful Press in March 2017. Janine has also had numerous novels and short stories published by Black Lace, Sweetmeats Press, Samhain, Nexus, Cleis Press, Ravenous Romance, Harlequin Spice, Xcite, Mischief Books, and Ellora's Cave, among others. She is co-editor of the nerd erotica anthology 'Geek Love'.

Janine is a prolific blogger and you can find her at http://janineashbless.blogspot.co.uk/

ELLA SCANDAL

Ella Scandal is a smut loving, sex-positive blogger from the UK. Her first story was born of an attempt to exorcise a recurring dream and she hasn't stopped writing since. When

Ella isn't keeping her family in clean socks and herding cats, she writes reviews and filthy short stories for her blog.

You can follow Ella on Twitter @ella_scandal, or check out her blog at http://www.scandarella.com/

SONNI DE SOTO

Sonni de Soto is a kinkster of color who is also an English major and graduated from the University of Minnesota. She also won the third place 2008 International Aeon Award story winner (Published in *Albedo One Issue 38*). Sonni has two BDSM erotica novels published, *The Taming School* with Sizzler Editions and *Show Me, Sir* with Sinful Press. She also has BDSM erotica short stories in Riverdale Ave Books's *First Annual Geeky Kink Anthology*, The Sexy Librarian's anthology *For the Men (and the Women who Love Them)*, *and* Sexy Little Pages' *Sacred & Profane* and soon *Rule #34* anthologies, as well and several others. To find more from Sonni, please visit

amazon.com/author/sonnidesoto

and sonnidesoto.blogspot.com.

JO HENNY WOLF

Jo Henny Wolf lives with her husband and two daughters in the idyllic Rhine Valley in one of the warmest places of Germany. She spent her childhood roaming the woods of the Black Forest, steeped deeply in myth and folklore and ingrained superstition, where her love for fairytales was nurtured and cemented.

She holds a B.A. in German Language and Literature as

well as Scandinavian Language and Literature. Tracing intertextual influences is like a treasure hunt and a fascinating puzzle to her, but it's not as fulfilling as writing her own stories, accompanying her heroines and heroes through adventures full of magic, love and melancholy, and lots of steamy sex. She writes Romance novels as J. H. Wolf.

You can find her at www.johennywolf.org

LILY HARLEM

Lily Harlem is an award winning, bestselling author of sexy romance. She writes for publishers on both sides of the Atlantic and has many titles to her name.

You can find her at www.lilyharlem.com

LADY DIVINE

Lady Divine is a professional Dominatrix living and working in Southern California, and that's where most of her writing inspiration comes from. She is also a wife and a mother, a classical musician, a photographer, and a greco roman wrestler, as well as an LGBTQIA+ advocate. Lady Divine can be found gracing the internet at www.lady--divine.tumblr.com

GAIL WILLIAMS

Gail B Williams lives in her own private dungeon populated with all the weird and the wonderful she can imagine. Some of it's very weird, and the odd bits and pieces are really quite wonderful. With a vivid imagination, there was no other choice for Gail than to write, something she's been doing her for as long as she can remember. Gail is English by birth, but lives in Wales, married a Welshman and have two fantastic children. They live with the worlds most imperious and demanding cat.

Enjoying the whole range of human experience, Gail has a collection of short crime stories out, "Last Cut Casebook", and a full length crime novel "Locked Up", and steampunk novel "Shades of Aether" both being published in Autumn 2017. For more information on the books, and her blog, find out more see www.gailbwilliams.co.uk.

SAMANTHA MACLEOD

Samantha MacLeod is the author of *The Trickster's Lover*. Her work has previously appeared in A Two Dame Production's anthology *Lustily Ever After* and *Typehouse Literary Magazine,* and her novella *The Night Watch* is forthcoming from Less Than Three press. Born and raised in Colorado, Samantha now lives with her husband and two small children in the woods of southern Maine. When she's not shoveling snow or writing steamy sex scenes, Samantha can be found teaching philosophy to undergraduates who have no idea she leads a double life as an erotica author. Samantha can be found at www.sammacleod.wordpress.com

TONY FYLER

Tony Fyler has been writing since he read the Ladybird 'Peter and Jane' books. In his mind, Jane was an alien princess sent into exile to save her planet, and Peter was an evil robot duplicate, secretly sent to wipe her out and begin a reign of darkness across the galaxy.

Pat the Dog was actually the President of the Algonquin Alliance of Shapeshifters, protecting Jane from Peter's evil intentions.

Surprisingly, Ladybird rejected his proposed plotline, and Fyler tasted the bitterness of rejection early.

At the age of 24, he began writing comic fantasy novels in earnest. His first completed manuscript was in re-writes for a year with HarperCollins, before being rejected.

He became a journalist to spite them.

He also started up a professional editing business – Jefferson Franklin Editing – and has since made a living telling other authors what's wrong with their novels.

Now, 20 years after his initial brush with writing success, he feels that the publishers have probably suffered enough from being denied his work, so he's started writing again. He also had a short story (based on fact) published in an anthology called Merthyr Writing, telling the story of his father. He has never tried writing erotica before.

ELLIE BARKER

Ellie Barker writes short'n'dirty flash fiction and short erotic fiction in any genre going. She prefers vampires over werewolves, and is always hot for a rainy night. Find out more at elliebarker.co.uk.

LISA MCCARTHY

Lisa McCarthy was born in the beautiful country of Wales approximately forty years ago. She holds an honours degree in Literature and an undergraduate diploma in Creative Writing. She currently lives in the Swansea Valleys with her two children, a handful of crazy cats, an OCD dog and a tank full of fish called Bob. When she's not writing about sex, or talking about herself in the third person, she is trying to make her own fantasies come to life.

OTHER SINFUL PRESS TITLES

PEEPER by S.J. Smith

BY MY CHOICE by Christine Blackthorn

SHOW ME, SIR by Sonni de Soto

THE HOUSE OF FOX by SJ Smith

A VARIETY OF CHAINS by Christine Blackthorn

IN BONDS OF THE EARTH by Janine Ashbless

THE LIBERTINE DIARIES by Isabella Delmonico

For more information about Sinful Press

please visit

www.sinfulpress.co.uk

Lightning Source UK Ltd.
Milton Keynes UK
UKOW04f2234310717
306398UK00001B/10/P